PRODIGAL
SPELL

ISBN: 978-0-9965378-0-3

Cover design by Rocking Book Covers.

*To my fairy godmothers- Gwen, Faith, and Tina.
You are the best inspiration.*

PRODIGAL SPELL

LILLIAN ARCHER

Chapter One

Richmond House, London, 1790

The thrum of witch power echoed and arched off the ballroom walls, swirling through the masses of dancers like their silk skirts in time with the music. My own magic answered the call, eager for release, but like most aspects of my life in London, I resisted that particular impulse, whispering the words to hide me from my brethren.

A witch without a clan was like having a death wish, something I managed to avoid so far.

I tightened my grip on my dance partner. "Do you find the evening entertaining?"

Lord Botetourt, leader of the largest witch clan in London, was a suitor of sorts. Ever since placing my dainty foot onto British soil, he had pursued, cajoled, begged, and pleaded for me to join his clan. "Do you find it so convenient to avoid me? I must dance with you in public to gain your attention. Join me, Lady Richmond. I urge you to consider my offer. Again."

I sighed, knowing it was the same reason they all wanted to keep me in the fold. I had something they thought they wanted.

"I do not practice, sir, as you know. I would be of little use to an active clan. Perhaps even a danger."

"I am not a man known for my patience," he replied. "I did not attain the position as head of my clan by waiting for wayward witches to come to their senses." He appeared irritated, wrestling with an unreadable emotion before continuing, "I do not like this situation, and it cannot continue."

"Ah. So now we have progressed to veiled threats as your latest attempt to frighten me into joining your clan."

He frowned at my words. His power rolled beneath his hands, the warm thrum of witchcraft pulsating with the rhythm of the music. I felt the other witches in the room pulling me, like shadowy blots of power in the mass of humanity, but was unable to discern exactly where and who they were in such close proximity to a man of Botetourt's circumstance. My own power stretched, racing to the place where his bare fingertips brushed my skin above the cuff of my glove, begging for release, like an urchin pleading for bread outside a tavern. My footsteps fell in line, never missing a turn of the dance, my composed appearance belying the turmoil raging beneath the surface of my silk gloves.

I breathed deeply, stretching the confines of my corset and thin silk dress, exhaling one rib at a time, wrestling for control, tamping my errant power from deep inside like a cloak into an overfull wardrobe. "I understand, Lord Botetourt. I have refused for three years, and must continue to do so. I cannot be a member of your clan."

He squinted his light brown eyes, making small creases blossom at the corners, while considering me like a hawk surveys a mouse. "You seem intelligent, Lady Richmond, which is at odds with your current stand. It is foolish to remain without allegiance to a house in these dangerous times." He twirled us in cadence with the music, his height no impediment, leading me fluidly through the steps of the dance. I held myself as far away as polite, but always remained wary. If he chose to press the issue, he could haul me into his clan house and force me to join his ranks. A simple joining of blood would suffice. I could defend myself, but not against an entire clan focused on beating me into submission.

I straightened my back, catching a glimpse of my husband across the room. I could not remember the last time I danced or talked, or anything else with my husband. I returned my gaze to Botetourt. "I do not fear the government, or the church. Or you."

"You should," he replied. "Almost as much as you need fear the witches in this room. Any one of them would exterminate you in the space of a heartbeat if they believed acquiring your power might give them an advantage over me."

There. The real issue. My ability. The thing everyone in the witch clans lusted after like a lewd for a virgin at Newmarket. They sought the promise of my pedigree, my talents, and my allegiance. I smiled and turned, my own feet quite nimble in their low-heeled shoes. "How foolish for any of them to think they could defeat me. If I chose to apply myself, of course."

He nodded his blond head, his wavy hair held in place with pomade. "Let us hope it does not come to that. I do not care for dirty duels, but I *detest* defeat. I am not the only witch at work in London." He added, "You cannot remain neutral forever."

That was unwelcome news to me. I thought Botetourt's was the *only* clan in London. Perhaps I was losing my touch? Or were my talents slipping because of my self-imposed exile?

We entered the final steps of the dance, now directly opposite from my husband and his new partner. My sadness at the state of our marriage notwithstanding, I missed Richmond's company as a friend. London was a cold, gray place in every sense. A difficult environment for a child of the sun.

I expected betrayal from a witch, infidelity from a trusted clan, humiliation on the dueling field with a loss, but never the marrow deep sorrow I felt now as I watched my husband looking so happy with another woman. To be fair, I did not think she was his mistress, but his public display of unbridled joy was damning in itself. And at odds with the sour expression he wore around me.

The music stopped. Richmond stood three feet to our left, extricating himself from his partner. Lord Botetourt glanced from Richmond to me. "One wonders if misplaced loyalty is worth the effort."

I could not meet his gaze, as I was unsure if I could prevent my tears from trickling down my face if I glimpsed any sympathy in his eyes. "It was at one time, Lord Botetourt, and that is more information than is proper for me to share." I curtseyed, signaling the end of the dance. "Merry Christmas."

"Merry Christmas, Lady Richmond. Consider my words. You know my direction if you change your mind."

"I will think about it. I promise." I preferred not to say why I would never join a clan, ever again. It felt like a betrayal of my own family, more of a transgression than marrying a human, or refusing to follow my father's orders. If I were to join another clan, join my blood to theirs, it would be tantamount to a declaration of war, and God above knew we could ill afford any more bloodshed.

A giggling couple pushed through the crowds, stumbling into Lord Botetourt, breaking me from my reverie.

"Hello, sir!" the young man in a green coat said, a glassful of brandy in his hand, the dark liquid sloshing over the edge to splatter Lord Botetourt's burgundy coat. "We are off to celebrate! Good things are afoot!" He clutched his female companion about the waist. "Come, Vivian, let us walk in the gardens."

The force of their power hit my gut. *Why are two young witches behaving so carelessly in a crowd?* Flaunting power was like asking for a duel, and they were in no condition to defend themselves.

Botetourt dabbed is sleeve with a plain handkerchief. "Take care not to offend the hosts, Jeremy."

"The gardens are closed." I added. "If you want privacy, the second floor gallery is less crowded."

Jeremy waved his hand, sending more brandy onto Botetourt's sleeve. "We need an audience, not privacy!" He staggered off, his companion in tow.

Botetourt dabbed at the dark blotch on his coat. It surely would cause a stain, and Richmond would be in fits if he knew his fine spirits were being wasted. "I bid you good night." He dissolved into the swirl of colorful ball gowns.

I searched the crowd for Richmond. He remained close, his head bent low to speak into his companion's ear, eliciting a laugh. I clenched my hands in the folds of my dress, shaking with the effort it took to restrain my power and keep it from bursting through my skin.

My father's words echoed in my ears, as if he stood beside me, instead of on our island home in the West Indies. *"Julia, you do not know this man. He is not a witch. How can you adapt? You were born to duel, born to lead, not to waste your time playing nursemaid to halfling children with no futures."*

Richmond smiled, his attention focused on the woman at his side. I smoothed my skirts, considering my options. Should I enchant him later in our rooms before demanding the truth from him? I had never crossed that line, but I certainly entertained it now. My fingers of my right hand, my casting hand, twitched, as if not knowing how to deal with the issue without blasting a spell and asking questions later.

Bespelling him is not worth the price. I am better than that. That is why I left home. As if telling myself made the truth easier to bear! A moral victory for sticking to an ethical code was cold comfort when your bed was empty.

I marched over to him and the woman, holding my head high. She saw me first, her black eyes narrowing before smiling at me. "Bonjour, Madame Richmond! Your husband has spoken of you often." Her voice lilted with a slight French accent, like the ones I remembered from French Islanders as a girl. Her hand tightened on Richmond's arm. I looked at her, then at her hand, then at her again, my right eyebrow arching askance. She dropped her hand from Richmond's arm, but kept her body close to his.

"Hello, and welcome to my home. Your accent is interesting. Are you from the islands?" I asked.

Richmond stepped to my side, draping his arm about my shoulders, and leaning to give me a kiss on the cheek. "Where have you been, Julia? I was looking for you."

I stiffened in his embrace, not from his kiss, but from her presence. In close quarters, I could feel power rolling off her, but it was different from any power I had ever encountered. There are only four elements, meaning four sources of power: wind, water, earth and fire. Those I knew. Hers, however, was none of those.

She replied, "I am from Martinique," while patting her hair, and piling the auburn curls higher to make her petite frame appear taller.

Richmond said, "May I introduce you? Julia, this is Madame Oualie. I met her on Martinique, a few months before I met you, dear. I did not know she was in London until she came to our ball."

A headache was starting behind my eyes, and its incessant throbbing prevented me from thinking clearly. There was something I knew I should be worried about, but it kept slipping into the corners of my mind.

An explosion boomed outside, shattering the glass of the French doors along the south wall. Guests screamed. Richmond tensed. "That sounded like a cannon. Impossible." A second boom ricocheted through the room, and bright flashes illuminated the line of tattered curtains blowing in the wind from the exploded windows at the back of the room.

"Fireworks," one man exclaimed.

"Let's go see," cried another.

The mass of revelers scurried towards the doors. We were caught in the queue, pressed together, Richmond on one side and Madame Oualie on the other. A thin stripe of skin between my glove and my sleeve touched her bare arm in the crush.

My head felt like it was in a vise as alien power rushed through me, dark as a bottomless pit. My body flushed against the unexpected onslaught, and the heat of my blood began searing my flesh. My power was recoiling from her contact, instead of defending me. Struggling against the wave of blackness, I wrenched my arm away from her, shoving her into the crowd.

With the loss of contact, my head cleared. I whispered to Richmond, "Did you arrange for fireworks? I did not see it on the plans."

He shook his head. "No. I fear this is the work of unsanctioned witches."

Witches were known, if poorly tolerated. If you outed yourself to the church, you were allowed to perform sanctioned spells. Exactly what constituted a sanctioned spell was up for debate, as no one ever lived to report about it after confessing to the church. Witches were disappearing at an alarming rate, and part of my mission in London was to find out what happened to them. However, it was not a mission from my father, or anyone else. It was just something to pass the time.

Another boom, this time followed by a collective "Ahh!" from the crowd outside. We squeezed through the doors with Richmond heading towards the east. I hugged the brick wall of the house, scooting westward behind the mass of bodies. I rubbed my arms against the cold, hurrying to an empty spot near the brick garden wall.

A pop sounded, and the fizz of fireworks exploded above our heads. The lights were brilliant white, like huge stars of glittering fire, and appeared rather beautiful against the night sky. Jeremy and Vivian, the drunken couple I met earlier in the evening, danced on the frosted ground, flinging their arms skyward, shooting jets of red power up into the night. Another explosion sparkled overhead, and the smell of brimstone was heavy on the breeze.

Botetourt slid beside me against the garden wall. "Fools," he said.

"Are they your clan?" I asked.

"No. They petitioned to join one month ago, but I never arranged a placing duel. I deemed them not mature enough for undertaking the task of belonging in my clan." He flexed his fingers, shoving his hands into the pockets of his coat. "As this is your house, it is your responsibility to contain them."

I shivered, not from the cold, but from his words. Any witch stepping up to stop them risked exposure. "I do not want to be known by the church. Or any of the other members of your clan. " *Or my husband*, I added to myself.

"Your husband may save you the trouble." He nodded towards the wayward witches.

Richmond and his brother, Sebastian, strode across the frozen ground, followed by Vicar Morris, our local clergyman. Sebastian was similar in looks to his brother. Both stood a shade over six feet tall, with gleaming brown hair, and had their pistols aimed directly at the couple. A formidable sight, they closed the gap between themselves and Jeremy.

Vicar Morris, hiding behind them, waved a Bible above his head, shouting, "Be gone, devils! Repent or suffer!"

Botetourt said, "When will they learn there is nothing to fear from the Bible? Honestly, the idiocy of it all! It is not God whom witches fear." He pulled his hands from his pockets, twisting the thin, gold ring on his right hand with his thumb. His clan ring.

My gaze returned to the macabre tableau: Jeremy and Vivian, still oblivious to the danger, and throwing fireworks into the air with careless abandon. "I have no stomach for this."

Richmond cocked his weapons, and spoke in a voice loud enough for all to hear, "We have no issues with you. Please leave my property. I have no calling with witches. We did not invite you." Shadows moved along the wall to his right, before the darkness flashed against the bushes; then it was gone. Richmond swiveled towards the disturbance, his gun held steady in his hand, a troubled look on his face.

The two night revelers stopped dancing, stumbling over each other before standing like petulant children caught eating treats without permission. "We meant no harm. Our mistress did not mean to offend," Jeremy stuttered, his previous bravado now very much absent. "Please put the guns away. We truly did not mean harm."

Sebastian replied, "Then leave." He waved his gun towards the back garden gate. "The exit is that way."

Vivian appeared confused. "You want us to leave? You don't like our fireworks?" Her voice sounded hurt.

"Yes. Leave. Please. Now." Richmond replied.

Vivian shuddered, as if against the chill she just recognized, and said, "I'll just get my wrap," before starting towards the house.

Sebastian stepped closer, his gun aimed steady at her chest. "We can forward it to your address."

Jeremy placed his hand about her shoulders, hugging her tightly. "We meant no harm. We are leaving now. Merry Christmas."

They turned, picking their way through the branches and stunted bushes of my garden, past my hothouse, to the back garden gate. They paused, and Vivian's gaze searched the crowd before exiting the garden.

Richmond turned to the gathered guests. "Thank you for attending our annual Christmas Eve celebration. Lady Richmond and I entreat you to make your way to the dining rooms for dinner."

The crowd murmured before seeping back into the warm house. Botetourt slipped away to join their ranks. Richmond glanced about, spied me, and gave a curt wave of his hand, motioning me to his side.

Vicar Morris was speaking when I reached my husband's side. "I will handle this, Lord Richmond. This is church business."

Richmond stared across the barren garden. "Thank you. I appreciate your help, but this occurred in my house, and I have resources as well."

He holstered his pistols, grabbing my arm. "We need to talk. Now." He moved towards the house, dragging me along behind him.

"Richmond!" I said. "What is wrong with you? Loosen your hand, it hurts my arm."

"We will speak inside."

His jovial mood from earlier this evening was gone. He pulled me up the stone steps to the porch. I stumbled, tripping on my gown. "Richmond, this is unnecessary. Tell me what is wrong."

We entered the back hall, away from the entrance to the dining room, and stopped at the door to his study. He twisted the knob, flinging me into the room before entering himself and slamming the door shut.

My power surged at his manhandling, imploring me to put him in his place.

His blue eyes blazed. "What is Alistair Dupont doing in my house?"

Chapter Two

My heart skipped a beat. "Alistair? Here? That is preposterous." I stepped away from him, rubbing my arm where it still throbbed from his unrelenting grasp. "The only person from the West Indies here tonight is Madame Oualie. And me."

"I saw him, Julia, in the garden."

"With the fireworks? How? It was too dark, and there was too much commotion. You must be mistaken." *I wanted him to be wrong. Alistair could ruin my life here in London.*

He stepped towards me, touching my arm. I flinched, as the skin was still tender. "I am sorry. I did not mean to hurt you."

"I know. " In his eyes, I saw the love and concern missing between us for the past weeks.

He dropped his hand to finger the pistols jutting from his trousers. One was hanging awkwardly from the thin waistband. A quick move and it might have hit the floor. He continued, "That man scares me, like no other. Vicar Morris says he is a witch."

I kept my gaze steady under his scrutiny. I had nothing to gain by telling my husband about Alistair. "Vicar Morris is a careful man."

Richmond pulled one of his guns from the holster, checking the priming pan, and looking down the wooden barrel before handing it to me. "Take it. Keep it with you at all times. He is not to be trusted."

I took the heavy gun, wondering if I would accidentally shoot myself. "I do not feel comfortable carrying this weapon around."

"I do not feel comfortable with unsanctioned witches slinking about our home." He curled my fingers around the barrel.

I walked to the mahogany desk beside the south wall, now covered with piles of papers, and placed the gun gingerly in the middle of the desk before wiping my hands on my skirt. "I will not carry that thing. I stand more chance of shooting myself than hurting anyone else with it." A gun was useless against a witch, anyway, but I could not tell my husband that. I sighed. There were so many secrets between us.

He approached, stopping just behind me. His finger reached out to trace the curve of my cheek, his skin touching mine in the barest hint of a caress. "Please, Julia. Do this for me."

I did not answer.

He dropped his hand. I longed for intimacy again, but I did not like being blackmailed with it. I stood still, waiting for his next move in this chess game that our marriage had become.

"I want you to be safe. Your well-being is my utmost concern."

I wanted to believe his words, but Stephen had grown distant. Late night discussions with his brother. Changing the conversation when I entered the room. Taking trips without explanation. I longed for the days when Alistair was halfway round the world, and Stephen and I shared everything. Now, we shared nothing. I turned to answer him. "I believe you. But having my husband's presence more in my life would keep me much safer than a firearm."

He glared at me, lifting a brow in surprise.

I drew a deep breath. "I do not know what to think, what with your midnight departures, and the rumors. You are so moody and angry when we alone. You seemed so happy dancing with that woman tonight. What is your connection with Madame Oualie? Why can she make you laugh? And all I can do is make you disappointed?"

He laughed. "Is that what this is about? Jealousy? My comings and goings are mandated by the Admiralty. By the job I took to stay home with my wife, instead of sailing off to sea again. As for the good Madame, she is an old acquaintance from Martinique. I met her months before I met you, as I previously stated. I wanted to be hospitable."

"I think your actions were much more than hospitable. It hurt me to see you with her like that."

He moved to the fire, bracing his arm against the mantel, and staring into the flames. "You do not trust me."

How could I when we live a life of lies?

"I wish I understood you better. Your work takes you away, at odd times, and I feel we never even talk anymore. I worry about you, Stephen."

"Worry," he repeated, his voice colder and harder. "I hope you realize the sacrifices I have endured to make you happy. To try and make a life here for us."

A tear slid down my cheek. "I have made sacrifices as well, Stephen. If you would just tell me why you are so unhappy with me, then perhaps we could work to make things right."

"Where are the sacrifices you have made?"

I fought back my tears. "None that I wish to share with you in this mood." *How can I tell him that I am a witch? That our children will have magical powers? Of the sacrifices I made in marrying him?*

"None you wish to share?"

"Not now."

He straightened, thrusting his hands into his pockets, and gazing hungrily at me. "We were married in haste in a port town by a drunken priest. I don't even know if he was ordained. But I loved you and nothing else mattered except making you mine." His voice softened. "That is still true three years later. I love you."

He moved to stand behind me, and the heat from his body delighted my power. He bent his head, his full lips a breath away from the shell of my ear. His breath tickled, sending shivers through my body, which had been craving closeness for months now. "What I need to know is if you still love me."

"Of course, I do." Like any good wife would answer.

"Good." Richmond stood, staring at the floor before focusing on straightening out the lace cuffs of his coat. "Take my arm and let's go to dinner." His offered his arm, waiting. "We can discuss this more after the party. There are a few things I need to share with you."

I was still too upset to eat, and just pushed my food around my plate. What if Alistair was really here? One tale to a newspaper, and my carefully constructed life here was finished. Sebastian did not show for dinner. Where was he? What about Vivian and Jeremy? Surely the church was out to find them. Could I help them without risk of exposure?

I hated feeling impotent; and I hated making small talk while feeling out of sorts even more. As soon as was proper, I excused myself from dinner and escaped to the gambling salon.

Games of chance and cards were all the rage, which was the only reason Richmond allowed a gambling room to be set during the party. It was the one place I could be assured that, at least, he would not bother me for awhile. I could be visible to my guests, while fulfilling my duties, and be able to *think*.

I paused on the threshold, surveying the room. I needed a table with no hint of excitement. I'd had enough turmoil for one night.

Several tables were stationed about the small room, offering Whist and Hearts, among other choices. Cigar smoke hovered near the ceiling of the salon, its wakes trailing like icicles around the chandeliers. I wrinkled my nose at the offensive smell. Craning my neck to see if any tables that met my specifications were open, I spied Lady Sutton playing with two older men. *Perfect*.

I threaded my way through the crowded room until I reached their table. She was a widow, who eschewed all the laws of fashion, and preferred puffing on a cigar and blowing smoke across the table, directly into the eyes of her opponent. Her dress was a concoction of red, green, and purple ruffles that was at least ten years out of date. Her hair was anchored by a poorly fitted wire cage, which towered a foot above her head, and was covered with powdered hair, replete with mistletoe and greenery. It listed to port under the weight of her festive decorations. Although her appearance reflected ineptitude, just sit across from her, and watch her astuteness remove coin from the pocket faster than a pickpocket at Covent Gardens.

"May I join you?" I asked. "Just to observe?"

She narrowed her eyes. "Are you familiar with the rules of Whist? Because I cannot tolerate an inept player at the card table."

I smiled at her honesty. "Yes, I believe I know the rules. But I do not wish to play."

The two gentlemen exchanged glances, then scraped their coins into pouches. They rose in unison, nodding and smiling.

Lady Sutton waved them on. "Nice evening, gentlemen." She collected the cards, shuffling them between her short, ringed fingers. "Nice to see you this evening, Lady Richmond. How was dinner? I remained in here with a few brave rakes and emptied them of their coin. Did I miss anything?"

"No." I settled in a chair with my back to the room, and concentrated on my cards before motioning to the two empty seats. "You need two more players."

"Let us play a variation I know. It requires only two players." She explained the rules as she dealt the cards.

I sighed, pulling a handful of gold and silver coins from my dress pocket. I never carried reticules, as they always got in my way if I ever *needed* to cast a spell. I flipped the coins between my fingers like a magician, the coins clinking into the pile from my supple fingers. I studied my cards. By her rules, I needed a better hand before even beginning to place a bet. I threw two coins in the center of the table. "I fear you have bested me, Lady Sutton. I must concede."

She slanted her eyes at me and smiled. "You are a quick study. Let us try again." Twenty minutes later, with considerably less coin in my pocket, I folded my cards, placing them precisely in the center of the table. "Really, Lady Sutton, I think you have a trick deck. I must concede again."

Coaxing a stray hair back into place, she said, "You remained at the game longer than I predicted, Lady Richmond. Not like that man from the West Indies I played earlier. He particularly stressed his connection to you, my dear. French-sounding name, Dupree? Devereaux? Odd-looking fellow with those mirrored glasses."

My hands stilled among the cards. There was only one tarnished soul I knew from those climes with a French name. I prayed to all the Holy Angels that Richmond was wrong. I felt much safer when half the globe separated me from Alistair Dupont.

I swallowed. "Dupont?" I offered weakly.

Lady Sutton snapped her fingers. "Yes! That is it! Of course, my dear, as he is an old friend of yours, I spoke with him at length. Awful about his lands, though."

Sweat trickled in a slow wake down my back, between my shoulders at the mention of his name. I was certain if he were to sit beside me, he could smell the reek of my fear. "His lands?" I repeated automatically.

"Yes! Some horrid affair with fire and savages."

As if conjured from the air, Alistair Dupont stepped from the crowd and began milling around the card tables. My worst nightmare incarnate was now embodied in the West Indies planter persona he held to the world. He was smaller than Richmond, with white-blond hair, bleached from the tropical sun. His coat was turquoise blue with a frothy cravat at his tanned throat. His hair was shorter than I remembered, but the coldness of his glare, and hardness around his mouth were more defined, if possible, from my last recollection. He wore a pair of small, mirrored, round lenses on his nose. Those were a new addition.

He leaned over Lady Sutton's chair, flashing a twisted smile, with his right casting hand twitching at his side. A thin, gold ring circled the middle finger of his casting hand. It signified his status as chief of his clan.

"Excuse me, ladies, but do you have room for another?"

I played with the coins in the pile until my fingers found a small one with sharp edges. My power thrummed with his close proximity. I doubted he would create a scene in such a public place, but Alistair's anger usually won over his common sense. That made him headstrong *and* dangerous.

I gazed into the mirrored lenses. "I'm sorry Mr. Dupont, but our game is full at this time. Perhaps my husband can find something to entertain you."

He adjusted the rims on his nose, draping himself in the empty chair. *Damn him*. I should have taken the seat with the better strategic position from the start. A mistake I would have not made in the past. My exile was making me careless.

"I will wait until you start a new round. I prefer to gamble with women rather than speak to your husband."

Lady Sutton replied, "That sounds rather like a disparaging comment." She fluttered her hand over her bosom. "I do hope Richmond doesn't take offense. He is a good shot."

I furrowed my brow and played with the coins, keeping my weapon at the top of the pile. "Mr. Dupont means no harm. How are your lands, sir? Lady Sutton told me of your unfortunate circumstances. Do you have enough coin to join our game?"

He clenched his left hand into a fist. "Quite immature of you, Lady Richmond. It seems marriage has increased your propensity to voice opinions others may not want to hear."

Lady Sutton appeared confused, darting her head from me to Dupont. "My dear, you said you were old friends?"

"No, Lady Sutton, we are old acquaintances, not friends. Mr. Dupont was once my fiancé. So you can now observe his bitterness in a new light."

She nodded in agreement. "Too right. There are a few bitter men in my past as well. Quite uncomfortable."

Dupont thinned his lips into a rigid line. "Uncomfortable or not, Lady Richmond, I came here with a purpose, and wish to speak with you in private."

I stared at his face, one I'd known since childhood. "I am afraid any audience with you must be in the company of my husband as well. I hope you understand."

"Need a bodyguard, sweet?"

Lady Sutton gasped, her cards forgotten.

"No. But I want him present."

"As you wish." He pulled a handful of coins from his waistcoat. "What is the minimum bet to begin?"

Lady Sutton licked her lips. "Ten pounds."

He counted ten pounds and placed them in the center of the table, his long fingers stroking the felt table covering.

My heart was thudding in my chest. A reasonable response to a man who never recovered from the humiliation because I deserted him. Lady Sutton shuffled the cards, placing a neat pile in front of each player. I rearranged the cards in my hand. "Same game, Lady Sutton?"

"Why yes, I have had such success, why change?" She placed her bet. "Now tell me why your engagement ended. Maybe I can help you overcome your disappointment, Monsieur Dupont."

Lady Sutton patted her hairpiece, cooing at her cards. I glanced at my own, certain to lose a majority of the coins in my pile. Dupont flicked his hand of cards open, threw them on the table, and glared at Lady Sutton. "I assure you, Lady Sutton, if your line of questioning is intended to diminish my concentration, it is an unsuccessful strategy. We are trained to succeed under many a stressful situation."

She asked, "Whom are you referring to, sir?"

"Why, myself and Lady Richmond, of course."

The audacity of the man. Talking about the witch duels our clans held in order to assign rank and power ratings to each member. It was an event every witch participated in on the first midsummer night after coming of age. Lady Sutton did not know what we were referring to, but I did not miss his intent.

I answered her question. "Our engagement ended when I met Lord Richmond."

Dupont parried, "Our engagement ended when you ran from your destiny. Richmond happened to be the one with the ship."

"So true love won the day!" Lady Sutton placed another bid on the table with a stack of coins.

Dupont wrinkled his nose. "The demise of our relationship began over a difference of opinion concerning a friend's illness. Love had nothing to do with it." His green gaze bored into mine. "You do remember Lady Penelope?"

God. How could I forget? My cards shook in my hand. "May she rest in peace."

"Your bet, Lady Richmond," Lady Sutton prompted me. Dupont stared at me, his gaze hidden from others. I hated that he knew things about me, secret things I'd rather forget, shameful things he threw at me as easily as a wager in a game.

Lady Sutton puffed on her thin cigar, lips pursed as she blew smoke in Alistair's direction. "Who is Lady Penelope?"

I swallowed the lump in my throat. I could not answer. The words would not come.

Alistair answered. "Lady Penelope was a childhood friend of Lady Richmond and myself. She suffered an unfortunate accident. Lady Richmond assumes a responsibility that is not hers." He glared at me. "Some believe she is not dead. Lady Richmond, however, labors under the pretense that she sent her to her maker."

How cold his description sounded in contrast to my memories of blood and screams.

Lady Sutton took another card before discarding it into the pile. Placing another bet on the table, she added, "Lady Richmond, in my estimation, has a charitable nature. Don't you help support the orphanage?"

"Yes." I wanted to cease this conversation, as well as the memories of my past.

A firm hand landed on my shoulder. Looking up, I gazed into the stern countenance of Vicar Morris. He maintained the parish church on the ancestral lands and traveled to London to preside over the Christmas mass. He preached in London often, trading gardening tips with the Bishop on occasion. "Sorry to interrupt, Lady Richmond, but I must speak with you."

Relieved at the excuse to leave, I folded the cards and tossed several coins into the pile. "That should even us out, Lady Sutton. Enjoy your evening with Monsieur Dupont."

She scraped the coins into a pile. "Merry Christmas to you both. Do not forget, my musicale is in three days and I expect you to attend."

I smiled, thinking of her previous outlandish fetes. "I will be there. Have a good night."

Dupont lounged in his chair, mimicking Lady Sutton. "Do not forget, Lady Richmond. We still have business to discuss."

I ignored him and followed Vicar Morris to an alcove off the salon. "How can I help you? Is all in readiness for the service tomorrow?"

He waved his hands, dismissing my comments, agitated, and glancing about before answering. "Yes, yes, all is in readiness. What I need to know is your attachment to Monsieur Dupont."

I considered my answer carefully before speaking. I did not want any association between myself and

Dupont, especially in the eyes of the church. I answered. "He is an acquaintance from my childhood home."

"There is something particular about that man I do not like. He is not godly in the least. I spoke with him before dinner. I think he was intentionally baiting me, claiming he was a witch. Do not fear, dear lady. I will send a messenger to the Bishop. He will direct us as to how to handle this situation. Until then, be wary of him."

I laughed, feeling uneasy. "My soul is not in peril from him, I assure you. This is the first time I have seen him in three years. Please do not distress yourself."

He hurried off, presumably to share with Richmond the same warning. I already knew what a deadly man Monsieur Dupont could be.

Slamming the door to my bedchamber hours later, I kicked off my heels, searching for Mary, my maid. I spied her robust form reliably propped in a chair by the corner, snoring softly.

"Wake up, Mary." I shook her gently, afraid a more energetic awakening might topple her from her perch. Stretching and yawning, she lumbered into a curtsey.

"Does my lady need help?"

"Yes, get this blasted dress and corset off me. I haven't had a deep breath all night."

I presented my back to her, fidgeting while she untied the intricate laces and fittings of my ensemble. Pushing the dress from my shoulders, I wiggled free of my stays. Goosebumps sprang along my naked flesh while Mary slipped a thick nightdress over my head. No frills and French lace for my husband! With the first snow, I always chose warm wool over frivolous fabrics. This was one of my favorites, for the peach color reminded me of the unfurled sails of a ship, reflecting the setting sun's rays.

Collapsing into a fireside chair, I propped my sore, swollen feet on the ottoman. I managed to avoid my husband for the remainder of the night. My body was exhausted, but my thoughts clashed in my mind.

I focused one-by-one on the mundane objects of my room: the painting of Mt. Nevis from my childhood home, and the center of this mess, hung above the marble fireplace mantel, an intricate clock depicting the late hour, perched on the bedside table, the candles burning low in the sconces flanking my four-poster bed, my telescope waiting in front of the balcony doors. Vases stood on every conceivable surface, filled with fresh blooms from my hothouse. And water.

Water, the essential element for any casting without a wand. No matter that I swore never to practice again. Or that I would never build a wand. Surrounding myself with ammunition was like an old soldier sleeping with his sword beside the bed. He may never have to use it, but it would be handy if he needed to defend himself from a thief. I scrunched my abused toes in the plush pile of the Persian rug under my chair.

The fire crackled in the hearth and a thick snow fell like feathers past my window. My maid finished turning down the bed, rubbing it with the bed warmers two extra times to ward off the chill of the night. She placed the device along the hearth. "Will you be needing anything else, my lady?"

"No, thank you. Merry Christmas."

She dipped into another curtsy. "Same to you, my lady." I waited until the click of the door signaled her exit.

The last guest had long since left, and the staff was attending to the flotsam and jetsam of debris downstairs. I opened my hand, allowing my power to burst from my fingertips, and pulling energy from the water in the vase next to my chair, as the liquid fueled my spell. The hearth roared with a shower of sparks and flames, pushing heat towards my chilled toes. I never adjusted to the cold climate here in London. The flowers closest to me, now deprived of water, wilted.

I fingered their blossoms, marked for an early demise when I selected them from the garden. *If stoking the fire did this to a flower, what must other spells do to animals? Or worse yet, to other witches? There were stories of some clans using other witches as vessels of power. Familiars.*

A draft blew into the room, dancing the flames higher. I felt a wave of energy hitting me. I knew I was no longer alone. And my visitor was not my husband.

"I thought your guests would never leave."

I turned to face the enemy, now in my room.

Chapter Three

I vaulted to stand, my right hand at the ready to cast a spell.

Alistair Dupont leaned against the panel that separated my rooms from Richmond's. The only exits were through the window to the garden three stories below, or through Alistair. I edged towards the window.

My power raced beneath my skin. "I knew you were reckless, Dupont, but this is ridiculous. Richmond will enter at any time."

Alistair touched the bridge of his nose, adjusting his lenses. "I hope he does. We have a few debts to settle."

His left hand whipped in an arc, causing the fire to leap in the grate.

Wonderful. I give him ammunition right when he needs it. I edged towards my writing desk where three vases of flowers stood full of water.

Alistair flicked his wrist, shooting a bolt of green light towards my heart. I flung my casting hand upwards, pulling water from the nearest vase, and forming a shield. His spell collided with mine, the impact knocking me off my feet. Reaching a hand behind me, I steadied myself against the wall, using it as leverage, as I scrambled to stand.

"Oh, do grow up, Alistair. That was years ago."

The fire flared, illuminating his form, and fueling his magic. The room glowed as bright as day when the flames leaped higher from the hearth.

He answered. "He ruined my life." His lips twisted as his casting hand glowed soft green. "You leaving Nevis did a lot of things, Princess, and none of them were good." Another bolt of green raced across the room. I ducked, breathless, as it slammed into the wall above my head before plaster bits fell onto my skin and eyelashes. "I came to give you news of your father."

I pulled water from the remaining vases within my reach. At the height of my powers, I could pull water from half a mile away. Now, the vases across the room seemed unreachable. "My father would tell me of his own news, I think." I concentrated on his hands, scrutinizing any twitch of light signaling a spell.

Alistair slid towards the center of the room, turning sideways to present a smaller target. "Under normal circumstances, yes. But these are difficult times." The thin gold ring on his right hand glowed. He could extract power from all the members of his clan as the head. Even across an ocean. I had no such reservoir.

Legs trembling, I pushed myself into a defensive stance. "I no longer practice. I cannot help you with your lands or sugar. Richmond will return at any moment. Be gone. Leave me alone. I'd hate to taint my floor with your blood."

I slid closer to the window.

Dupont flexed his hand. "You can make all the snide comments you want, Princess, but the words are no more than irritants, like mosquitos. Their bite stings for a moment, then they are forgotten." He regarded his cuticles, clenching his fist. "Your dad is currently possessed by a demon."

"Father calls upon demons frequently. He is always able to banish them."

"Not this beastie."

I chewed the inside of my cheek, my gaze never leaving Dupont. Demons were a natural extension of witchly power for a clan head. My sire was one of the most proficient demon masters. If he could not banish a demon, the whole clan succumbed to the infestation, no matter their location or distance from him. Even me. Miles were no safeguard from evil. *Blood calls to blood.*

I glanced at Dupont's clan ring. "You have the power. You are a clan master now. Why don't you banish it?"

Green fire erupted from both his hands before his spell hurtled across the room, catching me in the ribcage. The impact knocked out my breath. I collapsed over the back of the chair, my chest working, and my lungs gasping.

Alistair closed the gap between us, twining his fingers into my hair, yanking my head back. Pain laced through the tendons of my neck and tears welled in my eyes.

Adrenaline pulsed through my limbs, but I was exhausted. The few spells I had already cast were more than I cast in the last year. I could succumb to Alistair, let him take my life, along with my powers, and be done with all of it.

I rejected that thought, however. I was the heir to the wind, water, and fire clans of the West Indies. I would not lay down and die in a fight.

Alistair lay his casting hand along my neck, the heat and green flame burning my flesh. I tried to scream, but the sound choked as his hand closed around my throat. My mouth worked to fill my lungs with air.

"You misunderstand, Princess. I did not infect him with the demon, but I'll happily take advantage of it. I don't want to help your father. I want him to succumb to the demon. But I need someone to drive it out, for this beastie is one only you can remove for me. Then, when you are lying in the dirt, I want you to beg for my help. And I will refuse."

My vision blackened. I pulled the last aliquot of power deep from my core. I twisted my hand back, knocking his glasses from his face. Feeling the edges of the eye orbit, I pushed the last dregs of blue power into my hand, into his eye.

He yelled, releasing my neck.

I pulled energy from the water in the vases, mixing it with my own power, flinging more at the burning orbit of his eye, and digging my thumb deeper into the socket.

Alistair fell to the ground, breaking our contact.

I released the spell, scrambling around him to close the distance between me and the one remaining vase with water in the room.

"Why should I ask you for help?"

He clambered to his feet. Blood flowed from his right eye, and the socket was crusted with singed tissue.

First blood. My power rolled in my gut, satisfied. I choked down the bile climbing up my throat at the horrors I wrecked on Alistair's face.

He placed a glowing green hand over the wound, staunching the flow of blood. The crimson tracks bubbling through his fingers dried in the space of three breaths. "I have something to show you, Princess." He fished a thin, gold band from his pocket and placed it on his right hand to join his fire clan ring.

"I come to inform you, Princess, that I am your new master. I have defeated your father in a duel. I now head your clan." He pulled his hand from his face, and the metallic smell of old blood was overpowering. He took a handkerchief from his waistcoat, wiping the crusted mess from his hands before throwing the dirty handkerchief to the floor.

It was the same ring I saw on my father's hand for as long as I could remember.

Shock paralyzed me, slowing time so that each tick of the clock seemed like an eternity. "I don't believe you. He would die rather than allow you to gain his power."

"Yes, sweet, I agree. Which is why he is possessed." He bent, picking his glasses off the floor and placing them back on his nose. The frames were twisted, tilting the left lens higher than the right. A comical look. If the stakes were not so dire, I might have laughed at him.

He continued, "My house grows stronger with my boldness. The demon drains his power. I profit from it." He flung a shard of green power towards me.

I blocked it with a shield of blue, breathing heavily.

"But now that we are all one big happy family, I find that I require your help, or I, too will be affected; and I have waited too long for my rewards to botch it up now. And knowing this maudlin wallow of self-pity, which you call a marriage, is over, I knew you would be more open to saving the only family you have left."

"That does not explain why you are here. Father excommunicated me when I got married." The words still hurt after three years. "I am but one of two daughters. I have no clan allegiance to boost my powers."

Dupont chuckled softly, the sound chilling me. "What a sham, Princess. I know your ability, as well as your parentage." He circled in counterpoint to me, stalking me about the room until my back was at Richmond's door.

I shook my head. "I assimilate into London society precisely because I am weak. If I were strong of power, how could I exercise such gifts?"

"You always were a scheming miss. I'm sure you found a way to hide what you really are."

He waved his casting hand in a circle, dissipating the green light. Snatching his crooked glasses from his nose, he wiped the dirty lenses three times before settling them back in front his eyes.

I flattened myself along the wall. I was trapped between the door to Richmond's room and the fireplace, yet I needed to stay close to the final vase of water sitting on the mantel.

Alistair advanced, his arm outstretched, stopping four feet from me. He kept his back towards the fire. "Join my clan. Be honorable. Save your father, and yourself. All will be forgiven if you complete this task."

I did not hesitate. "No."

"You need my protection."

"I do not require anyone's protection."

"Then you leave me no choice." He stopped, bowing before me, the traditional opening for an invitation to duel. "I, Alistair Phillippe Louis Dupont, do hereby challenge you, Julia Southerland Nesbit Richmond, to a witch's duel. As challenger, I demand the terms. If I win, you will marry me, granting me full use of your powers at my discretion with no reservations. Refuse this challenge, and I will assassinate you and usurp your power anyway."

I raised my hand, blue light fluorescing along my fingertips. "I offer a truce."

"There are no options for truce or forfeiture."

"Then by the rules dictated for dueling, I demand my terms." My mind tripped over the possibilities. Alistair wanted me alive for his plans, or else he would already have killed me, collected my power, and be done with the problem of Julia. He wanted me to be the one who would suffer and dispatch the demon, so he could then swoop in and collect the spoils. My status outside of a clan limited my power, compared to his. Father always counseled me to work with my strengths. Nevis, with its pure water and constant trade winds, strengthened me more than dirty London.

The clock chimed thrice. Richmond might return at any moment. I did not have time to consider all the possibilities of this negotiation.

"My terms are these. The duel will take place on Nevis, in two months time. If I, Julia Southerland Nesbit Richmond, win, you will free my father, Malcolm Prescott Southerland Nesbit, and any of his clan from the demon. I will collect your power for my usage. I will consider terms for your forfeiture."

White mist encircled our casting hands, the magical equivalent of a legal document witnessed by a room of barristers.

Alistair laughed. "Enjoy your two months, Princess." He straightened his lace cravat. "How will you tell your husband, dear, that you are a witch? Or will you keep the truth from him to keep him alive, thereby protecting him from the assassins? How can you live with yourself knowing that your lineage is the cause for his death?"

My temper snapped. I threw a bolt of blue, draining the last drops of water from the vases. My spell caught him in the chest. He twisted and writhed like a man in a hangman's noose as the blue light snaked over the ridge of his shoulder to burrow into his neck. My anger fed the spell, a spell greedy for blood. It pierced his skin at the crook of his neck, and blood poured from the wound.

Fed by the magic in his blood, my power reveled, wanting to suckle the life from him drop-by-bloody-drop. His skin paled and he fell to his knees, stretching an arm to me in supplication.

He rasped, "Stop."

I did not heed his plea. My magic ran rampant, intoxicated with the violence, the blood, the euphoria of power. *The feelings I ran from years ago.*

I pulled back on the spell, tearing it from Alistair's skin, ripping its tendrils from his anatomy. I absorbed the energy, pain arcing through my body while trying to accommodate the excess power.

Inch-by-inch, I reeled in the spell. Stuffing it into my core. Burning my skin from the dynamic exchange.

Alistair clapped a glowing green hand to his neck, his clan rings blazing bright.

"Ruthless as always, Lady Richmond." Alistair stood, wobbling, his neck a bloody mess. I wanted to vomit.

The door connecting my chambers with Richmond opened, and my husband called softly, "Julia?"

"Christ! Of all bloody nights to visit me!" Flinging my hand towards Alistair, I whispered the words for invisibility. Alistair froze, his form disappearing like chocolate syrup covers a dessert.

I did not have a spell to mask the metallic scent of blood; or the energy for an illusion to mask the damage to the room. The fire had burned down to embers, cloaking the room in shadows. It would have to do. I hurried to meet him at the door to his room.

"Here, Richmond."

He stood in the doorway. In contrast to Dupont, he was tall, and his dark hair looked black in the low light. He approached, wearing the same clothes from the earlier festivities, his shirt opened at his throat, and cravat hanging loose. He regarded me for a long moment, then said, "I came to talk, Julia. Please listen."

I glanced at Alistair's hidden form, and felt the pull of my broken spell. *Good.* I hoped he ran from my house as fast as possible. He would pay for attacking me in my room. I turned to my husband. "I am weary, Richmond."

"It will not take long. I wanted to apologize for my behavior this evening. I should not have gotten upset with you. You are my wife, and had every right to question my behavior."

He took my casting hand in his warm palm, his thumb tracing the ridges of my knuckles. He turned my hand over, placing the cold barrel of a gun in my hand. "I want you to keep this with you at all times. Father Morris is concerned about us, what with the witches tonight and all. I know I saw Dupont in the garden."

I closed my hand around the gun. "I will keep it close." *I could have used it ten minutes ago to hit Alistair over the head.*

"I want us to reconcile."

I shook my head. "How do we reconcile, Stephen, when I cannot determine where we parted ways?" I desperately wanted to trust him, and believe his words. I laid my hand on his cheek. "What steals you away from me?" I whispered.

Stephen sighed, with sorrow and weariness evident in the sound. "Please trust me. I cannot tell you what takes me from your side. But it will be over soon. I promise."

He bent to touch his lips to my cheek, a tender caress that broke my heart. "Merry Christmas, Julia." He turned then and exited my room.

Chapter Four

Cold. I awoke to find my room dark, the fire no more than faint embers in the hearth. I shivered, my limbs stiff from sleeping on top of the covers, and was shocked the puddle of tears did not freeze overnight.

I scooted to the top of the bed, climbing under the blankets and fluffing a pillow to support my neck. Warmth returned to my body.

The door opened. Mary's plump form slid into the room, her brown hair tucked neatly into her starched cap. She carried a tray with a fat teapot and china cup, which she placed on the desk near the frosted window. She glanced at the bed, showing surprise on her face. "Oh," she said, "you are awake, Lady. Let me stoke the fire for you."

She took a poker from the holder near the hearth, bending down to tend to the fire. *What a weapon. Why did I not think of that last night?* I wondered. Mary jammed the poker into the pale glowing coals on the hearth. "Did you have a good night last night, Lady?"

Fear prevented me from answering. *My room. It was a disaster*. I had to get Mary out of there so I could clean up.

"I fear I have a headache. Could you go down and fetch me a tinsane for it?"

I knew she hated climbing the stairs more than necessary. Her knees hurt her in the colder months. She appeared irritated, then sighed. "I will be but a moment, Lady Richmond."

She lumbered out the door. As soon as I heard the click of the latch, I threw off the covers, rushing across the cold carpet to the teapot. I eased off the lid. Steam bloomed around my hand, scalding my cold fingers. *Water*. Exactly what I needed.

Fallen plaster from the walls, a dark stain on the carpet that had the metallic tang of old blood, and my chair had lost a leg in the fight with Alistair. Dead blooms from my sacrificed flowers littered the floor. I huddled in the shadow of the hearth. How Mary managed to not notice these things I could not guess, but I thanked providence for the small miracle. I rotated my wrists, working out the soreness in my casting hand, and a faint fizz of blue power popped around my fingertips.

I started with the chair, standing it upright, using the water in the pot to dab at the charred spot on its arm. I positioned the chair closer to the fire, repaired its leg, then used magic to pull the bloodstain from the carpet and burn the residue in the fire. Turning to the walls, I surveyed the hole Alistair blasted through the plaster last night. No fix for it, but a spritz of a spell. Dipping my fingers into the teapot, I coated my right hand with the scalding liquid, using the water to coax power into my skin. Last night, I fought to keep my power contained in my small frame. Today, I had to coax it from its lair like a puppy with a treat. I waited until enough energy lay under my fingertips to properly cast a spell, not wanting to rush the process, but afraid Mary would return before my restorations were complete.

But power has a mind of its own. Especially mine. So I sighed, and waited, keeping my fingers in the teapot, watching the water level drop as my fingers glowed brighter. At last, I threw the spell at the wall, the plaster smoothing into perfection as the light faded.

With no more water and no more magic, I glanced around the room, satisfied most of the damage was concealed. I curled onto the chair, tucking my legs up under my robe.

A knock sounded upon the door. "Come in," I called.

Mary shuffled to my side, balancing a tray in one hand, nudging the door shut with the other. She set the tray beside me on the table. A foul-smelling green concoction filled a pretty china cup. "Thank you for the tinsane, Mary."

"You are welcome, milady."

I cradled the cup in my hands, gulping the bitter liquid in one quaff. Coughing, I set the cup back on the tray, lining it up in the center of the tray's design.

"How was the party last night, Lady Richmond?" She busied herself about the room.

"Very well-attended as usual."

Mary threw two more logs onto the fire, rearranging them with the fireplace tools before replacing them beside the hearth. "All below stairs seems buzzing with news of those two witches causing trouble." She pulled a thin, peach-colored shawl from her apron pocket. "I found this when I was cleaning up this morning. One of the guests must have left it. I thought maybe you would recognize it and return it to the proper owner."

I took the garment from Mary, instantly feeling the witch power in its weave. Vivian's wrap, perhaps? "Thank you, and I will have this forwarded. As to the witches," I continued, "I do not recall them being on the guest list."

She wiped her hands on her white apron, leaving dark smudges on the starched fabric. "I knew you and the master would not tolerate such nonsense, and I said so."

Fear filled my chest, making my heart beat faster. "Who were you speaking with, Mary?"

She busied herself around the room. "Just the other servants, Lord Sebastian's man, the lower chambermaid." She fingered the dead blooms in the vase beside the bed. "You are the lady, and as such, you of course, can do what you want, but these flowers are not meant to stand the drafts in these rooms. It seems a waste of a fine flower, it does." She collected all the blooms, bundling them into her apron. "I'll just take these down to the kitchens."

"Thank you."

I pulled my thick wrap closer around my shoulders. Richmond, Vicar Morris and I were traveling in the coach to St. Michael's Church for Christmas service. The church was one mile away, but the streets were clotted with traffic, making the journey interminable. Richmond lounged beside me on the leather seats, the spicy cedar of his cologne a pleasant counterpoint to Vicar Morris's musty smell that was reminiscent of old books and damp cellars. The father's cloak appeared new, no doubt from our patronage, with shiny buttons at the throat showcasing his clean-shaven face. His lack of a beard accentuated the sharp lines of his cheeks. He clutched a small Bible in his slender hands, the edges frayed with use.

"I have never seen traffic as heavy as this for Christmas mass," Richmond said.

"It is a testament to these troubled times that people fear for their souls as never before," Vicar Morris replied, clutching his book tighter.

The coach lurched to a stop, and I braced myself on the seat to prevent my toppling onto the floor. Richmond curled his arm around me, keeping me perched on the seat. *He said he did not trust witches. How will he ever accept me?*

"Whatever do you mean?" I asked, fidgeting on the hard seat.

"You know of what I speak." He lowered his voice as if the holy angels took offense at his vocal volume. "It's the witches that are driving people to the church."

"Poppycock!" laughed Richmond. "It is the need to be seen in church with the newest bonnet, or the latest bauble that drives most to Christmas service. One does not need to worship on consecrated ground to be pious." He flicked a piece of lint off his pants. "The government has the witch problem under control."

"The government cannot save your soul." Vicar Morris wagged his finger at him. "Do not let the Bishop mistake your jocularity, sir. I know you and Lady Richmond to be God-fearing people, following the guidance of the church, but others are not so open at casual comments."

I shuddered. "You make it sound like the Inquisition has returned."

He nodded. "There are some in the church who believe those methods are needed to flush out the demon brethren." He ran his finger around the starched collar at his throat. "The two from last night would benefit from a strict lesson in morality. They were unsanctioned."

I answered, "We certainly did not invite them. I hope this does not cause issue with the Bishop."

He leaned closer, his gaze intent. "These are dangerous times, Lady Richmond. Care is required." He paused, drumming his fingers on his Bible. "Some persuasion is necessary to elicit a confession. I have seen the exorcism of two witches and cannot tell you the evils of what they revealed."

Richmond shifted in his seat, his arm tightening around me. "I would hope my work with the Admiralty would offer some protection from the church's interest."

I considered his words. *Exactly what was he doing for the government?*

The vicar wagged his finger, admonishing my husband. "All are in danger. It is our duty to turn in any suspected witch for questioning by more experienced authorities than we." His gaze, normally warm and inviting, frightened me now. "You are a trusting soul, Lady Richmond, but I caution you to remove yourself from all association with Mr. Dupont. He is currently under watch for suspicious activity."

My heart skipped a beat. Alistair in London was not only a physical threat to me, but his very presence was an opportunity to expose me to the church. One night in my house, one careless comment to Vicar Morris, and I would also be under suspicion.

"It is true that I do not care for Mr. Dupont, and I have dissociated myself from his company since our broken engagement. He spoke with me last night to tell me news from home. My father is ill, and on his deathbed." I clasped my hands together in my lap.

He nodded. "Thank you for clarifying your relationship. Remember the church's role in these times is for salvation and protection. Do not hesitate to inform me of any irregular activity."

"I will."

We alighted at the front steps of a tan stone building. St. Michael's Church dated from the 1400s, a testament to the beauty of medieval architecture on a smaller scale than the cathedrals of the time. Sculptures flanked the sides of the church, and the wooden double doors were wide open to receive the Christmas

Day worshippers. Throngs of people filed inside, a few flaunting new bonnets as Richmond suggested.

The original stained glass windows portrayed the usual characters, Jesus and Mary, in vivid colors, but there were twelve smaller windows along the east and west walls, chronicling stories from the Old Testament. My favorite was near the altar, beside Moses holding the Commandments. It was a depiction of David and Goliath, in beautiful teals, greens and golds, with Goliath tall and armored, appearing invincible. David was in the left corner, tiny in scale, with a small rock of brown in his hand.

Richmond guided me to our pew, three back from the front. The stone floors and plain walls were silent witnesses to countless baptisms, funerals and weddings. I loved this church more than the whitewashed wooden building on Nevis serving God's will.

Vicar Morris took his post at the altar, clearing his throat to quiet the talkative crowd. The service began, and as he directed us to remember the lessons of Jesus's birth, I surveyed the crowd.

There were the usual Sunday attendants, another day of improving upon God's devotion, as well as many faces I did not recognize. Lady Sutton sat in the pew behind us, with an enormous yellow hat, at odds with the winter colors worn by everyone else. I glanced over my shoulder as a murmur rose from the back of the church, a disturbance loud enough to cause the choir to start late into the hymn. However, the monstrous concoction on Lady Sutton's head blocked my view, and I craned my neck to see around her, not wanting to appear vulgar.

Richmond and I spotted her at the same instant. He stilled. My mouth dropped open.

Lady Sutton hissed behind me, "The nerve of her. She looks like she just left a brothel. I've never seen her in church before. I do hope she sits on the other side of the aisle."

Madame Oualie swayed down the center aisle, her black velvet corset tight enough to push her breasts over the bodice, globes jiggling with each step. Her black hat was jauntily perched on loose, auburn curls. Without a word, she captured the attention of every person in the room. I narrowed my eyes as she continued her steady sway up the aisle. Deep inside, my weakened power awakened, stretching within my bones.

She wiggled her fingers at me as she stopped at our pew. "Excuse moi, is there room for moi?" Her loud whisper turned heads all around. Madame Oualie tapped the wooden seat. "May I sit down? I do not want to miss any of the good father's lesson today."

Richmond did not look at her, but slid closer to me, making way for her to sit on the end of the pew. She sat closer to him than was proper, mere inches separating her and my husband. My power roiled to life.

"The nerve of her!" Lady Sutton whispered behind me, her finger jabbing my shoulder. "Are you going let her sit in your family pew and do nothing? After the way she threw herself at your husband?"

Richmond's back was a straight as a board, looking uncomfortable. He stared at Vicar Morris. I felt unsettled in her presence. *If only I had not dueled Alistair last night. If only I were in better condition.*

She smiled sweetly, placing her hands in her lap.

Vicar Morris cleared his throat from the altar. "We have a special service today on this day of celebration. As you are aware, we reserve time for baptisms and re-affirmations of God's hand in our life for this special day. Today, we shall witness the conversion of a witch to Christianity."

A collective gasp rose from the congregation. A muscle in Richmond's cheek twitched. I craned my neck, seeking another exit if I were the witch in question. After the vicar's words in the coach, paranoia caused me to panic.

From the other end of the pew, Madame Oualie' power stirred, rolling from her in waves, like the tide. I imagined a wall around me, like a breakwater, preventing her energy from touching my skin. It was a small spell, one children learned in elementary casting, and which did not require water for energy. It would not last long, but managed to give me surcease from her nasty assault. Her power felt *wrong*.

Vicar Morris announced, "Here is the heathen witch!" People in the front pew flinched.

A thin woman, no more than fifteen years old, was led from the sacristy between two portly men in brown robes. Her dress hung from bony shoulders, her blond hair greasy and unkempt. She stumbled up the steps, before being pushed into a kneeling position in front of the altar. I scooted to the edge of my seat, horror and fascination with the tableau on the altar capturing my attention.

Vicar Morris smiled, raising his hands above his head, nodding towards Madame Oualie. She waved at the father, giggling when the girl shrank from the touch of his hand to her head.

"Dearest Lord, please consider the plea for salvation of this wretched soul, Miss Chloe Longood, self-professed practitioner of witchcraft."

He paused, the uneasy noises from the congregation echoing eerily along the stonewalls. My stomach twisted.

"Stand, wretched one, and confess your crimes."

The friars pulled the sobbing girl to her feet. Her dress was too big, and the bodice gaped open at the chest. She pulled the dress closed, clutching her hands at her neck.

Her power hit me like a throw from a horse. Raw, sharp, and very earthy.

The friars jerked her hands cruelly behind her back. She shrank from them, crying out against their abuse.

Vicar Morris slapped her face. "Speak! Tell us, creature, what you have done?"

"I want to do the Lord's bidding. I am a child of the Lord, dedicated to this earth." Her answer was difficult to hear, her breath coming in great, raspy sobs.

What could she have done to deserve this?

Vicar Morris slapped her face again, the force of the blow snapping her head back. "Tell them where we found you, selling your evil!"

A trickle of blood from the corner of her mouth slid down her chin. "I do not know where you found me. It was somewhere in the city. I have never been to London before."

Vicar Morris turned to face the pews. "Brethren of the church found her walking the streets near the docks, offering her spells to anyone passing by. Evil spells, devoid of godly moderation." He paused, lowering his voice. "Spells of unspeakable intent on the corruption of the innocent. Unsanctioned spells."

Utter silence from the congregation.

He signaled to the friars, who pulled the girl to her feet. "Do you swear on the holiness of God's word contained herein that you will recant all witchcraft? Or face the gallows?" His face beamed with excitement, as if he hoped she chose the latter.

She straightened, her voice low, but steady so that I strained to hear her words. "I have sworn to lead a godly life. I will no longer offer my spells for sale."

Murmurs of unease rose from the congregation. He pulled back from the girl, brushing his robes and nodding to the friars. "In accordance with the church, we require Miss Longood to drink holy water. If she is insincere in her recantations of witchcraft, the holy water will reveal her true nature." He handed her a chalice. She clutched the cup between shaky hands, gulping the liquid in loud swallows. She handed the cup back to the clergyman, wiping the back of her mouth with her hand.

Miss Longood spoke. "I recant all practice of black magic and devilish witchcraft."

The church was as silent as the ancient stones lining its walls.

Madame Oualie rose and waved a handkerchief, as if hailing a cab.

"Excuse moi, but I have a comment, non?"

Vicar Morris squinted at the crowd. "Ah, Madame Oualie! What is your comment?"

"I think we need to have a Christian soul take in the chit, non? Teach her godly ways so she does not return to witchcraft. A mentor, I believe, is the proper English term."

Miss Longood froze, fear visible in her countenance. She clutched the arms of the friars beside her. "Please, allow me to choose my mentor."

Lady Sutton jabbed her finger into my shoulder, speaking loud enough for the entire pew to hear. "Since when is a French hussy a good Christian model?"

Madame Oualie grinned slyly. "I would be happy to take in the chit. I find I have much spare time on my hands." Her power rolled again.

"No! Not her!" Miss Longood turned her head from side-to-side, like a mouse trapped in the corner, trying to escape the cat. Her gaze landed on me. "Her!

The one with the red dress. I want to be with her!"

Chapter Five

I shrank down into the pew, wishing I'd worn a nondescript brown twill for the service today. It bothered me she could sense I was a witch; I worked hard to keep my nature a secret from everyone.

Vicar Morris shook his head. "Lady Richmond is very busy and cannot be bothered to rehabilitate one such as you."

"Please! I want Lady Richmond!"

"Hush, girl! You are lucky a good woman like Madame Oualie is willing to help you." He nodded to the friars, who grabbed the struggling girl and pulled her down the aisle. Madame Oualie stood and turned on her heel, swaying out of the church, ignoring the gasps and comments from the congregation as she passed. Their footfalls chimed like the beat of an executioner's drum on the marble floor. Miss Longood resisted, straightening out her legs to slow their progress, while pleading with her captors. "Please release me! I will go with anyone else, but her! She is a devil!"

I could not tolerate the girl's distress any longer. I stood, ready to do *something*, but Richmond wrenched me back into my seat, leaning over to scold me.

"Do not draw attention to yourself."

I regarded the struggling girl, concern knotting in my stomach. I wanted to help her, but I did not know how. Irritated at my impotence, I ignored the rest of the service, standing automatically with the rest of the congregants.

At the end of the service, the vicar waved us over to him. "Lord Richmond! Lady Richmond! A moment, please!"

Richmond replied, "We should speak with him." He guided me out of the crowd to an alcove off the western wall. Vicar Morris seemed ebullient.

"How did you like the service?"

Richmond replied, "Quite unconventional for a Christmas service. Or any service, for that matter."

Vicar Morris opened his mouth like a landed fish. "But, milord, with the government actions to round up the heathen brethren for exorcism, I though you would approve." His eyes were sly. "Being a government man yourself."

I remained still. The clergyman had always struck me as a kind, bumbling man of the cloth. My perspective now shifted, seeing instead, a man willing to disgrace Christmas service for a show of power and influence.

Richmond adjusted his cuffs, a picture of nonchalance. "I think the general public doesn't have the stomach for your display. That is why I object to your integration of this into the sermon."

"But, milord, it is a mandate from the Bishop. It is church creed. She is unsanctioned."

Richmond tightened his grip on my arm. "I understand. But the church needs to be cognizant of the appetites of the masses for its work. Slapping that girl only made the crowd more sympathetic to her."

The vicar nodded. "I see your dealings with politics is helpful in the presentation of our new church practice. These are things we did not consider." He narrowed his eyes at Richmond. "No one believed our congregation would be sympathetic to a witch."

"That is precisely why you need to keep these dealings in private. Control the public perception of what a witch does. Use your contacts in the witch community to secretly deal with the problem."

Infiltration into the London witch community? Secret church practices? Maybe my comment about the Inquisition was more correct than I knew.

Richmond placed his hat on his head, adding , "We can continue this discussion at another time. Lady Richmond and I have many visits to make today, so please excuse us. Merry Christmas."

"Good day, Lord Richmond, Lady Richmond." He hurried off into the shadows of the church.

Richmond pulled me towards the doors. I hurried to match his pace. Our coach was one of the last in line, the family crest on the side distinctive among the plain black vehicles. When it pulled up to the doors, Richmond vaulted me into the interior. He braced his capable hands on the frame, ready to pull himself into the carriage, when the coachman called out. Richmond turned to speak to the young man twisting his cap in his hands.

"Pardon, milord, but there is an overturned carriage on Wepping Street. We need to take the route closer to the river to get home." He peered at my husband. "If it pleases milord."

"Fine. But get us home as quickly as you can."

He was in a dark mood, and seemed pensive. I arranged my skirts meticulously on the seats, uncertain of what to say. The coach lurched, pulling into traffic. Richmond positioned himself to peer out the window. I closed my eyes, thinking of Nevis, and demons, and orphaned witches.

We rode thusly, quiet in our thoughts, until Richmond broke the silence.

"I do not like this, Julia."

"That girl's distress bothered me as well."

His blue gaze met mine, the force of his feelings staggering. "No. I do not like that she pointed you out to the congregation. It places us under suspicion."

I picked at imaginary lint on my dress. "I have nothing to hide. The church can investigate as much as it wants."

Richmond leaned over to me, grasping my hands and squeezing them tight. "Julia, the church does not make a full investigation into these matters. It is the words of a few minds against our protestations of innocence. We will not win such a battle. They are looking for examples, not necessarily the truth." He turned to gaze outside the window again.

"What in God's name?" he muttered. I leaned over to peer out the window as well.

Richmond pounded on the carriage wall, and John opened the panel between the post and the interior. "Yes, Lord Richmond?"

"Stop the carriage."

"Yes, milord."

John pulled the carriage to a stop, and Richmond flung open the doors, leaping to the street.

I followed him.

He shouldered his way through the gathering crowd. We were near the river, and the smell of sewage and fish mixed in the air to turn my stomach. A small crowd gathered at the edge of the road. I wiggled between the onlookers to get a view of the attraction.

Two bodies, those of a man and a woman, lay bloated on the ground. Her face was covered with stringy locks of wet hair. His face was frozen, eyes open, fear permanently etched on his visage. Their bodies were swollen, with little missing pieces of flesh where the fish had nibbled on their cheeks. They must not have been in the river too long, for their faces were still identifiable.

It was the two young witches from the party. The ones setting off fireworks spells in my garden.

Richmond knelt on the ground, unmindful of the stench or puddles of dirty water streaming from the corpses. He gently touched the girl's face, turning her neck from side-to-side, feeling along her limbs. He repeated the maneuver on the young man as the murmurs of the crowd grew louder around us.

He stood. "I am Lord Richmond. I have five gold pieces for any man who can remove these bodies for a proper church burial. I will pay the costs if their families are not located."

A slender man stepped forward, his waistcoat stained, with a new-looking watch hanging from a fob on his chest. A pickpocket, to be sure. He said, "I will be happy to assist, Lord Richmond. Five gold pieces is a generous offer for the transport of two bodies, but I must require a deposit against the funeral costs."

Richmond sighed, pulling more coins from his pocket. "Here are seven gold pieces, and please send a report to Richmond House when the task is finished. There may be more money for you if you can give me any information as to how these two ended up in the Thames." He clinked the coins together in his palm.

The man fingered the watch on his coat, eyeing the money. "Done." He held out his hand. Richmond placed the coins in his hand, and the pickpocket's fingers grasped the coins tightly in his fist.

With the exchange, the crowd dispersed, and we climbed into the carriage again.

"I need to go to the Admiralty office," Richmond said.

My teeth worried my lower lip, biting at the tender skin. "I hoped we could spend some time together."

He took his watch out of its pocket, flipping open the engraved cover, the inscription worn thin with the rubbing of his thumb over the lettering. A gift from his brother before he went to sea, it was one of his prized possessions. He consulted the thin hands before clicking the lid shut. "I have no choice in the matter, Julia. Forces beyond my control dictate my actions today."

He gazed out the window. "Stay away from him if you can, Julia."

"I have nothing to fear from the church."

He straightened his cuffs. "We all have secrets, Julia. I am charged with finding out some of them."

He rapped on the carriage roof, signaling the driver to stop.

Opening the door, he leaped into the foot traffic and snowy slush. I shivered in the draft of chilly air, pulling my wrap closer about me. I hoped my secrets were not the ones my husband intended to research.

I fretted about my room, pondering Alistair's challenge. Demons were best dealt with by the entire strength of a clan. One individual against a demon could fall prey to its siren calls, its promise of power, its devilry. A group of witches stood stronger when resisting the call to evil. That is why only the clan leaders typically called demons, and the actual process was a secret, handed down from generation to generation. It was too dangerous for any witch with a grievance to go sodding off and calling a dance of demons on their enemy.

My head pounded with the beginnings of a headache, and I rested it on my hands. How to banish a demon without the safety of a group? Except for another clan, the only other authority on demons was the church. I couldn't go to the church; that was asking for extermination.

Or was it?

Sebastian, Richmond's younger brother, attended Oxford and studied the religious arts, intending to enter the clergy. I certainly had access to his library; he lived with us. Now all I needed was to ensure he was absent to fully peruse his collections of books. I might find a volume to start my education on demons.

Energized by my plan, I hurried across the chamber to sneak open the door, peering into the gallery.

Silence.

I bustled along the gallery to the east wing of the mansion. Here, Sebastian maintained his bachelor quarters, remote from those of Richmond and me. Casting a look around, I opened the door and scooted inside his rooms.

For all his grandiose methods in dress, Sebastian was a spartan man. No Persian rug for him, just the enduring beauty of the hardwood floors. A simple cross hung on the wall beside sketches by Sebastian's hand. The west wall was covered in books from Sebastian's personal collection. These were my intended target.

I ran a finger along the spines, my heart pounding at the prospect of discovery. The last thing Richmond or I needed was the servants talking about me traipsing around his brother's rooms.

"Botany, archery, *The History of Rome*, Caesar's Gallic tales, Renaissance poetry. Is there any order to this man's collection?" I talked to myself, the cadence of my voice soothing my taut nerves.

"Geometry, really, Sebastian? Italian architecture, Homer, Life and Times of Egyptian Pharaohs, *The Taming of the Shrew*. This will take all day." The books, unlike the order of the room, were a mess, shelved in haphazard fashion, some upright, some lying on their sides, some stuffed behind others.

After twenty minutes of eye-crossed searching, I found a section with predominantly religious themes.

Three copies of the Bible, two treatises on the soul, and a collection of Sir Thomas More flanked a medium black book with gold lettering in the spine.

"*The Demonic Circles of Hell.* That sounds promising." I plucked the volume from the shelf and re-arranged the remaining books to disguise the breach.

Footsteps sounded in the hall. Panicked, I glanced around the room for a hiding place, but none were evident. The treads were heavy, steady, relentless, and coming towards my location.

Nothing a little witchcraft could not help. Clutching the book, I pushed power to my casting hand and swept it in an arc over my head and body. Before my eyes, my arms and bodice disappeared, my skirts turned transparent, and my shoes were the last to dissolve from sight. I plastered myself against the far wall, holding the book tightly to my chest. The key to invisibility spells was no movement. If I moved, it would appear as a shimmer along the background, and a sure invitation to discovery.

Sebastian entered the room, his boots crusted with snow, followed by his man, Phillip. "My Lord, may I help you remove your shoes? They are a mess."

Sebastian shook his head. "I know, I walked from the seminary chapel home. It is a bracing day."

"Sir! You will catch your death of a lung affliction! Please be more circumspect in the future of your health. You are the heir in line, as long as your brother has no issue."

"Stephen's issue is no concern of mine. I don't want the position. He and Lady Richmond can die childless. I will not take the earldom."

Phillip tutted and clucked as he worked to remove the dirty boots. "Milord says this now, but consider the future, sir. Anything can happen."

The audacity of the man! I wanted to put a power bolt through his throat for even thinking about discussing Richmond's or my circumstances. I filled my lungs with huge gulps of air to calm myself. Of course, people would talk about our lack of children. Richmond and I had not even tried to have a child. We were careful, not that it was Sebastian's business.

Calmer now, I concentrated on maintaining the illusion, for Sebastian showed no signs of exiting his room. Phillip fussed around him, offering him a velvet jacket and pipe. Sebastian settled the green coat over his shoulders, then shooed Phillip away. "Leave me, I have some correspondence to attend to this afternoon."

Phillip straightened his master's shirt cuffs with a tug before turning for the door. "Happy holiday, sir."

Sebastian nodded. "Same to you, Phillip."

My head ached from maintaining the invisibility illusion. On Nevis, my sisters and I held competitions to determine who could hold the spell the longest, like children holding their breaths underwater. I always won. It was simply a matter of properly applying the concentrative powers of the mind. I now focused on the cross opposite the room from me as a focal point, repeating words and phrases in my mind.

Sebastian settled at his desk, rifling through papers. The irregular, scratchy sound of his quill wrecked my focus, and the book weighed heavier in my arms with each breath. I glanced at the floor, the tips of my shoes now becoming visible.

Panicked, I pushed more power into my casting hand, and the shoes vanished from sight again. Richmond told me once of men in India, practitioners of yoga, who could contort their bodies into shapes and hold them for minutes on end, gaining peace and enlightenment from the exercise. He said it was a wonder to behold. I felt like one of those men, except I was certain neither peace nor enlightenment awaited me at the end of my spell.

Eyes locked on the cross, I pulled power from the marrow of my bones, my legs shaking. Most duels were a combination of quick bursts of power, tempered with spaces in which to catch your breath. This constant drag and consumption depleted me to the point where I wondered if I had any power left.

Sebastian continued with his scratchy quill, and I decided to buy him a new one for next Christmas. A knock sounded at the door, startling me. I juggled the heavy book in my hands, my elbow cracking against the plaster wall.

Sebastian stared at my location. I froze, my body awkwardly bent, holding the demon book.

Another knock sounded on the chamber door. Sebastian rose and opened the portal. Jameson stood there with an envelope in his hands. "For you, sir. Delivered by a runner a few moments ago. He said it was of utmost importance that you view it today."

Sebastian tore into the envelope. I could not see any address from my stance against the wall, but the missive must have been urgent, for Sebastian threw the letter into the fire. Stirring the ashes with a poker before cinching a brace of pistols around his hips, he rushed for the door.

With the click of the lock, I collapsed into a puddle on the floor. I thanked whatever immediate need managed to remove Sebastian from his quarters. Resting my head against the wall, I shook my arms and legs to drive out the tingling from my limbs.

Using the wall as leverage, I pushed onto my feet. Unsteady legs propelled me to the door. The hallway was empty. Hefting the tome in my hands, I returned to my rooms, thankfully, not meeting a servant or another soul along the way.

Once safely within my quarters, I searched for a place to hide the book. I promised to visit Louise today and the day was growing shorter. I fit the book with a modicum of difficulty into the drawer of my writing desk, easily pulling open the drawer with my spell this time. Flicking my wrist, a thin line of blue power settled into the lock, ensuring protection for the contents within.

Pulling the bell, I summoned Mary. She entered moments later, face red, and her chest heaving.

"You rang, milady? Those stairs will be the death of me, to be sure."

"I am visiting with Lady Gladstone this afternoon. What do you think of the green brocade?"

Mary removed the dress from the wardrobe, shaking out the folds. "A good choice, milady." Within the span of twenty minutes, I was redressed and ready for an enjoyable afternoon with my friend, if I could only leave my troubles at home.

I twisted Vivian's shawl tighter around my casting hand. Wind witches were almost extinct for several reasons, one being that they could track another witch by following the trail of a spell. I did not know what Vivian's shawl would reveal, but I had to try.

I stood in my back garden, reticule full, a goatskin of water for fuel, and soaked in the sensation of her power. It was fading with her death, so I had to strain to keep the tendril of energy in sight. A thin, red line smoked out from my hand, dancing in the breeze. I followed it, a trail that led out from my back garden, turning right, and towards the river. I tried to appear as if I were on a walk about the town, but the spell kept ducking in and out of alleyways. From that, I deduced

Vivian and presumably, Jeremy, must've been trying to stay hidden once they left my house.

Continuing thusly, down Wicking Street, I turned east along the river, several blocks from the wharves. This part of town was seedier and much rougher, and the trail led straight down the center of the road.

Until it stopped outside a tavern called The Prancing Pony.

Spinning in a circle, I concentrated on the shawl wrapped around my hand. It was cold, and a light rain had begun to fall. Redoubling my efforts, and using the rain for power, I saw a pink tendril, so faint as to be transparent, leaking from my hand and pointing across the street, to a boarding house.

I got out of the cold, and rang the bell. A child of no more than ten answered the door, staring up at me with round, brown eyes. "All we have is the one room, but it is being cleaned. You will have to wait." His gaze flicked behind me. "And if you have bags, you will need to bring them up yourself. Mama is in with a gentleman, and cannot be bothered."

I smiled at the girl. "I just wanted to return this to one of your boarders."

"Oh. Then come in."

Inside, the room was shabby, but clean, with beige wallpap-er barely clinging to the walls. A small fire burned in the hearth, and a single flight of narrow stairs curved upwards and out of view to the right of a desk. It was here the girl led me, her shoes catching on the hem of her too-long, wool dress.

"Here is the ledger. Tell me what room your friend is in, and I can take her things for you."

"Her name is Vivian."

The girl blushed, and pushed the ledger closer to me. "I can't read. You'll have to do it."

I glanced at the names, whispering under my breath a spell to locate Vivian. I found her name, Vivian Merchant, single occupant, room seven."

"Room seven."

The girl shrank back as if slapped. "Mama won't let me go in that room. You can take it up if you want."

I trudged up the stairs, stopping on the second floor. Room seven was down the hall, the last room on the left. A window at the end of the passage overlooked the back of the dwelling, and I could see the masts of ships swaying over the rooftops.

Touching my hand to the doorknob, a searing bolt of power shot down my arm, temporarily blinding me. Blinking my eyes, I sucked on my injured fingers and squinted at the doorframe. Etched in the frame were symbols I did not recognize, but knew they clearly meant "No witches allowed here." I dropped Vivian's shawl, and touched the knob again, receiving another shot of painful magic.

I studied the runes in the door, trying to dredge up any recollection of how to get past them. It was at times like this that I wished for a good, basic spellbook.

Sighing, I turned and went back to the desk. I dropped the shawl off on the ledger, saying to the girl, "No one was in. When she returns, please give this to her." I knew Vivian would never need it again, but I was not about to tell that to a little girl.

The girl nodded, glancing to her right. A door was open, and I could hear voices rising from inside the room. One I recognized instantly was my husband's.

"How can it be? This is supposed to be a safe house. Put the security into place."

"I will not have it with my girl roaming around. You can find another boarding house if those are your terms."

I smiled at the little girl, gently feeling for the thrum of her witch power. It was like a faint singing in a high wind, far off and protected. I doubt I could have felt it unless I was standing right beside her.

Satisfied, I thanked her for her help, and left before my husband realized I was there.

Lounging in Lady Gladstone's parlor an hour later, I noticed how the warm tones of the fabrics that covered the delicate furniture blended smoothly with the maize color of the walls. For such a frilly person, Louise decorated her private rooms with few knick-knacks except the porcelains she collected.

A small box wrapped with a festive bow perched on the table beside me, a holiday token for my friend. Louise sat across from me, allowing me the chair closest to the fire. On the coffee table between us, a mountain of warm scones and a hot pot of tea dispelled any sad thoughts from my head. I popped another bite of scone in my mouth, the confection melting into buttery goodness on my tongue.

"If we were not such close friends, Louise, I would have no hesitation in stealing your cook from your kitchens. Her scones are delightful."

Louise sat beside me, sipping her drink before placing it precisely on the saucer with a small clink. "One of the few good decisions my husband made was hiring her. Now, tell me what happened Christmas night. I have never seen you so upset."

I wondered how much of my tale to burden Louise with. I certainly could not tell her the entire truth. *My ex-fiancé hid in my bedroom to tell me my father is being possessed by a demon?* Not a proper topic for tea, no matter how dear the friend.

"Richmond ordered the staff to present me with my Christmas present moments before the party began." My voice wavered on the lie. "I admit I have a temper, and it got the better of me. I am ashamed I caused anyone distress over such a trivial matter."

She patted my hand. "I'd be upset as well. Men are obtuse unless it is discussing the best plans for investment, or the outfitting of a ship."

We sat in silence until the last scone disappeared from my plate. Licking my fingers, I continued. "Richmond wants a reconciliation. Perhaps an heir."

She nodded in agreement. "Very responsible of him. That is the point of marriage, after all. That's our Richmond."

"I want that too, but I can't see how to get there."

"Whatever do you mean? The mechanics of the situation should be obvious by now."

I snorted. "I don't mean *that*." I pondered the fire, searching for the right way to tell her how I felt. "I know a lot of marriages are arranged, but ours was a love match." I clenched my fist. "I expect arranged marriages to falter after the duty is done, but I eloped with him, at sea, in direct defiance of my father. I have never failed at anything in my life, and it makes me feel awful to know my father may have been right. What if I did make an impetuous mistake?"

Louise interrupted. "Falling in love with a good man is no mistake. That is providence bestowing a gift. Richmond is a decent sort."

Uncomfortable with my feelings, I steered the conversation toward lighter themes. I handed her the small box. "Speaking of gifts. I hope this brings you joy."

She ripped open the paper and cooed at the gift, a small painting of the roses in my garden, a spot she loved to visit in summer. "Julia, it is lovely! Now I can show my gardener why I love your rose garden so much. Thank you."

"You are welcome."

She placed the painting on the settee. "You seem distracted today."

"An unwelcome visit from my old fiancé, Mister Alistair Dupont, brought distressing news of my father. He is in poor health."

"I'm sorry."

"We did not part on good terms, you see, when Richmond and I married." Guilty anger and wounded pride colored my tone.

"Ah, and now the pangs of conscience infiltrate your mind. It is always so with unhappy partings."

"I feel I must go to him as a daughter's duty."

"Yes. The deathbed reconciliation. You are too nice a person to tell him to go to the devil and stay in London. It would be easier for you if he lived in Kent, instead of halfway around the world."

My heart felt heavy with her droll words. "Richmond will not approve of a visit to my family. I am afraid to ask his permission to go. If he says no, I feel I must go anyway. The strain will be too much on our fragile relationship."

"He would keep you from your father?"

"Yes. He is afraid of my family. They threatened him with all sorts of awful things for marrying me."

"But you are a woman, and something he wants. I see this as a capital time to ask a favor."

"I cannot!"

"Dear, it is not illegal to bargain with a spouse. You are not stepping outside the bounds of propriety."

"I do not think I can do that. I want things to be the way they were in the beginning, when we first married. Bedroom blackmail is not the way to achieve my goal." I plopped two spoonfuls of sugar into my tea, stirring until the gritty scrapes disappeared.

"Tell him you want approval to visit Nevis in exchange for an heir."

"That seems reasonable for you to suggest, but bargaining like that over a potential child is not what I envisioned."

Louise cocked her eyebrow. "Yes. But at least you have a husband who is willing to listen, and to try."

"As long as Madame Oualie is not in the room," I blurted out. "I want to tell her to leave us alone. I cannot abide to see her red hair, or even hear her name." I added in a whisper, "He seemed so happy with her."

Louise reached over, grasping my hand, and giving it a tight squeeze. "Listen to your words, Julia. You are distraught. I do not think this is the best time to confront an odious woman like her."

I thought of poor Chloe Longood. "It may be the only time to confront her. Louise, what did you think about the service today?"

Louise's face set into serious lines. "Appalling. I plan to write a letter to the Bishop."

"Richmond said much the same." We passed a few moments in silence before I added, "Would you forgive your husband's behavior?"

Her mouth thinned, and her lips pressed together before she answered. "My husband is a conniving bastard without any capability of remorse. Very different from Richmond." She stared into the fire. Shaking her brown mood, she continued. "When will you sail, if you convince Richmond?" A smile dimpled her cheeks.

"As soon as the weather allows. Mr. Dupont indicated it was a wasting disease in advanced stages." I drained the last drop of tea from my cup. "I do not know if Father will receive me."

"A father's love is greater than what you give him credit for, dear."

"No, I am a commodity in my father's eyes, one that did not behave properly. He would crow with his righteousness. I do not think I can stand it."

"Life is full of uncertainty. You must do what you feel is right."

"Then I will apply myself to persuading my husband to allow me to visit Nevis."

"I wish you safe journey."

I stood to leave. "Thank you for the lovely afternoon."

Louise grasped my sleeve. "Can you stay a few more moments? A man sent word he may have news of Lord Gladstone, and I want you present, if you would." Concern clouded her face. "I don't want to be alone if it is bad news."

"How do you keep hope alive?"

"I don't. Let us be clear, Julia. Ours was not a love match, and never could be. My husband would lie as soon as tell the truth. A part of me is ashamed that he is gone and hopes he stays away for good. Another, more Christian part of my soul, however, wishes him no harm, and hopes we could come to an arrangement."

"An arrangement?"

She sighed. "I know your feelings on infidelity, but is it wrong to want companionship? He's been gone three years. Three years of my life, wasted, waiting for a man that, in truth, I wish were dead. I do not fool myself to think he is waiting for me as well."

"What will this agent bring?"

"I do not know, but I hope it is the witness of his death or a decree for divorce. I cannot fathom tolerating anything else. I know you must think ill of me, but I am honest."

A sharp rap on the door. "Milady?"

"Yes?"

"A Lord Souter is here."

"Please show him in." She clutched my hand. "Please stay."

A tall man, slender, with a plain face was shown into the parlor. He gave a passable bow, then cleared his throat. His hair was ebony, falling straight to his shoulders, with a gray streak from the roots to the tips on the right.

"Welcome, Lord Souter. This is my good friend, Lady Richmond."

"Good day. Lady Gladstone, I hope you are well. I landed in Dover and sent word as soon as possible. I apologize for the rush, but I am pressed for time."

Louise inclined her head in acknowledgement. "I thank you for your promptness."

"I have distressing news, and want to caution you as to who may know." His gaze landed on me.

Louise answered, "Thank you for your reticence, Lord Souter, but Lady Richmond is my dearest friend. Surely, if you know this information, she can be privy as well."

"Certainly. I have returned from St. Christopher's on a trip for the West India Company. During a storm, we were blown off course. The ship was damaged, and we made port in a difficult place to make repairs."

"What place, sir? I am from those regions." I asked.

"Tortola."

"Oh. Rough indeed. It has a nefarious reputation."

"Well deserved in my estimation, Lady Richmond." His gaze returned to Louise. "I have seen your husband."

Her hands shook. "What are you saying, sir? He is alive?"

"Most assuredly." He handed a folio of papers to her, wrapped in leather. "He implored me to deliver these as expeditiously as possible."

Louise fingered the folio. "What are these?"

"A decree for divorce, Madame, if I may be blunt. You may need to make other arrangements." His gaze traveled around the luxuriously appointed room.

The fire popped and hissed in the grate, the sound roaring in the unnatural quiet. Louise read the papers deliberately, her brow wrinkling as the stack grew smaller. Finishing the documents, she handed them back to Lord Souter, who stuffed them into his coat.

"I understand. This house was owned through my mother, so it is not part of a dowry or otherwise entailed. But all the other properties belong to Gladstone. Thank you, Lord Souter."

Pity colored his gaze. "I understand the papers are not final until both parties are present to sign them in front of a barrister."

Louise clutched my arm. "Where, sir, do you recall seeing my husband last?"

Lord Souter cleared his throat. "Off Tortola, running from a Spanish galleon, flying the flag of a privateer."

"Dear Lord, how will I find him to finalize the papers? This is worse than before!"

Lord Souter glanced around the room, as if some chair or settee may have offered him cover from the emotional outburst. "I am sorry we met under these circumstances, but I felt it was the right thing to allow you some notice. I have orders from Lord Gladstone to announce the decree. It will be in the papers." He paused, considering the documents in his hands. "If you give me the direction of your lawyer, I can have these copied to him."

He tipped his hat to me. "Good day, ladies." He paused, considering me. "Ah, Lady Richmond. You are Lord Nesbit's daughter?"

"Yes."

"Forgive me for imposing, but I heard he is in poor health. I hope he recovers."

"Thank you. I plan on traveling to see him soon."

"It is a quick crossing this time of year, the trade winds favor a speedy ship. I wish you and your father well." He tucked a strand of gray hair behind one ear, shook out his cuffs, taking the time to arrange the lace over his wrists. "I hope Lord Richmond is well. I have worked with him in the past, a small affair in Martinique. He is a great leader among common men."

"Thank you. I will pass on your regards to him. He is working for the Admiralty in London."

He furrowed his brow at my comment, and cleared his throat. "Well, be that as it may, I look forward to the time I may work with him again." He bowed to us. "Good day, ladies."

Once the door shut behind him, Louise shook. "What am I to do?"

I hugged her close, muffling her sobs against my shoulder. "I don't know."

"Damn it! I want freedom from that horrid man."

"I know, " I soothed.

"If I understand the documents correctly, we need to sign the decree in person before a barrister, then apply to the church for annulment. How can that be possible?"

"I thought you wanted freedom."

"How can I divorce a man when he is never on solid land!" She wiped her teary eyes on a tea cloth. "I am sorry, Julia! We intended to solve your problems, and I have grown despondent with mine."

The ormolu clock chimed the hour. I stood up. "I must get back to Richmond House. Let me know if I can be of further assistance."

She stood and kissed my cheek. "Thank you. I shall be fine. That is the benefit of a sterling reputation, and a robust bank account. I need to arrange to speak with a barrister. Do you know of any?"

"No, but if the opportunity presents itself, I'll obtain a name for you."

Louise rose and hugged me. "Thank you. You are a dear friend. I trust you will keep this meeting private?"

I smiled sadly at my friend. "I am very adept at secrecy."

Chapter Six

It was three days after Christmas. Lady Sutton's house was decorated for her holiday fete with the same lack of taste as her wardrobe choices. Beaded strings hung from the transoms on the landing, with large pillows of discordant colors thrown about haphazardly to complete the Oriental theme. Her offerings of food, however, were legendary. On that reputation alone, all of fashionable London gathered for her ball and musicale.

Her ballroom was twice the size of mine, and dozens of dancing pairs twirled to the music of the small string ensemble perched on the mezzanine. Richmond was supposed to meet me here, begging my forgiveness as we left our house earlier, for being called away on "Admiralty business." I had no opportunity to tell him of my plans to sail for Nevis, or to ask him about the boarding house near the docks.

Two hours into the event, my patience grew short waiting for him. I tapped my foot to the cadence of the music, scanning the men in attendance to see if any could be persuaded to dance with a married woman of limited dancing ability. I hung to the edges of the ballroom crowd, smiling and nodding at the few who said hello. I feared my face would freeze with my fake smile in place, and the tiny lines of tension creasing my forehead would become a permanent fixture.

"Ah, it is as if the angels answered my prayers."

The hairs on the nape of my neck stood straight out. I turned to greet Alistair. He wore the same green velvet jacket and round lenses covering his eyes as on the night of my ball, but he seemed disheveled, and his hair was out of place. Uncharacteristic of him. He bowed, and I saw the corner of his mouth twitching. "You look lonely, Princess. Join me for a dance." His thin hand stretched for my arm, but I pulled my elbow out of his reach.

"I am waiting for my husband."

He nodded, nose wrinkling. "Ah, the staid Richmond. Tell me, Princess, does he ignore you often?"

"Leave me alone, Alistair."

His hand snaked around my arm, green light flickering to hold me immobile, the threads of his magic awakening my own power. My pulse quickened, flushing my skin with heat. Alistair pointed at my rosy skin, and said, "I think we need to dance, Princess, or people will talk."

He pulled me toward him, holding me close to his body, one arm securely around my back. My power oozed under my skin, pushing the limits of my control. I felt his power moving to meet mine, searching for a patch of bare skin. I thanked Mary for insisting on thick gloves tonight.

"Don't try to lead, Julia, I know you're a horrible dancer." He led us into the vigorous pace of the dance.

"I came here tonight to warn you that I have instituted a back-up plan for you, in case you do not come to Nevis."

I stepped on his toe with the heel of my shoe, satisfied at the look of pain on his face. "I will be there, Alistair; do not fret. I will take great pleasure in humiliating you in front of our clans."

"Like you did to Lady Penelope?"

"Will you stop talking about her!" I hissed. "That chapter of my life is behind me."

"Yes, you ran halfway around the world to put that behind you. Tell me, Julia, did marrying him help you forget what you are?"

Angrily, I pulled away from him, but his arms held me tight. "I will never forget my intent and purpose."

"Ah, the clan creed. How cute that you remember it."

"No, Alistair, my purpose is to defeat you, restore my clan, and return to London to continue my life."

"You always were a naïve dreamer, Princess."

We twirled near the entrance to the ballroom, a brilliant copper gown catching my eye. The familiar form dancing with the copper-clad woman made my blood boil. Blue fire erupted from my left hand before I could conceal it.

Across the room, my husband clung to an animated Madame Oualie. Blinking tears from my eyes, I wrenched free of Alistair's grasp, running for the nearest stairwell. I pounded up the steps, climbing higher, passing the second floor and careening up towards the mezzanine above the ballroom. Blue light flashed around my head, unchecked.

Stumbling, I fell to my knees and onto the floor. I waited for the blue light to seep back into my skin. Picking myself up, I spied a movement across the gallery in a darkened corner. No guests were on this level, although there was a retiring room further down the hall.

"Is someone there?" I called.

A shuffle and whisper of cloth revealed a thin form, silhouetted, that was crouching in the corner. I trod watchfully, power at the ready in my casting hand, eager for a fight.

"Hello?"

"Please do not hurt me." The shadowy form crawled out into the hall, illuminated by a sconce set in the wall. The form coalesced into the thin frame of Chloe Longood. She rubbed her hands over her arms, and her gaze seemed haunted. "Please do not hurt me."

Her hair, now shiny and clean, was pulled into a bun. Her red eyes were limned with fresh tears. Her arms appeared criss-crossed with cuts, some oozing blood. She dabbed a lacy handkerchief on one, staining the insubstantial cloth. It took me a moment to recognize her, so much was the disparity between her prior appearance and now.

She pressed the cloth hard against her skin. "It will not stop," she sobbed.

I took the cloth from her hand. "Let me see."

"No!" she exclaimed, twisting out of my grasp. "She said no one was to see. I need to stay here and wait for her." She wrung her hands together, scrubbing at the scabs on her arms, her eyes darting about the hallway.

"Let me see," I repeated, much sterner this time. I captured her hands in mine, pulling her into the light from the hall sconces. The insides of both arms were covered with straight cuts, like those made with a knife. Nausea roiled in my stomach at the undeniable evidence of her maltreatment. "How did you get these cuts?"

"*She* told me never to tell. I must not tell. No one must know." Chloe repeated the words in a childish voice.

Repetitive movements, shrinking from social interactions, loss of animation. Sure signs of enchantment. Possession.

By the trade winds! The pieces clicked together like the turnings of a lock. My feelings around Oualie, the interest in a young initiate. Madame Oualie was a practitioner of dark magic, using younger witches as familiars. I knew I hated Madame Oualie for her attentiveness toward my husband, but now I had another reason to hate her even more.

All dark spells were powered with blood. I'd never cast dark magic unless using my own blood as a tutorial by our father. Once. I was too scared to try after that. I looked at Miss Longood's arms again, arms riddled with cuts.

Dabbing the thin cloth against one incision, I was unable to staunch the flow of blood. If I remembered correctly, that meant continued drains from spells. Without an intervention, Chloe Longood would soon die, slowly drained of her life's blood, as well as her soul, by witches greedy for power.

"Chloe, how old are you?"

"Sixteen." Still not in her maturity as a witch.

"Where are you parents, Chloe?"

"They are gone."

"Gone? Gone where?"

"I do not know." She struggled in my grasp, trying to escape, but I held her tight.

She resisted, "No! I am to stay there!" Her voice broke into a sob just as the string ensemble played the chords of the next song. I hoped the music was loud enough to drown her harsh protests. "I am a good person. I have never done anything to deserve this. Why are my arms bleeding?"

I pulled her anxious form to her feet and down the hall to the retiring room, flinging a bolt of power at the lock to ensure our privacy.

Chloe's eyes widened and she held out her arm, making the blood flow faster down her wrist. Holding out the offering, she asked, "Do you want blood too?"

My power whispered yes, remembering the rush when I drained Alistair of blood in my rooms. Blue light flowed freely under my skin, lapping at the edges of my fingertips, waiting for me to utter my consent and strike at Chloe. To become like them, no better than Oualie and her ilk. I grated out my answer. "I don't need your blood, Chloe. I am going to help you, but I need a moment to think."

"She said no one would help me." My gaze focused on her wrist, the burgundy blood glistening, the promise of power contained in those few little drops. Power to defeat Alistair. Power to help my father.

No. I commanded my power to retreat to a space deep in my core.

"Are you going to help me?" Chloe inquired in a singsong voice.

"Hush!" Chloe was startled at my sharp tone. "I am sorry, but I need a moment to think." Madame Oualie must have been using a large amount of power to expend the amount of blood drained from Chloe. Or perhaps, multiple practitioners were using her. I could not leave Chloe in Madame Oualie' care. Already, she was at risk of never attaining her full powers.

How to get her away from Oualie? Without revealing my nature as a witch?

The door rattled. "Hello? Is there a problem?" A lady's voice floated from outside. "Is this room occupied?"

I answered, "I will be but a moment longer. I am having a problem with my dress."

"We will send a servant to assist you." Muffled sounds from outside sped my heart. I thought of Alistair downstairs, and Oualie with my husband. I could not fight them both with Chloe as a distraction. I needed to get Chloe out of the house now.

"Chloe, I am going to help you, but you must listen." I placed my hands on either side of her head, forcing her to look at me. "We are going to walk out of this house. I am going to take you down the backstairs to the garden. We will hail a cab and you will go to my house. I will take care of everything."

73

"She said not to go anywhere." Chloe remained stubborn.

My hands glowed soft blue. I pushed power into Chloe's skin, gently, searching for the key to open the lock of her enchantment. Dark red power, the color of old blood, moved like sludge from the light of my power, retreating to the corners of Chloe's body. A dim pulse of yellow light flickered from Chloe's fingertips, her natural calling, an earth color.

"Blue to red, yellow bright, give this one solace on this night." With the chant, I pushed blue power into Chloe, my energy encircling the malicious red sludge. Chloe moaned, trembling, then turned pale under the warring powers within her frame.

I soothed her. "I am sorry, little one. I wish I could make it easier."

She groaned again, yellow light flickering and fading from her fingertips. She was not strong enough to withstand the surge. I placed my hands on hers again, sending my power over her skin, searching for any aliquot of red to pull from her. I extracted the sticky barbs deep from her soul, yanking and tugging like an awful confection sold at the seaside. Removing a large glob, I swarmed it with my blue power, neutralizing it from Chloe. I absorbed the red glob into my core, holding my breath in an attempt to contain it all within my humble frame. My skin stretched, feeling taut and uncomfortable. Brighter yellow leaked from Chloe's skin and her color improved.

Her eyes snapped open, and were much clearer than before.

"Where am I?"

"In the retiring room at Lady Sutton's townhouse." Fear reentered her countenance, and I reassured her, "We are going back to my house. Do not fret. Madame Oualie cannot hurt you anymore." My breath rattled, and my chest felt tight. The power was too much. The red power fought back, pushing and beating against its coffin of blue. My head pounded so painfully, tears leaked down my cheeks, and it hurt so much, I wanted to bang my head against the wall to dull my senses.

The door rattled on its hinges, louder now.

"Come, we must go." I dissolved the enchantment on the door. It flung open, surprising the gathered ladies. We marched out into the small, waiting crowd in the gallery. Chloe pulled her ball gown sleeves lower to cover her macerated arms.

"Excuse us, we are very sorry. Must have eaten something off. We are ready for home." I repeated the excuses and apologies as I forced our way through the milling crowd, down the steps to the second floor, then along the gallery to the servant stairs on the south wall of the house.

Hurrying along the upper gallery, I indelicately pulled a stumbling Chloe behind me. Rushing around a corner, I slammed into a servant with a full tray of drinks. Instinctively, I flung a spell to stabilize the tray and erase the memory of the servant as we sped by.

"Years of relentless secrecy will all be ruined at this dreadful party," I muttered.

Finding a small door near the back of the house, I flicked a spell, opening it and pulling Chloe behind. She was breathing heavily, the blood from her arms trickling a warm path onto my hand. Like metal to a lodestone, my power surged to meet the offering. I pulled my energy away from the glowing yellow promise of Chloe's power. Panting with the effort, I restrained the blue power before it could feed off the girl.

Stumbling down the last turn of the step, we burst through the door into the kitchens. Never stopping, we exited into the night, and I rushed across the frozen slippery ground to the back garden gate. Chloe slipped, tumbling to her knees, and I hauled her onto her feet and continued. No sounds of pursuit were in evidence, but then again, a smart witch would disguise her steps.

I enchanted the back gate to open, moving quickly down the alley. Skirting refuse and the odd stray dog, we spilled out onto Welbeck Street, three blocks west of Cavendish Square. The traffic was brisk even for this time of night. I hailed a cab and reached for my reticule. Nothing. The cab careened across traffic, halting dramatically with two wheels on the curb. The cabbie peered expectantly at us, two women at night, clad in finery. I patted my dress for a pocket of loose change. Empty.

"By the tides. I don't have it."

The cabbie looked askance at me. "I need payment, ma'am."

"I dropped my coin, good sir. Give me a moment." I swiped my foot along the dusting of snow, to uncover a few pebbles. Bending down, I pressed the cold rocks on my hand, enchanting them to appear as coin of the realm and pressed them into the cabbie's hand. "Here we are, no problem. No other stops, sir, and there is a bonus for quick passage home." I relayed the address as Chloe climbed into the enclosed carriage, which smelled of cabbage and onions. I felt guilty at stiffing the cabbie, but there was no help for it.

"I must return to the ball. When you reach our home, tell Jameson you are my guest. He will prepare rooms for you." I squeezed her hand.

"Yes, milady. Thank you." She shivered in the cool air.

I patted her cheek. "I will come to you when I return home. I will take care of you, Chloe Longood, I promise." A mist of blue settled over her skin, sparkling for a short flash before dissipating.

"I trust you, Lady Richmond. Please, don't make me go back to her!"

"Shush, child. I will keep you safe."

The cabbie went off with a pull to his cap and a whistle to the horses.

I picked my way back into the garden, pausing to rest on a bench near the back entrance to the house. Twisted braches in rows revealed this was a rose garden, the vines empty of blooms so late in the season. I counted the passage of three waltzes, the music floating and sounding very beautiful in the winter night. My head ached, and my skin itched from Oualie's red, tainted magic.

I reentered the house through the kitchen. I needed to rid myself of this extra power, but my head pounded so that I could not think clearly. I knew there was something I had to remember, something I needed to do, but I could not identify it. Warn Richmond of Alistair? Warn Richmond of me? Thoughts swirled in my head. Dizzy, I plopped into the nearest empty seat, groaning with my head in my hands.

It took a moment to realize the crowd had parted, and I was the centerpiece. I lifted my head with great effort. Madame Oualie stood across from me, a vision in her copper gown. Alistair stood at her side, one arm on her waist. I forced power into my hand, becoming perplexed when it did not obey me.

She opened her fan with a snap of her wrist, a brittle smile on her face. "Ah, Lady Richmond. Bon soir! That dress is an unfortunate choice for you, but you are not known for your taste in fashion."

I glanced down at my navy blue silk gown. It was a lovely dress. I glared at her. "And you are not recognized for your manners." I thought of Chloe, resting in my house. My fingers twitched to send a spell at her. Alistair remained silent. The crowd pulled closer, sensing a good bit for gossip on the morrow.

"The lady's tongue is sharp tonight." She waved her fan twice, and thin rivulets of red witchcraft, twisting in the lace of the fan, imbued it with the appearance of animation. "I want you to meet my new charge. She is a delightful girl."

Alistair added, "You would do well to study Madame Oualie and her methods. They may prove useful to you in the next months."

"I don't need to capitulate on the unwilling offerings of innocents to perform my best, Mister Dupont. Surely, you know that." The music, the dancers, and all the activity of the evening swirled around us, while I focused on the danger in the copper dress. "I met Miss Chloe Longood earlier, on the balcony. She felt unwell, so I arranged passage home for her."

A shiver passed through Madame Oualie. "How dare you! She is my charge. MINE." Red light flashed on her fan. I stood to meet her challenge, my legs unsteady. *What was wrong with me?*

"I understand the ways of Martinique are different than London, but if you take the responsibility of a young girl, you must treat her properly. Or risk ruining her reputation forever." I grabbed Oualie's arm, my fingers digging deeply into her flesh, sending her globule of red energy back into her skin. Her body resisted. I forced her power back deep into her flesh over the protests of my own body, and my own power, begging to keep it with me. I refused to listen to my traitorous witchcraft, determined to push the red out of my body, down my arm, and back into her body.

My hand burned with the transfer of energy. It took the space of three heartbeats, but it felt like an eternity touching that woman.

Ripping my hand away, I resisted the effort to wipe my palm on a napkin. "I hope I did not offend you with my concern for her welfare," I panted, out of breath. "If I can be of further assistance, please, I am at your disposal." Turning to Dupont, I added. "I thought you had better taste in companions, Mister Dupont. I am disappointed in you."

Madame Oualie remained still on her spot, disbelief etched in her features. She glared at her arm, then at me. "I will wreak my retribution on your skinny frame." She lapsed into a flurry of French. I was positive it was not polite.

I chuckled, "Have a lovely evening."

Dupont glared at me, pulling Madame Oualie away from me. "We will settle this in a more appropriate setting later, Lady Richmond." Whereupon, they melted into the crowd.

I traveled to the refreshment table, swallowing three glasses of champagne in swift succession to calm my nerves. The bubbles tickled my throat as I swallowed.

A warm hand cupped my elbow, turning me away from a fourth glass. Richmond stood there, appearing happy. My agitation at the confrontation lessened under his smiling gaze.

"Lady Richmond, I have searched the entirety of this property for you. Where were you hiding?"

"In plain sight. I saw you dancing with her."

"I know how it appears, but I was truly just reminiscing about old times."

"Stephen, there is something I need to tell you."

"Is it a matter of grave importance?" He glanced at the crowded room.

"It might be."

"Then let us move to a more appropriate setting." He offered me his arm. I curled my fingers around the crook of his elbow, following him to a corner of the room near a drafty window with lavender drapes. He leaned against the wall, tensing in the way he held his shoulders, as if he were afraid of what I had to say. "Go on."

"I offered Chloe Longood an invitation to stay with us."

"What!?"

I rushed to explain, using my carefully rehearsed and orchestrated reasoning, which was now forgotten in the face of his response. "I literally ran into her, and she had cuts all along her arms, definite signs of maltreatment. She asked for asylum and I gave it. I plan to notify Madame Oualie on the morrow."

He remained silent.

"I'll fix everything, I promise. But I could not let that poor girl go home with her if the cuts on her arms were signs of abuse."

No response.

"It's not right, Stephen."

"We will offer her a place to stay for a few days, then speak with Madame Oualie regarding a permanent solution. I do not welcome any situations that might spark the interest of the church. And I do not want a witch living in my house."

"I think the girl deserves better treatment than having her arms cut to ribbons, whether she is a witch or not."

"I do not care for witches and you know it."

My temper flared. "No, I do not know, Stephen, as we have not had any conversation of import in quite some time."

"Then let me educate you, wife. I abhor witches for their lying, mercenary ways. I do not want them in my house. I do not want them in my club. In fact, I wish the church would remove all of them and we could be done with this mess."

My heart pounded. "Are you sure about what you are saying, Stephen?"

"Certainly."

"Because I like to think I measure the worth of a person based on God's teachings. It is not my place to judge. It is my place to help those less fortunate than me, and Miss Longood definitely falls into that category."

"I do not want her in my house."

"She is staying."

"We are already under suspicion from the church, Julia. You are under evaluation because of your association with Dupont. I do not want you to draw any further attention to yourself by fostering this youngling."

"Then I will go to Nevis and visit with my family until this all blows over."

"What? Where is this coming from? Is this why Dupont has been slinking around, to tell you to go home?" He scowled. "I do not want you to leave London. It is a dangerous time for travel at sea."

"Pirates and Spanish galleons seem safer than the scrutiny of Vicar Morris. By the way, whatever happened to the couple from our garden? The ones with the fireworks?"

His face blanched before he answered. "I do not know."

"Do not lie to me, Stephen. I can tell by your face you know their disposition." I continued, "Did you get them a church burial at least?"

"Yes. But I have no ken as to how they died."

I fingered my dress. "Thank you for telling me." I turned to go, my mind racing with possibilities for Chloe and me. I would not leave her to be picked over like a carcass by Oualie.

Richmond reached out, his fingers brushing my dress. "Julia, I worry about you. We can keep the girl for a few days, but she needs to be gone from our house by

New Year's. I do not care about her. I only care about keeping you safe."

I left his side, seeking the butler to ask for my cloak. Richmond followed me to the door.

I did not ring for Mary when I returned to my rooms. My dress was easy enough to remove on my own, and in truth, I wanted a few precious moments to myself.

"Julia?" Richmond called softly from the door. "Are you still awake?"

I stood in my corset and stockings, debating whether to reach for the robe lying across the foot of my bed. No, I thought. I am a lovely woman, even if I am a bit on the short side. I have nothing to be ashamed of.

"Yes."

He walked closer. "I want to talk about the girl."

I reached for my robe. This was not the conversation I hoped we would have. "Then let us talk."

"Jameson approached me, and although I do not make it a habit to listen to servants' gossip, I heard the man out."

"Go on."

"The servants are afraid to be in Miss Longood's presence. One of the chambermaids is wearing a clove of garlic around her neck. Another refuses to go in to her rooms without a Bible. Really, Julia, her presence is turning the house upside-down."

"The girl needs a place to stay until she is well. She has suffered great mistreatment. I will consider an alternate placement for her when she is better."

"Then we are agreed she cannot stay with us forever."

"Yes."

"Then that brings me to my next point." He reached out, his hand cupping my cheek. "I think you looked lovely tonight, Julia."

"Thank you." I refused to think of the events of the last days. "I was hoping we could have spent more time together tonight."

"I was too."

We stood, neither knowing exactly what to do. Richmond broke the silence. "I have missed you, Julia." He bent his head to slant his lips across mine.

Chapter Seven

"Jameson, please tell Miss Longood we will take breakfast here this morning." I sat in a small salon on the east side of the house, a room filled with sunlight. The butler did not acknowledge my request, turning on his heel to leave the room.

I inhaled the scent of chocolate from my cup, my fingers curled around the china. Hot chocolate in the morning was one of the benefits of a colder climate. I sipped the delicious brew, savoring every swallow. We could not keep chocolate on Nevis; it melted in the tropical heat. I would definitely miss hot chocolate when I returned there.

Chloe entered the room with a soft tap on the door. She looked better than last night, the blood having scabbed over on her arms, but the color of her skin remained a sickly pallor. She wore a brown, woolen dress of mine, but it only reached the tops of her ankles.

"Good morning, Chloe. Did you sleep well?" I drained my cup, setting it down on its delicate saucer.

"Yes, thank you, Lady Richmond."

I motioned for her to sit at a small table. "Please eat. Then we can talk." She ate in silence, devouring three scones, two pieces of buttered bread, and finishing off the hot chocolate in my pot. Sitting back with a satisfied grin, she said, "That was the best meal I have ever had. Ever. Thank you, Lady Richmond."

"Come with me, there is something I want to show you. Your ankles will be chilled for a few minutes, but I think it is worth the discomfort."

Exiting outside near the kitchens, we walked along a small porch running the length of the house. At the far end, a glass enclosure rose into the air. Chloe gasped in surprise. "It's a hothouse! Here in London! I've only read of these in the papers!"

I opened the metal handle and a cloud of warm, moist air wafted out. Fragrant waves of plumeria, pine-apple, and gardenia mixed in a floral mist, permeating everything. Green blooms and thick vines climbed to-wards the heavens. I breathed deeply, the smells exotic and comforting at once. Shutting the door behind me, I fingered a stand of foxglove. "I think this is a more ap-propriate place for us to chat."

Chloe pushed her dress up her arms, the scabs a stark red against the paleness of her skin. Pausing above a large palm, she questioned, "May I?"

I nodded. "Of course! That is why I brought you here."

She plunged her arms to the elbows in the dirt, moaning in pleasure. "This feels heavenly." Pale yellow light filtered through the dirt to illuminate her enrap-tured face.

I propped my hip against a wooden shelf beside her. It was filled with pottery bowls for the plantings in the hothouse. "Chloe, where is your clan?" I pointed to the dirt. "You have had some training."

Her brow furrowed. "Gone, mostly. We were from Northumberland. Our clan numbered thirty. One night, armed men on horses stormed our house. My dad was the head of the clan, you see, and the men demanded we join allegiance with a fire clan or risk exposure to the church. My father refused. They threw fire from their hands, igniting the house and stables. We lived in a small, remote village. There was no one to help us. We were weak, with no water witches among us to counter the fires." She wiggled her hands deeper into the dirt. "We fled, my sister and I, into the fields. My father and mother were smote down protecting us. We never thought to fight."

She stared at the dirt. "The church finished off the rest of us. I was transported in a coach to London, imprisoned in the dungeon of an Abbey, I think. The men who brought us food were dressed as friars. My sister died a few days after we reached London of a lung ailment. I lost track of time. I think you know the rest."

My mind reeled with her story. What if Madame Oualie, whose magic matched that of a fire clan, was behind this? What if she played both sides of the coin? Pushing smaller clans to join hers, increasing her power, and if not, turning them over to the church? Lord Botetourt mentioned there were other clans at work in London now. Perhaps he meant Oualie'? Despicable, in my opinion. And not a whit of evidence to support my supposition. Chloe dug in the dirt, her yellow light increasing in strength.

"Chloe, have you thought about carrying a small pouch of dirt with you wherever you go? If you are captured again, at least you could replenish your power, and cast spells."

She cocked her head. "I've never thought of that. What a good idea." She rubbed dirt along her arms, sighing with the contact. "What kind of witch are you?"

I pointed to an orchid across the aisle. "I am like that flower, Chloe. My mother was from a wind clan, my father a water clan. I am a mixture, with powers from both."

"You know wind spells!"

"A few. There are not any wind witches left to teach me. My mother died in childbirth before my coming of age."

"Where is your water flask?"

"I do not carry one, a situation I plan to change. I am an oddity, Chloe. My father suspects it is from my mixed heritage, but the truth is, no one knows the answer. I tell you this because you need to consider carefully if you want to stay with me or join the London clan."

She traced a path of dirt along the tendons of her arm. "I don't trust the London clan. Where were they when I needed to escape? The only hope we had of release was from an English gentleman others whispered about in the dark. But he never came for me. No one helped me or my sister." She dug her fingers into the pot, wiggling them until her wrists were covered. "It's a dark place to be without any friends. Or any hope for rescue."

I waited for her response. We stayed thus, with her playing in the dirt, for ten minutes before she broke the silence.

"I want to stay with you, Lady Richmond. My clan did not protect me before; a clan will be of no use to me now."

"Very well. As your protector, is there any information you would like to know?"

"I never got to enter the duels. Did you?"

"Yes, but I stopped. I hurt a very nice witch, and did not have the stomach to continue."

"I never got the chance to duel. I think if we'd had the training, my sister and I, we could have fought. And possibly resisted."

I rotated my wrists. "Then let us practice, Chloe. These are dangerous times." I pushed a bolt of blue into a shield. "Make a shield, Chloe."

She pulled her hands from the dirt. They glowed a soft yellow. She rotated her wrists, and a small disk of yellow appeared in the air.

I clapped my hands. "Brilliant! Now make it bigger."

The light grew brighter, but the disk size remained the same. Crestfallen, she plunged her hands into the dirt again. "I can't."

"I cast spells differently from my sisters, because of my water clan and air clan parentage. Do all earth witches cast the same?"

"Mostly." Chloe pulled her hands out of the dirt again. "I'd like to attempt another shield." She rubbed her hands together, loosening the dirt to pile into her hand. Throwing the dirt into the air, she aimed a bolt of yellow at the matter. A bright disc, as yellow as a Saharan sun, erupted between us. Chloe giggled.

"Chloe! Wonderful! You simply need a bit of dirt to cast. Now, practice hitting targets. I've used the palms before; they grow fast and their trunks heal well." I dusted my skirts.

"Chloe, I need to ask something important of you. Do you remember anything about your stay with Madame Oualie?"

Her hands remained in the dirt. "I was blindfolded mostly, whenever anyone was around. Everyone spoke in a different language. French, I think. Two men held me while they cut my arms." She threw a sprinkling of dirt onto her bodice.

I pointed at the dribble of dirt on the front of her dress. "It is unfortunate you cannot submerge yourself in dirt. I do not have a pot big enough to hold your frame."

She smiled at the comment, but her eyes were downcast. "They did not enchant me while they cut me. It hurt." Her gaze pierced mine. "I will never be put in that situation again. Teach me what you know, Lady Richmond. Please."

I fussed with a hibiscus bloom on a nearby plant. "How did you know I was a witch in the church?"

"I felt your power. It was stronger than any other pull in the room."

Interesting. An uncommon talent. Perhaps that is why Oualie wanted Chloe so badly. We remained thus, with me assisting Chloe on her basic spells for shields until the sun rose higher in the sky. I wiped my hands on my skirts.

"I need to run an errand and make a few visits today. Do not leave the grounds or my spell of protection is lost. I'll return this evening. Neither Lord Richmond nor my servants know of my witch powers. Be certain it stays that way."

"I will not reveal anything, Lady Richmond. I promise."

"Then I take you at your word, Chloe Longood. Make yourself at home."

"Can I work with your plants? Some are in dire need of attention."

The plants looked fine to me, but I was not an earth witch. "Of course."

She practiced throwing her shield in the air, whizzing it among the fern fronds. "Thank you."

"Chloe? Remember, no one here knows I am a witch. Please practice discretion."

"I will, " she answered, her dirt disc racing among the flowers.

Hours later, I waited at a most unlikely place. I stood on the stoop of Madame Oualie's home. I was never good at confrontation, growing up with the idea that a knife in the back was a more successful method of conflict resolution than a conversation face-to-face. In respect for the conventions of our kind, tradition dictated that I notify her Chloe was now under my protection.

I imagined a depraved black witch living in a dilapidated property, not a respectable house of sturdy white brick and yellow shutters. A small, iron gate encircled the property. A perfectly unassuming home.

I rapped on the knocker harder than necessary. I flexed my hands, my power ready at my fingertips. Convention and rules dictated this should be a bland exchange. I did not think I would escape so easily. I rapped again, turning my back to the door to watch several coaches roll down the thoroughfare. A flower girl hurried down the street, her arms laden with greenery, calling for customers.

A skeletal butler eased open the door. His hawkish nose overpowered the remaining features of his face, with no pleasing attributes, evidenced from his high dappled forehead to the sneer upon his lips. "Yes?"

"I am Lady Richmond. I wish to see Madame Oualie."

"She is not receiving visitors today."

"You misunderstand. This is not a frivolous call, and I will wait on your stoop until I have a word with her."

He glanced at my clothes, and the coach waiting in the street. I may have been of average height, but there was nothing average about my clothes or coach. "Who are you again?"

"I am the wife of an acquaintance."

He didn't even blink. "Follow me."

He showed me to a room at the left of the hallway. The furniture was made of black wood, and dark red upholstery covering the chaise and chair. A curio cabinet with delicately carved legs housed a macabre collection of bone bracelets and a small shrunken head. Dante's *Inferno* lay on the settee, and I tried to remember if there was a level of hell for black witches. A large oil painting of Hades handing Persephone a pomegranate was framed in gold gilt above the mantel. *She is French. Maybe this is the fashion given the Revolution.* I poked at a bone bracelet in the curio cabinet with my gloved finger.

The door to the parlor flew open. My power surged, hungry for release. I flexed my casting hand, turning to greet my hostess.

"Oh, Lady Richmond! I wondered who could be calling at this hour. What a surprise!" Madame Oualie swayed into the room, a pink silk robe cloaking her figure, her auburn hair falling beautifully around her face. She clutched a gray cat in her arms. "When my man tells me it is the wife of an *acquaintance*, naturellement, I am intrigued. It could be many people, of course."

"I will not take but a moment of your time. I wish you to decease all association with my husband immediately."

"Oh, la, la! How direct you are!"

"I do not wish to be in your presence any longer than necessary."

She laughed. "And because you wish it, it must be so, non? This seems to be a character flaw with you, Lady Richmond. We women are demanding creatures." She sauntered closer, stopping only inches from me, our bodies barely touching. The cat hissed at me, and a paw swiped at my face. Her power reached out, lapping at the air around my body, threatening in its proximity.

"I would not dare if I were you," I warned. I pulled my power away from her, not wanting to start a duel in her drawing room. I did not know how many of her staff were aware of her powers, and I certainly did not want to notify all of London that I was a witch by blasting her in her nightdress.

Scratching the hissing cat, she ignored my threat and continued, "What if your husband wants to continue our relationship? I find him rather entertaining."

"He does not." I backed further away from her, my head aching with the effort to restrain my magic.

She smiled. "So certain of him! You understand, I wish no harm to you or to him, but if he beckons, I cannot deny him. He is very charming, your husband."

"Yes, he is. But my husband is mine and I do not intend to share him with you."

"Yours? We do not own people, cherie. A man like him, you cannot hold away, or deny him, but only threaten the rest of us to stay away."

My hand twitched with the desire to slap the smile from her face. Clutching the back of the settee, I struggled for composure. Dark energy snaked like tendrils of ivy along an old wall up my arm. I breathed deeply, tugging my hand away from the couch.

It would not budge.

Pulling again, my hand wrenched free, throbbing from where it contacted the settee. I reconsidered the room, the furniture, the fabric, the curios. All natural substances, all capable of bespelling.

"Trouble, cherie?"

"Non, Madame." I sent a frisson of power to my casting hand, walking toward the center of the room, to avoid letting my skirts brush against the furniture. Or her. "You are so beautiful, it must be difficult to choose among all your admirers."

She twirled an auburn ringlet around her finger. "Yes, of course. But your husband, he is the best prize."

I closed my eyes and thought of the many reasons it was ungodly to imagine the ways to kill her.

She continued. "I wonder what it feels like to be cuckolded? Is that the correct word?"

"Betrayed is a better choice of words, I think." *I wonder who is telling me the truth? Richmond, who swears his fidelity, or Oualie?*

"Yes, betrayed. What it must feel like to know he has been with another, the natural human tendency to compare, and find lacking in some category. The despair."

"It must be a heady brew for you." I hated her more than was reasonable, and a primitive call to hurt her made it even more difficult to control my temper.

She twisted her lips into a grin. "We must all feed in different ways from the fruits dropped on our paths. I think that is a quote from the Bible."

"I wonder what type of deranged sensibility allows one to sleep at night knowing you have lain with a married man. I think that is decidedly not Biblical. In fact, it breaks several of the Old Testament commandments."

"Ah, French literature is full of such questions. I do not think much of these things."

"Perhaps you might ponder these ethical dilemmas if you slept alone."

"Of course! But I am busy most nights and have little time for introspection that yields nothing. Leave daydreaming to poets and philosophers."

I switched topics to the second reason for my visit. "Miss Chloe Longood is under my protection. Any attempt to harm her will be viewed as an act of aggression."

She narrowed her eyes, and her skin turned blotchy. "You awful woman. She was MINE."

I wagged my finger at her, gaining confidence by the moment. "We do not own people, Madame Oualie. You are quite unattractive when you are angry."

"I pledged to help Monsieur Dupont, but I will hurt you for the insult you have dealt me. This is like stealing from my garden." Her accent thickened with her rising anger.

I studied my cuticles. "Do not put much trust in Dupont. He is a fickle ally. Ask my father."

She worked to compose herself. "I wish a *leetle* we met under different circumstances. I may have liked you. Richmond is so delightful, I cannot agree to leave him alone. Take the girl; she means nothing to me."

"Well, my husband is no longer your entertainment, and Miss Longood is no longer your source of nourishment. Consider yourself warned."

"Ha! What are you, little one, going to do to me?"

Burn your skin, drown you in your own fluids, as a start. "I would like to scratch your eyes out and feed them to your annoying cat, but I have another engagement. Please consider my words seriously. I shall not ask so politely again."

She clasped her hands. "I am delighted! If we were men, we would duel over pistols and swords to right our honor."

"Ah, yes, Madame, but as women, we must fight our battles in different ways."

She nodded in agreement. "Just so."

"I must be off. Miss Longood requests my company this afternoon."

Her mouth formed a moue of discontent. "Did she tell you anything?"

"Why, yes. Yes, she did." I did not elaborate.

"It is dangerous to be in the company of witches, Lady Richmond. Anyone can befall the accusation of witchcraft."

"I agree. But I am not of a house, nor do I have any artifacts or talents to lend to you. One word of my heritage to anyone, including my husband, and I will strip you of your power and drain your blood drop-by-drop.

I will gladly burn at the stake knowing you are burning in hell."

"You cannot possibly hope to best me in a duel. I am aligned with the great witch houses of Europe."

"It is inconsequential whom you've bedded, Madame, as long as it is not my husband. If your intelligence on my ability hails from Mister Dupont, think again before believing him. This is your only warning."

"You need to be put in your place, you who believe you are so powerful. How can you be anything without your clan?"

"I do not require a clan." I thought of the gun still on my bedside table. Perhaps I should have brought it with me. "I bid you good day. If Miss Chloe Longood so much as suffers a cold, I will take it as a personal threat from you and deal with you accordingly."

She wiggled her fingers in a wave. "Tell Stephen I said hello." Her French accent made his name sound carnal.

I marched from the room, muttering a spell for cold drafts to aggravate her in her thin chemise.

Chapter Eight

Our box was stage left in the opera house. I held my opera lenses to my face again, surveying the crowd. Richmond studied the stage, a pensive look upon his face, one I knew well. It was no use talking to him in one of these moods. So, I searched the theater for my secondary target.

My intended mark was Lord Botetourt. My maid, whose cousin worked in Lord Botetourt's house, told me on good faith he would attend the show this evening.

I was worried about the meeting, to be frank. I needed a library, a practice pen, and an introduction for Chloe into the London houses. She knew nothing of my intention to travel, and I did not know if she would be well enough to live through an ocean voyage to Nevis. Earth witches and ocean travels do not mix well. I needed options for myself and Chloe.

I circled the house again, peering through the opera lenses, my view distorted from the myopic perspective. Few spectators were focused on the stage. Most were socializing, or traipsing from box-to-box. I felt sorry for the performers as I panned my glasses over the theater seats again. An uncommonly tall gentleman with blond hair brushing the top of his shoulders settled into the box across the house. He wore no jewelry, except a thin gold ring on his right hand. It was Botetourt. I lowered the glasses, planning my entrance.

"Do you enjoy the opera?" Richmond patted my hand, pulling my attention back to my husband at my side.

I resisted the temptation to cover my ears when the soprano hit a high note, since Richmond loved the music. "I like this one better than the last one."

The curtain fell on the first act, silencing the ringing in my ears. People began milling about, vendors snaking through the standing room of the theater floor, selling drinks and meat pies. Richmond stood to stretch, his broad shoulders rolling under the fine fabric of his evening coat. "Would you like some punch?"

I was reminded of the rum punch on the islands. "No, but a glass of champagne would be nice. I'm going to the retiring rooms."

"Consider it done. I'll meet you back here for the next act."

We exited the box in different directions, and I wove through the crowds with a single purpose in mind. I needed to speak with Lord Botetourt alone. Walking as quickly as I could without raising eyebrows, I hurried up the stairs leading to his box. Pausing to catch my breath, I pushed power into my casting hand. As my father often said, it is always better to be over-prepared. Satisfied, I knocked on the door.

"Enter."

I swept inside, giving a customary curtsey. A thin man with a turban stood behind the door, the tint of his skin belying his Indian roots. Lord Botetourt remained seated with his back to me, turning as I approached. His gaze flicked to my hands, then back to my face. His hands remained on the arms of his chair, his casting hand drumming the melody to the last song.

His voice was soft. "It is past time you gave me your answer, Lady Richmond. Your insolence is unappreciated. After our discussion at your home, I expected a call within a day. Maybe two. I do not like to be ignored."

I kept my gaze downcast. "I do not adhere to all witch customs. I am not required to respond to your summons."

"Common courtesy demands a response, not witchy rules. You are rude."

I clasped my hands in the folds of my skirt. His power ran as deep as the marrow in my bones, calling my own. "I am sorry. I did not mean to offend." I cleared my throat. "I am in a predicament."

"Is this in relation to your trip to see Madame Oualie?"

My mouth dropped open. "How?"

"How did I know? My dear Lady Richmond, do not insult me so."

"I was referring to a separate predicament."

Interest sparked in his eyes. "Ah, yes. The orphan witch. Is it true she is an earth witch?"

"I cannot let her remain in my house for long. She has not attained her majority."

"I am not a nursemaid."

"I only ask what is your protocol for entering the duels." Duels were employed to place witches within the clan. As you gained power, you continued to challenge again in order to increase your standing within the clan. Most clans enforced specific rules for entering the duels, to prevent any mishaps or mismatches.

"We duel new initiates on the summer solstice."

"What about new members with experience? What is your policy in that instance?"

His fingers ceased drumming and he shifted his weight in his chair. "That depends on the witch."

Drumming his fingers again, he asked, "Where is your wand?"

"I was never granted one by my house."

"Fascinating. A lesson to all that when they are headstrong and marry outside the clans, there is a price exacted. Yet you dueled without a wand."

"Yes."

His gaze flicked to the Indian beside the door, who melted into the crowd outside the box, shutting the door with a click. "Hadgi is a loyal servant, but I wish to speak plain with you. You are a difficult conundrum, Lady Richmond. You defy all the conventions of the houses set down for generations."

"I have good reason, Lord."

His brown eyes limned with red. "I did not ask your opinion, Lady. Firstly, you did not present yourself to me when you entered my territory, an omission worth the cost of your wand. A wand, which you do not have."

"I meant no offense."

"But I take offense, Lady. Secondly, you married outside your house, and I am duty bound by the laws that govern our lot to return you to your house for reckoning."

"I plan to return home soon to visit my family and make amends."

"*Soon* is not *now*. I was happy to ignore your existence, until your presence in London made it difficult for my clan. Thirdly, you ignore my attempts to corral you into a clan, consorting instead with the English assassins. What am I to do? Others have petitioned me to eliminate the problem, but your father and I have a trade agreement, which I do not wish to test. I lost enough witches to our bloody brawl ten years ago. So you see my dilemma."

"The problems you outlined are mine to negotiate, Lord Botetourt. I come here for a proposition."

He smiled, his fingers beating faster. "A proposition implies you have something of worth to bargain. What can you offer in return?"

My stomach turned queasy. "I can give you a plant seedling from Nevis, one of two I brought with me from the islands. Very useful in many a potion."

He flicked his tongue to wet the edge of his lip. "That is all? You offer a plant in exchange for a wand? How inadequate."

"I apologize, sir. I do not know what you may find valuable."

"Valuable? What a decidedly interesting choice of words." He sat up straighter in his chair. "I find information the most ethereal item of value. Do you have any information to offer one such as me?" He stretched his legs in front of him, the muscles in his thighs visible against the tight cloth.

"I am sure you have the most information at your fingertips, but there might be a small bit I have." I considered my answer. "I know the fire clan in the West Indies has a new leader."

"Bah! I knew that weeks ago. You must do better than that, Lady Richmond. I grow bored quickly with this game."

"I am set to duel him in six weeks. I have no desire to rule his house once I defeat him."

His eyes brightened with hunger. "Can you beat him?"

"Most assuredly. With practice." *I think. If I can exorcise a demon from my father first and get reinstated into my house.*

His fingers resumed their drumming on his chair. "Come to my home on Tuesday next. We can practice dueling, and I can evaluate your abilities then. If I feel you are capable, I can give you and yours amnesty while in my territory."

"Thank you." I rose, shaking out my skirts. "I am humbled by your generosity. Are dueling witches allowed the opportunity to explore your library, perchance?"

"No. Only clan members of certain rank." His gaze flicked over my form. "But there are exceptions to each rule."

"Then I await your decision on the matter."

"Does he know?" He strained his head across the theater to Richmond, who was just entering our box.

"About my heritage?"

"About your plans to duel."

"No."

"My, what a tangled web you weave, Lady Richmond. Even I would not have the constitution to lie at night with the admiral's assassin."

"Whatever do you mean?" My voice sounded surprised to my own ears.

"Dear Lady Richmond, tell me you knew." False sympathy rolled off his tongue.

"Knew what?" I whispered.

"Your husband is the chief witch assassin for the government. I've debated throwing him on a ship and ridding myself of his threat, but then, he is a cracking good sailor, and would probably end up in the moat around my summer house. So I watch and wait for now."

"I question your intelligence on the matter." *It has to be a lie.* If it were true, Richmond and I had no chance for reparation, no chance at long-term reconciliation.

"I interrogated the last survivor myself."

The orchestra raised their instruments, playing a few bars of the melody. Panicked, I rose. "I must return. You are wrong about my husband."

"We shall see, dear. If I kill him, consider myself your first caller. You intrigue me."

"If you try to hurt my husband, I will retaliate. I do not wish to damage our arrangements with death or disability." I moved to the rear of the box. "Good evening." I exited the box, nodding to Hadgi as I passed him in the hall. I hurried back to my seat, upset and nervous with the whole exchange. Reaching my seat, I hastily settled myself beside Richmond to endure the second act.

He handed me a glass of champagne. "It may be too warm now. Where did you go?"

I sipped the fizzy liquid. What to say? "I wanted to speak with Lord Botetourt. He has extended me several invitations to his home, and I have not replied. I wanted to assure him there was no offense."

He nodded absently as the largish woman began to lament in song. A soft rap on the door caused the hairs on the nape of my neck to stand on end. Calming my power, stuffing the blue deeper into my core, I turned to greet Sebastian. I smiled, nervous in his presence, and uncertain why he was so unsettling to my powers. Since Lord Botetourt's words, I wondered how I survived this long in London. Sebastian nodded to me, then leaned over, whispering into Richmond's ear.

Richmond kissed my hand. "I must leave for a few minutes. I'll return before the end of the act." He rose and left with his brother without a backwards glance. Across the theater, Lord Botetourt winked.

I looked at Richmond's empty chair, then back at Lord Botetourt. He lifted his opera glasses to his face, concentrating on the stage.

I cast my mind back over his words. What if his words were true? What kind of man was my husband? I looked at Richmond's chair again, remembering his pledge to keep me safe, and his presence in the boarding house where Vivian lived. A safe house where the witch ended up dead.

I made up my mind. I was going to find out exactly where my husband spent his time away from me.

I left the box without another thought, and rushed down the stairs, hurrying through the few couples still talking in the foyer. The doorman lounged against the wall, sipping from a small flask. As I approached, he tried to put away his flask, but dropped the cap on the floor in his haste.

"Sorry, ma'am. I will call your coach immediately." He stood at attention, the flask now held behind his back.

"Do not bother. I am only going out for a bit of air."

He glanced at my bare shoulders in my blue silk gown. Already, goosebumps puckered my flesh. "Those gloves are not enough, if you beg my pardon. Let me call for a cloak."

"Of course. Thank you. It's under my name, Lady Richmond."

He ducked through the archway on his left leading to the cloakroom. I slipped outside.

Haymarket Street remained clogged with coaches, even at this late hour. Few people walked the sidewalks because of the cold rain falling, creating great puddles of mud and slush. I sighed. Witchcraft could make me invisible, but it could not save silk slippers from the mud. No matter.

I walked around the corner, shielded from view of the passersby. The alley stunk of urine and garbage. I pulled my gloves from my hands, my teeth chattering. Glancing about again, I braced my back against the rough bricks of Her Majesty's Theater, opening my magic to the world. I felt my power swelling, blossoming like a flower with my permission to infuse my limbs with energy.

Breathing deeply, I used my power to feel my surroundings, searching for other witches in my proximity. I felt a faint thrum, three of them, from inside the theater. Satisfied, I threw a warming spell over me, heat settling like a blanket to cocoon my body. Around me, the piles of snow left from today's earlier snowfall melted as I pulled energy from the water around me to fuel my spell.

Now that I was warm, I cloaked myself with invisibility, concentrating to keep both spells energized simultaneously.

My toes, however, were still visible.

Frustrated, I closed my eyes, struggling to maintain heat and invisibility. I imagined my blue witchcraft partitioning into four portions, one element aimed at my heat spell, one at my invisibility spell. I turned my attention to the third element. This aliquot I commanded to find Richmond.

Tracking spells worked best when cast by earth witches. Through the dirt, a decent earth witch could track anyone or anything touching the ground. Wait patiently enough, and eventually, the prey would touch ground, alerting the tracker to its presence. Water witches, like myself, could track anything through water. We were useless on land, unless that land were a swamp or marsh. Or covered in snow. Or of it were raining. I did not have a personal item to track like I used with Vivian.

My power leaked out of my fingertips, mingling with the rain soaking my clothes, sluicing down my sodden dress to puddle in the mud at my feet. I scanned the circle of blue, searching for any sign that my power had found its target. The circle of blue pulsed with the rhythm of the rain. As the rain splattered, the blue retracted, coalescing into an arrow pointing towards Haymarket Street.

"Yes! By the tides! It has his direction!"

I hurried down the street. Her Majesty's Theater stood on a respectable corner of Haymarket, but it was not far from the less fortunate areas of London. I followed the pulsing arrow, heading south. The going was more difficult than I estimated. Between avoiding the street traffic, tromping in silk slippers through snow, and glancing at the arrow to ensure I was on the right track, I quickly developed a headache.

I passed the corner at Charing Cross. The Thames was close, but her dirty water did not call to me on this dreary evening. I scooted among the coach traffic, attempting to cross the street.

A coach and six turned the corner. The horses were wild-eyed, and the coachman was hauling on the reins. "Look out!" he cried. "Beware!"

Coaches veered towards the sidewalks as walkers leaped for the safety of the few doorways in this section of street. I was caught in the middle, unable to negotiate the traffic from the middle of the street, and unable to call for help. He could not see me.

The horses barreled down upon me. I crouched in the muck, shaking. Pulling water from the rain around me, I directed my magic to create a ramp. The thin slick of blue started at the ground, rising a few inches above the ground.

The near horses snorted and reared, wary of the eerie blue light. They veered right, their hooves landing only inches from my barrier. Mud splattered over me, dirty water splashing my eyes. I dared not move my hands, afraid to disrupt my spell, so I blinked the water from my eyes.

The first wheels hit the ramp, careening over my barrier of witchlight. I grunted with the impact, the crushing force of the carriage pushing me and my frame deeper into the muck. I pushed back, elevating the ramp, gaining clearance.

My arms shook, and my skin grew hot with the energy transfer required to maintain the spell. The front wheels over, I breathed deeply, bracing for the impact of the back wheels.

I lay on my back, flowing energy into my spell, an act that became easier with each beat of my heart. My father's words echoed in my mind. "Julia, you are a natural. Develop your skills with my tutelage, and we will be the leaders of the West."

The back wheels hit the ramp, and I grunted, my father's words forgotten. The final wheel over me, I extinguished my spell. Struggling to extricate my gown from the muck, I staggered to the sidewalk.

The arrow pointed at the departing coach, headed down Whitehall Street.

"By the tides! I should have held on to the axle and saved my ribs from a second bruising." My body was sore; magic could protect me from the worst of the impact, but the bruises were mine to keep.

I hurried after the coach, less cautious now. As I closed the distance between myself and the coach, the blue of the spell brightened. The coach pulled to a stop in front of a butcher shop. The sign indicated the store was closed. A light in the second-floor window flickered from a single candle. Laundry hung from the sill, a small child's white shirt bright against the dingy bricks of the building.

The street here was narrow, the sidewalks full of garbage piles and empty gin bottles. Shadows flitted in the doorways, then melted away into the dark night.

I chose a spot across the street from the coach, maintaining a direct view of the shop. The horses pranced, steam rising from their flanks. The door to the coach crashed open. Lord Sebastian, my brother-in-law, was the first to alight. He pulled his cloak closer to his throat in the pouring rain, looking left and right. My husband was next, and by the tilt of his head and the set of his shoulders, I knew something was amiss.

I crept closer, crouching behind a pile of garbage. Safely in the shadows from the flickering lamplights, I released my invisibility and warmth spells. No sense wasting magic.

A third occupant exited the coach. If I'd been a dog, my hackles would have risen, for it was none other than Madame Oualie.

"This is the house." She pointed at the window. "We are being watched."

A ragged curtain twitched. A small boy pressed his face against the glass.

I did not like this.

"Wait here, Madame Oualie. We will be but a moment." Sebastian pulled a pistol from his belt. "Follow me," he said to Richmond.

Sebastian pounded on the door, not afraid to attract attention. "Open up on order of the King."

The door remained shut.

Sebastian pounded again. "We wish to speak with you."

Oualie raised her nose, like a dog on the scent. "Sebastian, do any others know of our intent tonight?"

"No."

I felt her power oozing across the ground, the strange mix lapping at my toes. I scooted my shoes out of the flow of her red magic. It receded, snapping back into her frame. I shifted, trying to allow more blood to flow into my cramped legs. Sulfur tinged the breeze.

Sebastian banged on the door again. Richmond grabbed his arm, preventing him from hitting the portal. "Let us go. No one is home except a little boy."

"Excuse moi, but let me try." Madame Oualie swayed to the door. Gripping the handle, red flashed about her fingertips. She twisted the knob, and the door swung open. "See, gentlemen? The door was unlocked. Now, go get the boy."

Sebastian entered the shop as Richmond remained on the stoop. I strained my ears, trying to hear what was happening inside the house, but the street noise and sounds of the city were too loud.

A few moments later, and Sebastian exited the shop, the small boy held under his arm like a sack of potatoes. The boy had a dirty rag stuffed in his mouth. His legs kicked as he struggled in Sebastian's arms.

"Excellent!" Madame Oualie clapped.

"What are we to do with the boy, Sebastian? We do not collect urchins for the government."

"We can use him as collateral."

Richmond pointed to the shop. "Collateral for what? His parents run a butcher shop a few blocks from the Thames. What do you think they can do for the government?"

"They may have valuable information about the trafficking of witches through London."

"And they may not. I do not approve of this, Sebastian."

"Always the one with a soft heart, brother. Watch your back, Richmond. One of your charity cases may stab you right there."

I had heard enough. I opened my power, my goal the slick sidewalk between Sebastian and the coach. As long as I commanded the water, there would be minimal witchlight to give away my presence. He stepped onto the sidewalk. With my power, I slid the film of water between his foot and ground.

"Oh!" he cried, losing his balance.

I threw a spell at the rain around him, pelting him with sharp points, slicing his cloak. The spikes of water penetrated his clothing, landing in his arm, spilling blood on the ground.

"I've been stabbed!" he exclaimed, dropping the little boy. He landed in a heap in the mud, then spit out the rag, stomped on Sebastian's toes, and ran for his life.

"There is someone in the shadows." Oualie peered through the dark towards me.

The little boy disappeared in the alley behind the shop. Doors opened, and the street was illuminated with the light.

Sebastian stood, holding his right arm. "Let us go. We can return another time."

Oualie climbed into the coach, Sebastian behind her. Richmond went to follow.

A bellow sounded from the alley. A large man, his arms thick with muscle, burst from the shadows. "Get out of my shop! Leave us alone!"

He closed the distance to the coach in two strides. His arm swung down, a cleaver glowing dully in the weak light.

Richmond turned, throwing his arm up to block the blow. He swung his foot, sweeping the butcher off his feet.

Oualie appeared from the coach, gazing at the fight below her in the slush and garbage. Waving her hand, I felt the energy leaving her fingers to cast a spell.

The shop burst into flames, and the first floor was quickly engulfed. Heat rolled in waves through the air. I flung out my blue light, searching for life inside the building.

Richmond yelled. I turned to see him clutching his leg, blood flowing from a cut to his thigh with the cleaver. The butcher raised his arm, ready to cleave Richmond's head in half.

Richmond put his hands above his head, bracing for the blow.

Red witchlight erupted from Oualie's hand. The butcher screamed, falling to the ground. The red light travelled over his skin as he lay twitching in the offal on the street.

"Collect him, Sebastian."

Sebastian climbed from the coach. He and Richmond struggled to lift the butcher to the coach. His head lolled on his neck, his arms and legs without strength.

They rolled him into the coach.

I felt a pulse of life.

I turned to the blaze. Again. A pulse of life. The second floor.

The coach pulled away from the curb. I stood, unafraid of the gathering crowd. I headed for the alley beside the shop.

It still rained, but the steady drops were unable to keep the witch flames at bay. I pulled water from the air, coalescing it to ensconce me in a globe of protection. I hoped it would be enough to resist the flames.

I plunged into the fire, entering from the back alley. Great hulks of beef and pig hung from hooks in the ceiling, charred from the flames. The smell of roast meats mixed with the scent of burning wood and clogged my nose.

I dodged the carcasses, headed for a flight of stairs visible along the east wall. Sweat trickled down my back, collecting under my arms.

Flames licked the stairs. I could not put out the fire; and there was not enough moisture in the burning house to fuel any spells. My own watery encasement was thinning, evaporating in the heat. I hurried up the stairs, feeling with my power for the pulse of life.

To the left.

I sensed the child inside the room. I kicked the door down, my silk slippers offering no buffer. Thick clouds of smoke billowed out of the room. I coughed, my eyes watering with the sting of sulfur.

A child, no more than five, lay in a heap on a make-shift bed. No flames engulfed this room, but the smoke was dense. I hurried to the child and reached out my hand, touching her shoulder.

No response.

I felt for a pulse, my hands searching for the bend of the girl's neck. It was there, but weak.

I scooped the unconscious child into my arms, pulling her arms and legs within the protection of my watery circle.

A rag doll dropped to the floor when I stood. I hesitated, then shifted the girl in my arms, squatting to pick up the doll.

I stood with the girl in my arms, searching for an exit from the room. Flames licked the door frame. Heat warmed my feet through the soles of my shoes. No exit there with my thinning shield. I surveyed the back wall, spying a window. It was no more than three feet in its widest measurement.

For once, I was happy for my petite stature.

I gently placed the girl on the ground and pushed against the sash, the window opening halfway. I cradled the girl in my arms once again.

I pulled the cocoon of water from me, swirling it into a disc of blue. I placed the girl on top of the watery cloud. Pushing the cloud through the window, I hung over the sash, guiding the girl to the ground. I tilted my hand, and the girl slid off the disc onto the ground.

Pulling water from the falling rain, I blasted a hole in the wall, stepped onto a platform of water, and floated to the ground. I released the water from the spell, and the discs dissolved into puddles on the ground.

I knelt on the ground beside the unknown child. If I knew any wind spells, I could have pulled the poisonous gases from her body. But I could not call on the wind. I cradled her thin frame in my arms, hurrying through the back alley away from the blaze.

This cross street was seedier than the last. I looked up and down the alley. The third doorway on my left was lit with a lantern. A sign above the lintel indicated it was a bakery. I crossed quickly to the doorway. Peering inside the glass, I spied small wooden toys scattered about the floor of the shop. A person with small children, owning a shop in the neighborhood. I hoped this would be enough to reunite the child with her remaining family.

I pounded on the door until a light flickered in the back of the shop. Laying the girl on the ground, I tucked her doll inside the crook of her arm.

I hurried across the street, hiding in a block of shadows. The door flew open to the bakery. A thin woman, her hair in a neat cap, stood holding a candle high.

"Who is there?" she called into the deserted street.

The child coughed. The woman knelt beside the girl, stroking her head. Satisfied I had chosen as well, I threw an invisibility spell over my head and hurried into the night.

I had to get back to the theater before the end of the third act.

Chapter Nine

A cold draft twirled around my ankles as I stood outside Her Majesty's Theater. The glass doors twinkled in the lantern light. No queue of coaches, no crowd pouring out the doors.

I made it back in time. I peered at my dress, which was ruined, and still smelling of the garbage I rolled in this evening. No choice, but for a spell.

I pulled power from a patch of snow at my feet, cloaking myself in an illusion spell. I was never very adept at cloaking smells, but I could always blame any stench on the crowded theater.

Starting at my toes, my muddy, ruined slippers transformed into perfect, glowing silk. My dress appeared full, the bodice unmarred by the splotches of mud. Although I could not see it, I imagined my face reflecting a clear complexion and my hair, a perfect coif.

I sauntered across the street. The doorman from earlier spied me, and tipped his flask as he held the door open for me to reenter.

He wrinkled his nose. "No wonder you wanted some air, ma'am. Pretty rank in the theater this evening, if you beg my pardon." He pulled on the brim of his cap.

"No offense taken, sir. Thank you."

I walked as fast as I dared to over the plush red carpet, climbing the stairs to the box level. I cracked open the door to our seats, fearing the scene that, no doubt, awaited me.

Empty.

I scooted inside, planting myself on my seat, and arranging my skirts. The elegant feel of the silk was as perfect as the illusion, but my skin felt cold and wet. I scanned the audience again. Lady Sutton was still snoring one level below me. The same soprano continued to sing. In fact, it seemed as if I had never left.

Furrowing my brow, I gazed across the room at Botetourt. He pulled his watch from his pocket, making a show of opening the device, and tapping the face as if it were not working.

He can manipulate time. Oh, dear God, what a terrifying gift!

He tapped the face of the watch again. The room blurred, like it does when you spin too fast on the dance floor. I clutched my chair, closing my eyes to the dizzying tableau.

The spinning sensation ceased. I cracked open one eye. Two baritones, men, were swaggering on the stage. Lady Sutton was awake, and fanning herself. I looked at Botetourt again. He smiled and tipped his head.

Cold air chilled me and I became anxious for Richmond's return. I twisted in my chair to see Alistair Dupont settling in beside me.

"What are you doing here!" I tried to rise and face the threat in my box, but his hand snatched mine and held me in my chair.

Dupont raised opera glasses to his face, reviewing the characters on stage. "I am warning you again, chit, that you are wasting time. I will not practice spells on you here, as I've been called to task for our engagement in your rooms the other night. Put away your power before you hurt yourself."

I looked to Lord Botetourt, who gazed intently at our exchange.

Dupont continued, "It's been one week, and all you seem to do is consort with the enemy."

"My husband is not the enemy." I leaned as far away from him as possible without toppling out of my seat. I doubted he would try to exterminate me in a theater full of witnesses, but I could never be certain with him.

"Do you know how he spends his time away from you?" A long finger that looked like a spider leg probed and adjusted the opera lenses.

"He works for the Admiralty. I imagine he does whatever they ask of him." *Including the torching of butcher shops.*

"He is on a witch hunt, my dear, and I do not jest." He lowered the glasses, peering at me with his cold eyes. "He is out now, under cover of the opera, and searching for a particular informant. Be careful, dear. You may be next."

"How melodramatic. Forgive me if I don't believe you."

He stared at me, his nostrils flared. "Let me elaborate, Princess. When you are crawling into bed with him, keep your witchy ways under control. If he finds out about our arrangement, and kills you before we get to Nevis, I will exterminate him and his family for wrecking my plans."

"What do you want from me, Alistair? I can't work out why you so desperately want me alive, when it is far more expedient to expose me to the church, as well as my husband, whomever, and let them do the dirty work for you. That is what you prefer, isn't it? To keep your hands clean?"

His gaze darkened, and anger practically oozed out of every pore. "You will go to Nevis, or I will take you there myself. It was not my intention to reveal you to your assassin husband, but I will if I must, if only to provide the proper inducement to get your pretty, little self on a boat headed west. I will not warn you again. More people than you know are watching our little drama."

I clenched the arms of my chair, restraining myself from sending Alistair Dupont to his maker. "I will leave in good time. I have work left to do in London first."

"Yes, I heard you and Richmond were reconciled. Pity. It will hurt you more when he turns on you again. But such is the denouement of falling in love."

I turned from his gaze. Hadgi stood up straighter behind Botetourt. *I bet he never had unwanted guests in his box.*

"I wish you would leave, Alistair. I understand your words and will heed the warning."

"I hope so, Princess."

He left as quietly as he came, and the seat was cold when my husband returned. With all the comings and goings, the opera was almost over. Richmond settled into his seat stiffly, his leg held out at an odd angle. He massaged his left thigh, and blood trickled from a cut on his hand.

I whispered in his ear. "Where did you go? What happened to your leg?" I wanted to see if he would tell me the truth.

"I tripped on the stairs and landed awkwardly. It is not a serious wound." He wrapped a white handkerchief around his palm, staunching the flow of blood.

I reached for his hand, capturing it in my own palms. "Here, let me see." I removed the handkerchief, and examined the cut. It ran across his palm, starting below his thumb and ending underneath the little finger. Whispering a spell of healing, I blew on the edges of the wound. A thin, white ribbon, like a wisp of smoke, rose from the bleeding edges.

A sure sign of witchcraft. *Maybe the butcher was a witch after all.*

I rewrapped his palm. "I am sure it will heal just fine. I have a poultice I can make at home."

He smiled, and the threats to our happiness seemed like a distant twinkle on the horizon. "I'd like to see the last act, but I also want to beat the crush home."

I bolted upright. "Do not concern yourself with my disappointment at leaving the performance early. I assure you I will survive the loss."

Placing his arm around me, he leaned heavily upon my frame as we slipped out of the box.

He sat stiffly in the coach, cradling his hand.

"Stephen, what really happened?"

He gazed out the window into the night. "I went on an assignment with Sebastian. It went wrong."

"How were you hurt?"

He remained silent for several minutes. I thought he was either ignoring my question, or possibly had drifted into sleep.

"Enchanted blade. That is how I was injured."

"Is that the real reason you want Chloe gone? Because of your work with the Admiralty?"

"I chose my position with the Admiralty because of you, Julia. It has evolved into the activities of this evening. Activities I am not proud of. Things that are best forgotten. I do not want you to suffer because of some foolish chit in our home. That is why I want her to move."

He groaned when the coach hit a pothole on the road. "I want to rest, Julia."

I needed to think in the meantime.

• • •

Once we were home, Jameson helped Richmond settle into his rooms. I bundled myself in a cloak, grabbing a candle from my room and scurrying outside to the hot-house. I never healed a cut that was laced with a witch-fire curse, and certainly never without a spellbook, but the basic tenets were the same in all spells. It was a form of chemistry, in which opposites balanced each other out: dark intent was neutralized by pureness of heart, and loyalty negated betrayal. The trick was not creating a basic antidote. No, the true kernel of witchcraft was in knowing your enemy. If you knew your enemy, you could properly guess the components of a curse: greed, avarice, prejudice, and hate were as much ingredients of a spell as the plants and animal bits.

I surveyed my stockpile, tapping my finger against my chin. The problem here was the unknown identity of the curse. If I had to make a curse for a blade, I'd have laced it with a plague to sour the wound, and added evil intent to retard healing. I debated on the inclusion of avarice, in case the blade was intended for a robbery, but the plants to neutralize avarice did not mix with the herbs for inducing plague. I settled on the willow bark and juniper, a pinch of moonflower pollen, and two white rose petals. Placing a candle on the wooden workbench, I gathered my mortar and pestle.

Taking a pinch of moonflower pollen, I cupped it in my hand. Focusing on the small pile, I tapped my fin-ger against the grains. Blue light trickled out, drawing water from the pitcher to power the spell.

I peeked at the pollen in my palm, now glowing a soft blue. Tapping the small particles into a glass mortar, I collected the willow bark, chewing it in my mouth to soften it before spitting it into my hand. Again, I sparked blue witchlight that glistened in the poultice.

The mix of spittle and bark heated my palm, and I added it to the pollen. When the two substances met, pink smoke wafted up from the bowl to tickle my nose, its sweet smell the sign of a good spell.

Taking the pestle in my right hand, I pulled water from the pitcher again with my left, condensing the humid mist into drops of pure energy to drip into the mortar. The addition of the water turned the poultice into a thick white mixture that had a salty smell. I tasted the mix with the tip of my tongue, until I was satisfied it was correct.

I cleaned the area, washing the tabletop with water to absorb any magical excess, and hurried back to Richmond's room.

Sprawled on his bed, the white of the sheets seemed much darker than his pale skin. He was stripped bare, and a small cloth was draped over his hips. A jagged gash swept across his left thigh, the edges dripping with blood. Clotted scabs floated like ice floes on the river within the gash. Sweat glistened on his body and his face contorted with pain. He groaned when I touched his leg.

"Julia, leave me please."

"Let me clean these cuts; then you can rest." His skin was warm, but not hot like a fever. He suffered from the curse of witchcraft.

I cleaned the wound with strips of linen and hot water. Smoke curled at the edges, rising from the surface of blood like mist on a lake in fall. With each press of the cloth, Richmond thrashed upon the bed, muttering obscenities between clenched teeth.

"God, Julia, make it stop!" he groaned, arching his back with pain.

"I am almost finished." I spread the poultice into the raw flesh of his thigh, eliciting a great shout and protest from Richmond, as fresh sweat began beading on his brow.

"God, is it over? It hurts worse than a bullet."

I finished wrapping the wound, pleased with my herbal selection. "I am finished." I held a glass of water to his lips before Richmond collapsed back onto the sheets. I inspected his palm, repeating the ministrations until I was satisfied that this wound, too, was free of any curse.

I felt his forehead. Already, the heat of his skin was cooling.

"I have heard, husband, that you hunt witches for the government. Is this true?"

His eyelids squeezed shut. "Do not put me in a position to choose between you and my duty, Julia. I do not have the liberty to choose freely at this time."

"I do not see any difficulty. The proper choice is clear to me."

"Julia, there are things bigger than us that need to be resolved."

"Then I will bid you good night. I put herbs in the poultice that will help speed the healing. You won't even limp by tomorrow."

He reached out a hand, his fingertips brushing the fabric of my dress. "Please do not be cross with me, Julia. I have one more element to secure, then we will be free of this mess."

"I hope that is true, Stephen. I hope you are correct. I'm leaving for Nevis in one week. With or without you."

A hot bath is a particular treat of living in a cold climate. I sank lower into the heated water, which managed to turn my skin red, and scrubbed my body until it felt raw, and the rose-scented soap was merely a sliver in my hands.

Propping my ankle on the side of the tub, the cool porcelain was a nice contrast to the heat of my skin. I worried about Alistair. For all I knew, he was practicing daily at a secret dueling pit in central London. Technically, I did not have to be in Nevis until the day of the duel, so I had time to prepare here. But my anxiety increased my agitation, and I soon felt like I was swimming in circles. I needed to complete my research on demons and board a boat to Nevis.

Tilting my head back, with the crook of my neck resting on the lip of the tub, I surveyed the plaster ceiling, as my mind now switched to Richmond. I felt foolish trusting a man I'd only met a few days ago over the man I'd known for years, but one thing I could not deny were his injuries. Injuries that were bespelled with witch curses.

A knock sounded on the door. "Lady Richmond?" Mary craned her head around the door.

"Yes?"

"I'm sorry to bother you, Lady, but Vicar Morris is here to see you. He says it is a matter of great urgency."

I emerged from the tub, grabbing a fluffy towel, and wrapping it around my body. I stepped out. "Please help me dress, Mary. I do not want to keep him waiting." *What is he doing here at this time of night?*

As Mary pulled and tugged my body into a suitable green woolen dress, I prepared my defense, for I knew this was not a friendly visit. With my hair twisted into a simple bun, I spared one last glance in the mirror before leaving my rooms. I wished I could have finished my bath in peace. "Mary?"

She paused in her work, her arms full of wet towels and discarded underthings. "Yes, milady?"

"Is Lord Richmond awake?"

"No, ma'am."

I nodded. "Good. Please do not disturb him."

"Yes, milady. Vicar Morris asked to see Miss Longood as well. Should I send for her? She retired to her room two hours ago. As frail as she is, she needs all the rest she can get, if you pardon my saying so, ma'am."

Remembering the look of terror on Chloe's face at her last meeting with the church on Christmas Day, I shook my head. "No. Let her be, Mary. I'll retrieve her if necessary." I exited the room, leaving her to her duties.

A few moments later, I sailed into the parlor, a cheery room with a high fire in the hearth. Two candles burned in sconces on the mantel, casting shadows about the floor. Vicar Morris paced in the center of the room, his Bible in his hands. Upon seeing me, his brows lowered and a stern look came over his face. "Lady Richmond, I have much to discuss with you."

I sat in the chair closest to the fire, and motioned for him to follow suit, as was proper. Here was the need for manners, the time to practice all the arts of cunning, daring and bluff Father made us practice as young women. *Manners are your best friend. Societal rules will save you many a time, and give you room for a retreat, as necessary.* I employed his recommendation, greeting the visitor with a sincerity I did not feel. "It is good to see you, sir. I hope the New Year finds you well."

He sat across from me, his hands on his splayed thighs, somewhat severe in his posture. "My year would be better if not for your meddling, good lady."

I raised my eyebrows in surprise. "Meddling? If you are referring to offering a home to Miss Longood, something I view as my Christian duty to lead her back to the proper ways of the Lord, I must object."

"The Bishop and I both determined Madame Oualie was best suited for that task."

I clucked my tongue in disagreement. "She escorted Miss Longood to a ball, and Miss Longood was never presented. That is simply not done, sir. If she is to have any hope of redemption, it must begin with the resurrection of a good reputation. I have discussed it with Madame Oualie, and she and I have an arrangement."

"It is that arrangement that brings me here today. It is unsettling for me to admit this, Lady Richmond, but you yourself have been under watch by the church, for having links to witches."

I placed my hand over my heart, gasping. "How absurd! And just who are these witches I am allegedly cavorting with?"

"Rumors of your family being one of the clans of witches in the Americas have reached the Bishop's ears." At seeing my astonished face, he continued, "I do not think they are correct, dear lady, and I do not mean to worry you, but that is why the Bishop feels you are not a worthy sponsor for the chit."

"My family is beyond reproach! What must I do to reassure the Bishop? You have no idea how this distresses me."

He rose, approaching the fire, and ran his hand along the fireplace mantel, then inspected his finger, wiping it on his frock coat. "I recommend that you continue your good works, Lady. Perhaps, if I could see the girl, then I could reassure the Bishop her rehabilitation continues at a proper pace."

"She is resting, but we plan to attend services this Sunday. You are most welcome to visit at any time and assist her with her scripture lessons."

"I will speak with your husband and arrange a suitable time. I am sorry to bother you at this late hour. In point of fact, I am relieved to find you at home."

I furrowed my brow. "Why?"

"Government men captured a coven of witches tonight. Several escaped, but not without suffering injury. This will help you in my petition to the Bishop on your behalf. Good night. I'll show myself out."

Stunned, I remained standing in the parlor long after Vicar Morris departed. My plans to leave for Nevis now had to include Chloe, for I could not leave her in this house alone. Or in London, without the protection of a clan.

The next morning, my eyes were gritty from fatigue. I could not sleep the previous night, what with my fears and concerns over Richmond, Chloe, Nevis, and everything too great to allow my mind peace. I rubbed my eyes, and resumed my search about the house for my young charge.

I entered the fragrant hothouse, my tension melting away with the humid air. Chloe wore a yellow dress of mine, the lace hem brushing the tops of her ankles. A bougainvillea plant curled around her arm, its leaves a vibrant green. She hummed, and a smile was on her lips.

"Chloe, you have done wonders for my plants."

She blushed. "I hope you do not mind, Lady Richmond. This one needed more light and attention."

"I do not mind in the least." I pointed at her dress. "We must go shopping today, Chloe, and I have sent a letter to Lady Gladstone to see if she will meet us at Madame Mincer's."

"You do not have to purchase extra things for me, Lady Richmond. I am happy to borrow your older garments."

"But I am not happy with the arrangement, Chloe."

Her face fell with my words. "I do not want to be a burden, Lady Richmond, honestly, I don't."

I considered my next words. "Chloe, you are not a burden. We must travel to Nevis, and you need more appropriate apparel for the voyage, that is all."

"We are going to Nevis? How exciting!" She danced around the plants, their leaves bending towards her as she passed. "All the tropical dirt I require! Think of the spells I can cast outside of dirty, sooty London! I will do well on the ocean journey, I am determined. I will not be afraid of the water."

I let her dance two more circles around the hot-house. "Chloe, it is a secret."

She stopped. "What?"

"Lord Richmond forbids me to go because he does not approve of my family. My father is ill, and I am the only one who can help him."

She circled her fingers in the fronds of a fern. "What is wrong with your dad?"

In for a penny, in for a pound. "He is possessed by a demon. I must duel Alistair Dupont in six weeks time on Nevis. So despite my husband's obstinence, I am compelled to go to Nevis."

She threw her arms around me, hugging me tight. "Lady Richmond, I'll go wherever you go. I'll keep your secret."

I squeezed her tight, then pushed her an arm's length away. "I am concerned you may not fare well on the voyage. Think about staying here with the London clan, if I can broker your security."

"I do not think I want to stay, no matter what the arrangements."

"Think on it." Switching topics, I continued, "We must board the ship in disguise. I want to get enough of a head start that we can make it to Nevis before anyone can come after us."

"Brilliant! A new spell to learn!"

"There is one more reason you must consider before you come with me."

She stilled. "What?"

Of all the things, this was the most difficult to tell her. "Vicar Morris visited late last night. I am under suspicion by the church for being a witch." At seeing the horrified look on her face, I rushed to continue. "Do not fret, Chloe. I assured him you were learning scripture, and we will attend church services on Sunday. But I cannot leave you here without protection; for once I sail for Nevis, I am unsure who would look out for you. Under the present arrangements."

She dug her fingers into the dirt of a potted palm. Brilliant yellow light flared around her wrist. "It seems I am a burden after all."

"Chloe, stop it! You are not a burden. I plan to petition the head of the London house for time in his library, as well as practice time for me in his pen. If his mood is right, I will approach him about offering his protection to you."

Chloe launched herself into my arms, her voice muffled against my hair. "You are all the protection I need. Wherever you go, I go. I'll be a great help, do not worry."

"Then come with me. I have several errands to perform. I will send a note for Lady Gladstone to meet us at the dressmaker's."

An hour later, I instructed the coach to halt. Chloe peered out the window. "Why are we near the docks? Is this the dressmaker? She must be good if her clients travel to this part of the city to consign her."

"No. This is not Madame Mincer's. This is a charity stop."

The street appeared very different in the light of day. The buildings were poorly constructed, crowding up three storeys, blocking out the natural sunlight. I entered the bakery.

The floor was scattered with wooden toys as I remembered. The counters were worn, but clean. Chloe peered at a selection of glazed buns.

"It smells wonderful in here. Can I have a pastry?"

I opened my reticule. "Of course."

The thin woman I recognized from the night of the fire entered from the back room, wiping her hands on a white cloth. "Can I help you ladies?"

I smiled. "I am Lady Richmond. I heard through the papers that there was a fire in the neighborhood?"

She adjusted a tray of sweets. "Yes."

"Were there any displaced persons from the fire?"

"I do not understand you, ma'am."

"Let me ask another way. Were there any people who lost their homes?"

The woman pressed her lips into a thin line. "I took in the only survivors. A girl, and her brother. She was the only one at home at the time, according to Missus Lovey."

"Well, I am inquiring if there is any help I can offer. I have charitable interests in the city, and I am always looking for new cases to aid."

"The little one is a friend of my own Henrietta. I have taken her in until her relatives can come to collect the girl. The boy, however, refused my help."

I hefted my reticule, the coins clinking. "May I offer a contribution to assist you until her relatives are located?"

The woman eyed the purse, then shook her head. "I do not need your charity. Thank you."

I pulled several coins from my purse. "I am sorry, I did not mean to offend you. May we have two of the pastry buns?"

The woman rolled the purchase into a waxed paper. I handed her the equivalent of a year's earnings in coins. She felt them, placing them one-by-one in her mouth and biting them. "Thank you, but I do not have change. Business is slow today." She selected two coins, equaling less than the amount of the buns. "Pay me the remainder next time you come into my shop."

I shook my head. "Please keep the change. Let me help you."

She nodded, a sad look on her face.

I continued, "I noticed the streets were not crowded."

She replaced the tray of sweets in the display case. "Them government raids have people too scared to come here. People are going over to Reading Street to the bake shop. Too frightened to come here."

"Government raids?"

"Yes. Looking for witches, or people suspected of helping witches. Silly business, really. I worry more about the pickpockets outside the gin houses than the butcher they took the other night. He never did nothing to me except buy my bread."

"If you require more assistance, please let me know."

"Stop these incessant raids into my neighborhood that keep driving my customers away. That is real assistance!"

We left the store, Chloe chomping contentedly on her pastry. "I need to stop eating or I will never fit into any dress."

We met Louise at Madame Mincer's, a reasonable dressmaker without the fussiness or airs surrounding many on Bond Street. She was a young woman with three daughters who played in the back rooms while she attended to customers. Louise was sitting in the small lounge, drinking a cup of tea, examining a red silk dress with less bodice than most. She pointed at the dress when our greetings were complete.

"What is your opinion, Julia? Is that a fine dress to wear to your divorce?"

I looked at the dress again. It was divine. "I think it is a smashing dress. Have you found your errant husband yet?"

"No." She put down her cup, placing it precisely on the saucer, as a good lady with manners would. "But I have retained the services of a barrister who is willing to travel with me to find him once the weather clears in the spring."

The dressmaker's assistant folded the dress carefully. "Would Madame like to have this added to your bill?"

Louise corrected her. "Please add it to Lord Gladstone's bill."

The girl nodded and bustled away. Madame Mincer appeared, clapping her hands when she spied me. "Lady Richmond! How nice to see you! Was your dress the sensation at your holiday ball?"

"Yes, It was. Madame Mincer, I'd like you to meet my charge, Miss Chloe Longood." Chloe dropped into a proper curtsey.

Madame Mincer turned a business eye to the girl. "She is very skinny. And tall. How many dresses do you require?"

"Two dresses of wool for now, and six dresses of a lighter weight for the spring. Pastel fabrics, please, and minimum lace on the hem. I want them delivered by Friday."

Madame Mincer appeared outraged. "I cannot possibly have that many dresses completed in that time! You know what a busy woman I am!" She pulled a measuring tape from the apron about her waist and started voicing numbers to her assistant. She turned Chloe to the right, and then the left, as she answered. "I can have one dress for now, and two for the spring ready in that amount of time."

Chloe stood stoically under the ministrations of the dressmaker. "Really, Lady Richmond, there is no need for the rush."

I rolled my eyes and popped a small biscuit in my mouth from the refreshment table. Pausing to chew, I swallowed the sweet bread before answering. "I can pay you double, and even a bonus for early delivery for half the order."

Madame Mincer held a length of pale green silk against Chloe's chest. "No, too light." She handed it back to her assistant. "Get me the length of yellow from the shipment this week."

The girl hurried to the back of the store. Madame Mincer turned to me. "Done. What do you think of the yellow?"

The assistant hurried from the back, with a bolt of soft, yellow silk, the color of butter. Chloe sighed. "Yellow is my favorite color."

Madame Mincer cooed, "Silk is the most expensive fabric."

I looked from one to the other. "I love the yellow. Put it on Lord Richmond's tab."

Chapter Ten

"Chloe, you are eating as if you will not see any food again." Chloe sat across from me, shoveling eggs into her mouth, her plate piled high with buttered bread and ham slices. It was the day we were to meet Botetourt and his clan.

"They did not feed me much in the dungeon. I am merely taking advantage of a good situation."

"How are you this morning?"

She glanced at her arms. "Almost normal." She tapped the cover of a leather-bound book sitting beside her plate. "I hope Lord Richmond does not mind, but I wanted to borrow this."

"Which title?"

"Caesar's *Commentary on the Gallic Wars*. I am curious about the defeat of the French, no matter how long ago."

I chuckled. "I think he won't mind. My father made us read *The Art of War* when we were younger. Living in the West Indies, one year, you are allies with the Spanish, next year, it's the Dutch, although the English have been on Nevis the longest."

She dabbed a napkin to the corner of her mouth. "What is your home like?"

"Beautiful, green, like you can only imagine, covers everything in sight, Mount Nevis rising into the clouds, never far from the rush of ocean waves. I miss it." I realized as I described it how much I did. I missed the island, for all the nostalgic reasons one longs for a toy you can never play with again as it is unseemly, or that time in your life has passed.

"I miss Mom and Dad." Chloe's eyes filled with tears, and her words sounded raw. "If they were better, or more powerful, or if they loved me more, they would have fought to protect us. But they were weak, and here I am." She pushed away her plate, crumpling to the table. Her shoulders heaved with her sobs.

Shocked by her rapid change in mood, I hesitated a moment, unsure of what to do. When I cried, I wanted no one near, but my heart ached hearing the bare emotion in her yearning whimpers. I rushed to her, engulfing her in my arms.

"Chloe, I will do the best I can, I promise. I cannot offer you the security of a clan, but I will do my best." I knew how precarious her situation was. Until she entered her full powers, she was like a rare fruit, just ripe for the picking by any cruelly intentioned witch.

She raised her head, and her tears flowed down to dribble from her chin. I wiped the excess off with a napkin as if she were a toddler. "I don't want to leave you. For the first time in months, I have faith I'll live to see my next birthday."

"I want to introduce you to Lord Botetourt."

Her hands clutched me desperately. "I will not leave you. I am afraid he will misuse me like *she* did."

"I promise you that will not happen. I trust he is a man of his word. If he does not pledge to foster you, we will leave. I will take you to Nevis with me. I will make it right with Lord Richmond."

She sniffed. I handed her the napkin from the table, which she swiped below her nose. "You'd do that for me?"

I hugged her close. "Of course. I will not let anyone harm you."

She pulled away, wiping her nose again. "I want to be strong. I do not want to be weak again."

"Then I have a proposition for you. I must visit Lord Botetourt today, and you may accompany me if you promise to observe. Do not speak unless spoken to. I do not want you provoking anyone." I had no inkling about who might have been at Lord Botetourt's, but I did not want to leave Chloe alone in the house. I dabbed her cheeks again. "So dry your eyes, and wear a loose skirt."

Her face lit up. "I'll be ready in an instant! I mean, your home is lovely, but I want to get out and see more new sights."

"I understand. We leave in twenty minutes." I followed her up the stairs. Chloe actually skipped to her room.

I closed the door to my quarters, turning the lock before opening the massive wardrobe containing my clothes, and shoving aside the tulle, silk and lace gowns. Clearing a path, I sent a thin line of blue out from my casting hand, rotating my wrist to set the spell to unlock a secret compartment of the wardrobe. Most well-crafted furniture had a secret compartment, and mine was no exception. It was on the small side, measuring two feet-by-two feet. An issue arises when the presence of the secret compartment is known by all and sundry. I enchanted mine to appear as if the lock were rusted shut. The spell complete, the lock popped open and the hatch squeaked on the unused hinges. Reaching inside, my fingers brushed the soft sensations of leather and linen.

I tugged out a white linen shirt and black leather pants from the compartment, my dueling clothes. I certainly hoped they still fit. Wiggling into the leather pants, I secured them at my knees, with my stockings remaining in place. A long-sleeved shirt followed, held up with a leather belt studded with pouches for potions, vials, dirt, whatever I needed. A knife scabbard remained empty. I hated knives.

Black, supple, leather boots covered my calves, ending just below my knees. A coat similar to a gentleman's duster completed the outfit. The coat, being wool, was a good buffer since it could absorb energy, thereby lessening the impact of any spell.

I covered my ensemble with a cloak. Glancing at the clock, I estimated a mere ten minutes until our departure. I rushed outside to the hothouse. The warm humidity caused a trickle of sweat to fall between my shoulder blades. Working quickly, I gathered leaves of thistle, willow tree, and heather. I placed each sample in a separate pouch, leaving two empty. Pausing in front of the pineapple tree, I debated the virtues between the acidic juice properties of the pineapple leaf versus the toxicity of the foxglove flower. Both were transient reactions, and each would be necessary in a pinch. I decided to take both, packaging them with care in the remaining two pouches. I uncorked a small goatskin, and filled it with water, securing it inside my belt. Satisfied with my preparations, I headed back into the house. I had one more stop to make before meeting Chloe.

I continued to Richmond's study, where he kept a small collection of pistols in a cabinet. They did not have ammunition, but I wouldn't need bullets. I only used a gun for threats. If threats failed, a swift hit to the head of a properly balanced pistol solved many a dueling conflict. Hefting a small handgun in my hand, I balanced it between my thumb and forefinger before deciding it was big enough for my purpose, yet small enough to fit into the holster on my belt. I shoved it into my belt, then hurried to meet Chloe in the foyer.

Her eyes widened when she saw my outfit. "That is not entirely proper for a morning visit, is it?"

"It is for this one."

We climbed into the coach. Along the way, I briefed Chloe on the salient features of a practice duel. "The head of the house dictates the rules and the partners. This is to protect the weaker members, while offering them an opportunity to practice."

Her eyes were huge. "I'll stay out of the way, I promise."

I adjusted the buckle on my belt. "Once the pairings are complete, in my clan, any new members must be ranked into the grid. This is at the sole discretion of the master. He might direct a new initiate to duel with the lowest member of the grid, or the second lowest. The rules of the duel may also differ between houses. In my house, anything was permissible. Lord Botetourt may set different guidelines, however."

"Have you killed anyone? I mean, in a duel?"

Her simple question hung heavily in the air. I could not meet her eyes. "I might as well have separated her neck from her head." My voice choked and I swallowed, trying to compose myself before I continued. "If you mean, did I suck the life from her? No. But I permanently maimed her casting hand. She cannot spell. I maimed a perfectly nice witch for the sake of a higher notch on the grid." *For no good reason except that it was expected of me.*

"You can use both hands for a cast. I felt it myself."

"One of the gifts from my mother. It is unusual. My victim did not have the good fortune of having a wind witch for a mother."

We traveled in silence, the tall mansions of Edgeware Street, north of Hyde Park, passing by the window. We turned right onto Queen Street, with a quick left onto Horace Street. I chuckled. The head of the London house lived scarcely a stone's throw from St. John's Church and the Bishop.

Our carriage was the only one in evidence when we alighted moments later. I adjusted my cloak. Chloe shuffled her feet, scuffing the gravel. She placed both hands palms down in the exposed dirt, and scooped up two handfuls with which she filled her pockets. Brushing the excess dirt off her hands, she smiled and pointed to the door. "That is different."

The front doors were carved wood, and stained dark. Where the neighbors' doors were straight rectangles and lined squares, Lord Botetourt's front door was covered in chiseled, sharp lines that intertwined in complex patterns. They were so intricate, I could not decipher the picture. Before I could peruse it any longer, the door opened. Hadgi stood inside.

"Come in. My master is expecting you." His voice was lilting, like a beautiful melody floating on the air. He reached for my cloak and coat.

I shrugged out of the cloak, but stopped him from touching my coat. "I will keep my coat, thank you."

He eyed my wool duster. "If you wish. It is of no import. Follow me."

We trailed Hadgi down the hall. The house was larger inside than it appeared from the outside, and each room was decorated in a similar classical style, making it difficult to identify any exits or distinctive features. After two more turns, we clambered down a flight of stairs.

Most larger homes had the kitchens on the ground level, or separate from the main house. Where the stairs to a kitchen would normally end, we continued downward, a full forty steps from the landing. Chloe placed her hand on the dirt walls.

"It must have been difficult to dig so far below ground."

Not if you were an earth witch, I mused. We followed Hadgi deeper into the underground of London. The tunnel gradually tilted downward, ultimately leveling out in front of an antechamber thirty feet across. I had certainly never seen any room this large excavated so deeply into the earth. At the far side, a door gleamed in the torchlight, its panels as black as onyx, and smooth in the flickering torchlight with no apparent locking mechanism. Hadgi glanced at Chloe and me.

"Stay here." He left us at the other side of the dirt chamber. I could not see well in the dim light, but I imagined the earth animals: worms, beetles, and shiny, crunchy insects, burrowing above us. Those animals I did not mind. Spiders, however, I hated. I patted my head, feeling for cobwebs, reassuring myself that I only imagined the eight little legs creeping up my arms. Chloe scrabbled her fingers in the dirt wall behind her, sighing with contentment.

Hadgi placed his hands on the smooth metal surface, with fingers splayed. He chanted in a sing-song voice, a beautiful tenor at odds with his usual silence. A teal glow flickered in a maze across the panel, spraying out bursts of light like little fire sparks into the air. The light swept from his hands, extending to the four corners. Brilliant green light joined the teal, and a passage opened in the middle of the metal. I marveled at the skill necessary for an illusion of this level. Master level, at the very least.

Hadgi turned, motioning us through the multicolored opening.

I went through first, with Chloe only a few steps behind me. Her hand gripped mine, and the dirt from her palm wiped onto my hands.

The practice pit on Nevis was located on our property in the middle of a cane field. We changed it each season to follow the fallow fields, using enchantments to ensure the slaves stayed away. The areas were isolated, and unless one clung to the top craters of Mount Nevis with a spyglass, our identities remained safe. Our duels were held in the bright sun, or under moonlight, with plenty of open space.

Here, the setting was as contrasting as a bright diamond on a dark facade. The floor was dirt, with shadowy patches of what I suspected was blood. A wooden wall, rising five feet tall, formed the perimeter of the practice pit. Wooden chairs were arranged on two elevated rows, which encircled the ring. Most of the chairs were full, and the men and women intermingled. No one wore masks, but the flickering torches offered little illumination to delineate their visages. I felt like a Christian about to be fed to the lions in the Roman Coliseum.

So much for using their identity as a blackmail tool. Lord Botetourt stood on a dais at the extreme opposite end of the room. He tipped his head towards me in greeting. He was dressed as I, in traditional dueling garb, but his was all black. Hadgi pointed to the center of the ring. "Stand here. Wait." He broke into a run, raising his hands above his head before somersaulting into the air, and clearing the wall to land on his feet in front of Lord Botetourt.

"Showy."

Chloe shivered beside me. "I don't feel the warm welcome I was wishing for in a new clan."

I squeezed her grubby hand.

Lord Botetourt clapped his hands for attention. "I hereby convene this practice session. In accordance with our laws, we must allocate a hierarchy level to Lady Richmond. I will open the challenge. The rules are as always. No death. Maiming is permissible, as long as a healer is present, and one is today. No assistance from the audience in the form of spells, potions, curses, hexes, et cetera." His brown eyes met mine, and I could glimpse his amusement with this game. "Are you prepared, Lady Richmond?"

I presented a one-legged bow, a parody of those Lord Botetourt gave each day. "I, Lady Julia Richmond, await my worthy opponent." I spoke the traditional words of the practice duel. The crowd murmured as a lanky man with red hair stood four chairs down from Lord Botetourt, signifying his place in the clan as fourth in line.

"I'll put her through her paces."

The crowd murmured louder. He descended into the dirt. My head barely reached his shoulder; so to keep a tactical advantage on the flat floor, I kept a cushion of distance between us. I turned to Chloe who clung to my side.

"Take a seat wherever Lord Botetourt indicates. Do not try to help me. I'll be fine."

Chloe eyed the gentleman. "I've seen him before. At Madame Oualie's house."

Lord Botetourt interrupted. "Miss Longood, please take a seat as you have forsworn all practice of witchcraft to the church." He motioned to a seat on his left, in the front row.

"All manner of dark spells. Not all witchcraft," she mumbled as she took her place. Hadgi extended his hand to help her scramble up the wall to the dais.

The gentleman presented himself in the light of a circle of torches suspended from the low ceiling. He bowed. "I am Lord Fairfax. Are you ready, Lady Richmond? I've wanted to toss you on your backside for awhile. Your husband irritates me."

I eyed his garments. Pockets everywhere, and a knife in his left boot. No telling what he had hidden in the pockets, but the knife belied a weakness. He was a right-handed caster. No witch would put a weapon on the same side as his casting hand. I rolled my shoulders, stepping back three paces. "I am ready."

"Begin," Lord Botetourt commanded, and a thick column of purple fire erupted from Lord Fairfax's right hand. I dropped to my knees, ducking under the shot. Before I could stand, another blast hit the dirt beside me, blowing a cloud of dust into my eyes. I rolled, throwing a shield of blue with my left hand, and digging into my pocket for the pineapple leaf. Lord Fairfax appeared smug, cracking his knuckles.

"Is that all you can do, little witch? I heard you were extremely talented. I suppose gossip is always fraught with half-truths."

I circled him, keeping my shield in place. His words were telling, not that his comments deflated my confidence, but in the amount of pride they suggested. I turned again to Lord Fairfax, letting down my shield. "You need more than harsh words to best me, sir. I am not an orphaned witch without proper training." I formed a ball of blue in my hands, cupping the leaf between my palms. Blue mist erupted, the smell of fresh pineapple infusing the air. I blew the mist towards him.

Lord Fairfax laughed, a harsh sound. "A bit of a mist? Slow mist? Where is the power in that?" The gallery erupted in laughter. I dug a bit of thistle from another pouch as he taunted me for the crowd. He pointed at the floating blob.

"Stop it! Send me something to test me." He threw a bolt of purple at the spell. When the purple met the mist, the mist separated, engulfing the purple bolt and expanding to twice its size.

He threw a succession of power bolts at my left hand, any one of them capable of separating my hand from my arm. I dodged each one, keeping close watch on my spell. Picking myself from the dust, I tutted at the shocked look on his face. "I was hoping for a challenge as well. I fear there is no diversity in your repertoire, sir, and I grow bored. You are all power, and utterly without finesse. It is a wonder you rank fourth in your clan." My mist reached his head, hovering just above it. He swatted at the nuisance, but the mist floated and remained out of reach.

Ignoring the spell, he pulled a huge circle of purple on his palm. A fireball. Agitation and irritation warred for control of his features.

"I am done playing nursery games." He heaved the energy at my head, throwing a spell to rope my feet. I ignored it, and threw up a shield to deflect the fireball.

The impact of the rope snaring my ankles knocked me off balance, and the purple bolt deflected into the stands. Screams and the smell of burning timbers clogged my nostrils. The power rope remained around my ankles.

I stilled. Rope spells were tricky. Once released, they relied on the return of energy from the wiggling captive to fuel the tightening coils. Staying still sapped the energy, and eventually, the coils would fall apart. However, one needed to simply stay alive until that occurrence.

I lay in the dirt, clutching the thistle. Lord Fairfax strode to stand over me. His eyes were green, with pupils dilated, and all of his features seemed taut with excitement.

"Now to finish you, witch. Let this be a lesson to your husband." He grabbed my casting hand, twisting it cruelly while holding my elbow firm.

He was trying to break my arm. I blinked against the pain as tendon and muscle stretched unnaturally. Sweat beaded on my brow, but I remained still, hoping the rope spell would loosen in time to prevent Lord Fairfax from permanently injuring me.

The ropes, however, remained taut.

Nausea rose in my throat as he forced my wrist to pop. Pain shot up my arm. I cried out in anguish, struggling to stay still, while blinking tears from my eyes.

Fairfax leaned his weight into my wrist, forcing the broken bones farther apart. I could hear the crunching of bones against bones. I choked down bile, panting with the effort to remain still.

Time to end this. Collecting my thoughts, I pushed some power into my wrist, to initiate the healing process. Thrashing my hips and legs, I threw Fairfax off balance. The rope spell tightened around my legs, but now, my right hand was free.

I pushed my hand into his face, rubbing the thistle over his skin. Eruptions covered his flesh, and the burning caused him to drop my hand. He yelled as the thistle burned into his face.

The rope gave way at my ankles, and I scrambled to my feet. Swaying on shaky legs, I snapped my fingers, activating the spell.

The blue mist pulsing at his earlobe expanded to engulf his head. It was a simple cloud of mist, but once the power was applied to the spell, the drops coalesced inside the lungs and mouth. He would drown ten feet below the surface of the earth in a dirt cave. He struggled to pull the mist away, but wherever his fingers touched, the mist separated, only to form again once the passage was complete. It was like trying to hold water between your fingers.

The crowd was silent, their earlier chattering drowned by the gulps and gurgles of Lord Fairfax. He dropped to his knees, signaling his surrender with crossed arms. I kept a safe distance between us, my casting arm still energized. I asked, "Are you surrendering, Lord Fairfax?"

He nodded, his face as blue as the spell surrounding it.

I snapped my fingers again, and the mist fell like water to the floor. Fairfax collapsed to his hands and knees, gasping for breath before vomiting into the dirt.

My casting hand throbbed with pain. It would be another three hours before it healed under my powers.

Lord Botetourt stood. "Lady Richmond, I pronounce you the winner of this practice duel. As it was with a ranking member of our house, you are thusly allowed membership."

A cry came from a full-figured woman on the second row, "She was brilliant! She deserves his spot. Those are the rules." Other voices joined her protest.

Lord Botetourt raised his hands for silence. "We have a prior arrangement." He gazed at me. "You are granted amnesty while in London. You may keep your wand. You don't need one anyway. So it is of no use extracting it from you." He winked at me, laughing at his own joke. I turned to Lord Fairfax, noticing the blisters and pustules erupting on his face. He looked miserable. Nothing like being emasculated in front of a crowd. I knelt beside him. "Do you want me to take those off?"

He shook his head, scratching at his neck like a dog with fleas. "I deserve them. I am an embarrassment to my clan."

"No one deserves more punishment than they need." I handed him a piece of the willow bark. "Take it. It will help."

He paused only a moment, eyeing the brown glob in my hand before popping it into his mouth and chewing. "What was that spell, anyway?"

"Common thistle, indigenous to these lands. Appalling, isn't it?"

"Very." He stood, brushing the dirt from his trousers. "You could have finished me off, you know."

I gazed into his eyes. "That is not the point. What good is it during a practice round? There is enough bloodshed between the houses as it stands. I have nothing to prove by permanently harming you."

He blushed, glancing at my wrist.

"What has my husband done to warrant your anger?"

"He helps hunt us down and drives witches into the waiting arms of the church. It is a wonder you can sleep well at night."

By the tides. "I am sorry. I had no idea."

Chloe hurried to meet me on the dirt floor, hugging me close. "Are you all right?'

"I am the picture of health." I cradled my throbbing wrist. "How did you enjoy it?"

"It was wonderful! Your spell was magnificent! Simple, yet elegant, just like the perfect dress for a ball."

Lord Fairfax grimaced. "Defeated by fashion. Even worse." He bowed to me. "Your reputation does not do you justice, Lady Richmond. I apologize for the slurs on you and your house."

"Thank you. I hope my husband has an opportunity to redeem himself in your eyes as well."

He stiffened, and the blisters began receding on his face. "Doubtful."

He strode off to follow the columns of people exiting the ring. Lord Botetourt approached us, eyes twinkling. "Well done! And you left my fourth intact. Thank you."

"May I peruse your library, as a boon for good behavior?"

His mouth quirked, suppressing a smile. "Yes. One hour. Let me know when you want to visit. Some things are off limits."

"I'd rather like to visit now. The tenacity of my position deems it necessary to carpe diem."

He laughed, but the laughter did not reach his eyes. "You are an impertinent miss."

"Yes." I met his gaze.

He checked his watch, motioning for Hadgi. "Hadgi will escort you to the library. I will chat with Miss Longood. You have one hour."

I hesitated to leave Chloe in his care. He continued, "Come, now, Lady Richmond, surely you do not question my motives towards this delightful girl?"

"Yes, I do."

"Good. Then you are not a fool. I swear I will not harm her in any way."

Chloe gave me a stern look. "I'll be fine, really. I am not without powers."

I looked at her arms, the healing scabs a reminder of her worth. "Be careful."

She hugged me. "I will."

I left Chloe and Lord Botetourt chatting in the practice ring before following Hadgi into the bowels of the house.

It was too many turns to follow. The pain in my wrist had diminished to a searing burn by the time we reached two double doors. Hadgi threw open the doors.

"What? No secret incantations to unlock the entryway?"

Hadgi ignored me, and stepped aside so I could enter the room.

The doors slammed shut, plunging me into utter darkness. The scurrying sounds of small animals, expected in a large house, did nothing to ease my fears. I wasted a few minutes searching for a light before realizing I had no need of one. Pushing a blue orb for illumination, I held my hand high to survey my surroundings.

When I think of a library, the images of great stacks of books, with a table or chair for quiet repose come to mind. Lord Botetourt's library was more like the British Museum: a catalogue of interesting things, loosely grouped by themes. A monstrous armoire with glass doors of a yellow-tint housed row upon row of magic wands, from the infantile twigs of saplings to the intricate wood and precious metal of a master witch.

The tile floor was concealed by jars like an Egyptian funerary, except they were filled with dirt. I presumed they were from different locales around the globe. Rack upon rack of lumps of rock and stone covered the western wall. I proceeded among the disparate things, looking for a traditional book or even a collection of scrolls. I couldn't even find a parchment. All too soon, a shaft of light pierced the blue-tinted gloom. My time was up.

"Come, Lady Richmond." Lord Botetourt himself called from the doorway, and appeared cheerful as he greeted me. "I hope you found your hour educational."

"I learned to be more specific in what I ask for. A mistake I will not make again," I grumbled. "Where is Miss Longood?"

"Ah, the stings of defeat." He fell in line beside me as we traveled through the house. "She is enjoying a light repast in my study. I swear Madame Oualie must keep a poor table to whet a girl's appetite so."

"It is probably from so much bloodletting."

"Pity the girl didn't have better sense than to fall into a stronger witch's web."

"I was hoping you would foster her. She is a good soul. I cannot teach her properly in my current situation."

He paused in the hall. We were alone, and for the first time, I thought of how attractive he was. His eyes were creased with the lines of responsibility. "Lady Richmond, I cannot extend a place to Miss Longood. Madame Oualie is a," he paused, allowing his tongue to touch the corner of his mouth before continuing. "A competitor. Protocol dictates she has first say in Miss Longood's disposition."

Irritated, I snapped. "Then you are a lame leader if you would allow a witch beneath you to determine your clan's personnel."

"Don't be cross. With your defeat of Fairfax, you are technically fourth in line for my throne. You could challenge Oualie and the terms of the challenge could include acceptance of Miss Longood."

"No." I stepped back from him. "My father often spoke about the strain of leadership. Your position must be easy, as you determine everything with a duel when you need to decide an outcome. It is a wonder any witches with two hands are left in your ranks."

He stiffened, and his hands clenched into fists at his sides. "You know not of what you speak. The issue of Miss Longood is not negotiable at this time." He visibly relaxed, mastering his emotions. I am sure the last thing he wanted was to deal with me or my problem ward.

"How is your hand? Fairfax likes to immobilize his opponents. His spellcasting is, frankly, quite lackluster."

I flexed my fingers, a shot of pain lancing up my arm. "It feels better than an hour ago."

He cradled my hand between his, teal light surrounding our joined palms. I felt the light probing my wrist, gently, offering peace and surcease from the pain. I held my power in check, allowing his to dip into the bones and tendons, knitting them whole again. As the light receded, he dropped my hand, and a smile played about his lips.

"Forgive the impertinence, but I could not let you leave unhealed. Your husband might grow suspicious."

"So you were the healer present at the duel."

"No. There is another."

He spun on his heel, and I hurried behind him.

He flung open a door, expecting me to follow. The proportions of the room were geometrically perfect, from the fireplace to the chair sizes to the balanced windows on the wall. Shelves were stacked against two walls, floor-to-ceiling, with leather-bound books of all shapes, sizes and colors. An Oriental rug of silk covered the floor, and I itched to take off my boots and scrunch my toes into the plush pile. The room was warm, and I threw off my coat, wishing I could peruse the book titles. I bet there was a volume on demonology.

"Where is Chloe?"

Lord Botetourt nodded to Hadgi. "Please escort Miss Longood here."

Hadgi nodded and left.

"These are your private rooms." My white shirt was damp with sweat and stuck to my skin, while my breeches revealed the womanly shape of my figure. Lord Botetourt glanced down at my form. He wandered to the bookshelf, pulling a plain book from the collection.

"This is the spellbook of a deceased master of London, the man here before me. I understand he had an affinity for demons." He placed the book on a large, wooden desk. "Do you have anything with which to bargain, Lady Richmond?" He leaned against the furniture, his body taut with energy.

I tugged my blouse from my skin, hoping for modesty as Lord Botetourt shifted on his feet. I answered, my voice strained. "I do not. We have already discussed this."

He approached, stopping inches from me. My skin heated from the rush of power in standing so close to him. Blue tingled in my fingertips, and a teal tinged his skin. He was flushed. I could see the his pulse beating in his neck.

Desire unfurled in my core. I took a step backwards, seeking distance from his suddenly irresistible attractiveness.

Lord Botetourt remained still.

"Do you ever wonder what it is like with another of your kind? The freedom of expression, the knowledge that you can release your power without being chastised for it in the morning?" His voice was rough.

I imagined what it would be like to melt into someone's arms, to be accepted for who I was and what I could do. I ached for the freedom to be myself. Freedom I thought I had when I married Richmond. Freedom I did not have now.

"I am a married woman, Lord Botetourt, and I took a vow of loyalty to my husband. One I fully intend to keep." I pressed my palms together, praying for strength,

"I have no problem with your marriage vows. To me, they are null, as you married outside a house of witches." He stepped closer, reaching a finger to touch the middle of my lower lip in the barest of gestures. "I want you, Julia Richmond, marriage or no. I am willing to bargain, and I am a man of my words. That book on demons for a kiss."

I swayed closer to him, studying the contours of his lips, and the small scar on his cheek. I wondered if his kiss would be rough. My power swelled, excited at the possibilities. My breasts burned under the fabric of my shirt. His brown eyes lit with victory as I inched closer to him, to meet his embrace.

I stopped.

I repeated in a ragged voice, "I am a married woman, and I took a vow of loyalty that I intend to keep." I slid from his grasp, clasping my shaking arms around me as a feeble shield. "I thank you for your generous offer, but I must decline."

He stood silent, a muscle twitching twice in his cheek before he answered. "I will have Hadgi take you to Miss Longood."

He closed the distance between us, grabbing my casting hand with his. Energy thrummed between us, and a pure jolt of power and desire emerged from the depths of my body. A body that ached for release. He bent over my hand, planting a kiss on the ridge of my knuckles. "Good evening, Lady Richmond. Consider my offer open for renegotiation." Straightening, he continued. "I hope you find the peace you seek."

He turned and left, taking the demon book with him. I collapsed onto the nearest chair, my legs shaking with the adrenaline of the day. Botetourt offered me peace. Freedom. And was willing to bargain a book for my body. I valued my pride, my loyalty, my marriage vows, more than a stolen kiss for a book.

But I was tempted. That is what unsettled me the most: the depth of my loneliness. Shaking my head, I hugged myself closer. The door opened and Hadgi ushered in a chattering Chloe.

"Lady Richmond, what a wonderful house! I am sure the gardens are magnificent in the spring. Lord Botetourt was especially polite. I wasn't scared at all!"

Hadgi escorted us to the front stoop, shutting the door behind with a solid thump. I shivered under my layers, not from the cold, but fear. Fear at how close I came to breaking my vows. With a witch!

Chapter Eleven

We stood on the front stoop, with the darkness falling blacker around us, and the few lanterns sputtering in their sconces along the street.

"If our coach does not come in a few moments, we will walk to Queen Street and hail a cab. It is unusual for John to be late." I shivered in my dueling garb, pulling the cloak closer about my frame. A steady stream of traffic continued on Horace Street, most paying us no mind.

"All right," Chloe agreed. She peered down the street. "Is that your coach?"

I looked at a long line of dark coaches lumbering down the street. "I believe so. I think that is the set of John's hat. But why would he leave?" Richmond's servants enjoyed their position with a good employer. Most strived to exceed our expectations in their daily duties.

"I'm getting chilled. If it is the wrong coach, I do not care. I'm climbing in anyway."

The coach maneuvered closer to the curb, the Richmond family crest in bold, gold paint identifying it as our ride. Chloe clapped. "Look! It is your coach! At last!"

John pulled the horses to a halt, vaulting from his perch to open the door for us. "Sorry, Lady Richmond, but I was delayed near the cathedral. Bad accident." He kept his eyes downcast, holding the door as we climbed into the warm interior. Chloe settled herself on the seat as John slammed shut the door.

I sniffed the air. "Does it smell like mold to you in here?"

She sniffed, wrinkling her nose. "No. Maybe it is from your exertions at Lord Botetourt's house?"

I breathed deeply again, the musty scent tickling my nose. I was positive someone else had been in the coach, and recently. I fingered my belt: all the pouches were empty, as well as the water vial. The familiar sooty streets passed outside the window, failing to calm my nerves.

We rounded Queen Street, a few blocks from St. John's Church. The coach's speed increased, and the figures on the street soon became a blur.

"Ow!" Chloe cried as she fell against the leather squabs.

I braced myself in the corner, pounding my fist against the door connecting the interior to the coachman's box. "John!" I cried. "Slow down!"

He did not answer. The coach careened around a corner, sending me tumbling into Chloe.

She grunted, rubbing her head.

The coach stopped, toppling us into a heap on the floor. I picked myself up, untangling my legs from Chloe's skirts.

The door banged open. A man stood at the door, his form blocking my view. A musty scent wafted on the cool winter air. Warning bells pealed in my head. Chloe cowered behind me, her fingers digging painfully into my arm.

"Lady Richmond, by order of the Church, you are to turn yourself over to the Bishop for questioning,"

I recognized the voice as Vicar Morris'. I sat on the leather seat, refusing to exit the coach. "On what grounds? As you can see, Lady Chloe is here and in good health." Chloe shrank further away from the door.

The vicar reached into the coach, his fingers wrapping around my ankle. "The request of the Bishop is reason enough. Get out."

Chloe scrambled for the opposite side of the coach, shrinking from his grasp. I kicked, screaming, "John! Move!" I aimed my boot at his elbow, and the kick landed true. He grunted, his elbow buckling, but his grip tightened around my ankle. He heaved, pulling me towards the coach door.

"No!" I yelled. He pulled me prone, my arms flailing, and trying to find purchase within the coach, while my fingers groped to find any leverage that might halt my slow slide into the embrace of the church.

Chloe clutched my arm, pulling against the force of the churchman. "Lady Richmond! NO! Don't leave me!"

I kicked again, feeling the crunch of my boot heel connecting with his nose.

"I'll make you pay for that, demon woman," he snarled.

Chloe's voice keened, "I can't go back! Don't leave me! Where will I go?"

"By the grace of God, release me! My husband will hear of this!"

"Richmond has his own problems to deal with. You will be interrogated and exorcised before he realizes you are gone." He tugged again, relentless in his grasp.

Chloe's grip slipped. He encircled my waist with his arm, hauling me out of the coach with a grunt, and throwing me onto the ground. The cobblestones of the street bit into my flesh.

He rolled me onto my stomach, his breath hot and hissing in my ear, his knee grinding my hips into the uneven ground. My breath left me in a whoosh, and the cold seeped into my skin.

"Chloe! Run!" I grunted. Hearing a scuffle behind me, I prayed it was Chloe escaping. I did not think she could hear me.

"Let the girl go. Madame Oualie can find her for us. Secure Lady Richmond," Vicar Morris directed. He shifted off my back, allowing some air to return to my lungs before he was replaced by another set of knees in my back.

I raised my head to see shoes only inches from my nose, and bright red drops of blood plopping onto the cobblestones and staining the ground. My power swelled at the scent of blood, flowing and stretching my skin like meat on a spit. I closed my eyes, blocking the lure of power, and finding control. My power could not help me, not if I ever wanted a life in London with Richmond.

Rough tugs pulled my hands behind my back, tying them together, the rope biting into my wrists. "Bring Lady Richmond."

Two men pulled me to standing. We were in front of St. John's Church, the familiar forms of the saints staring down at me from their lofty perches within the stained glass. A few people, bundled up against the cold, scurried across the square, refusing to look in my direction.

The coach melted into the falling night with a crack of John's whip. I prayed Chloe was not inside.

We entered the church, and continued through the sacristy out the back, into a small alley.

"Where are we going?" I asked.

"To dine with the Bishop." The men laughed at my question, their unbridled cruelty stamped in their tightening grip. I was not fool enough to think we were eating together.

We entered the garden of Bishop House from the alley. A brick wall denoted the perimeter of the property, taller than was usual in the city, a full six feet. The garden lay dormant, twisted branches of shrubs that appeared ghoulish in the fading light, casting shadows across the gravel path.

I hesitated as we approached the house. *Should I try to cast a spell?* There was certainly enough snow present in the little piles beneath a stand of rosebush shrubs along the western wall.

The man on my left jabbed me in the back. "Keep moving." His voice was rough, like metal scraping across stone.

The gravel crunching under my boots soon turned to flagstones. A stone mansion rose from the perfect orderliness of the winter plantings, warm light in the windows making the house appear rather charming in its proportions.

"Is this Bishop House?"

"Yes. Where you will meet justice."

"Over here. Bishop says to bring her into the study." A small wooden door opened at the east end of the house, where a young man waved. "Hurry. The Bishop leaves for his engagement within the hour."

We filed through the hedgerow to follow the young man inside to a room filled with light and warmth. A fire burned high in the grate. A silver tea set graced the desk, the aroma of fresh scones and steeping Darjeeling causing my stomach to growl.

The young man, arrayed in clerical robes, motioned for me to sit in a chair by the fire. "Please, Lady Richmond, sit here. The Bishop will be with you shortly. I will let him know you are arrived."

He left the room. Vicar Morris squeezed my shoulder, sending tingles of pain lancing down my arm. "He said to sit here, witch."

I sat in the chair, eyeing the teapot. "May I have a cup of tea?"

The vicar peered at his reflection in the silver teapot, his nose distorted in its convexity. "You may have a cup of tea when my nose heals."

"Do not threaten Lady Richmond. She may be more amenable to pleasant coercion."

The Bishop of London leaned heavily on a cane as he ambled into the room. He was known for having an agenda designed to rid England of all forms of malice against the church, lumping in witches with the lot. He ran thin fingers through his gray hair before adjusting a large ruby ring on his left hand. He eased himself into an armchair closest to the fire.

Vicar Morris knelt before grasping his hand and kissing the Bishop's ring. The men who escorted us disappeared into the garden, one shaking his finger in front of his nose, as if to warn me not to try to escape from that direction.

He rose. The Bishop ignored him, turning to me. "Lady Richmond, what a surprise. I admit, when your name was turned in, I was shocked. You have lived among us, posing as a righteous woman, attending our church, and all the while worshipping a demon master."

"I am a child of God, sir, and follow the Lord in all things."

"Interesting. You do not hesitate to mention God. Perhaps your sources are incorrect?"

"I have no doubt as to my sources. The truth will come out on the morrow."

The Bishop nodded. "An astute point. Please fetch my assistant, and escort her to her rooms."

The vicar bowed, fingering his nose as he rose. "Sir, I do not wish to disagree with you, but she broke my nose. She is violent, and not to be trusted. I hesitate to leave you alone with her."

The Bishop smiled, showing perfect, little, sharp teeth. "I will be fine. Go, fetch Alexander."

He left with a withering glance my way. The Bishop continued, "I hope your accommodations meet with your approval . As you know, we will post the notice of your interrogation tonight, and begin in the morning. Any witnesses testifying on your behalf must present themselves on the morrow."

"May I send a note to my husband?"

He blinked. "Of course not. That is not the purpose of our discussions. We are not looking for the truth. I could care less if you are a witch or an angel with wings hidden beneath your dress." He leaned closer, firelight dancing in his eyes. "What I want is information."

"I have no information to give you, sir."

"Oh, dear. Then I think things will go badly for you."

The churchman returned with the young man, Alexander. "Where shall we put her, sir? The underground is full."

The Bishop poured himself a cup of tea, blowing on it before taking a sip. "I think the outdoor area is required. I want her separated from the others."

"A capital notion, sir." Vicar Morris beamed. He jerked me to a standing position. "She will do nicely in the outdoors."

"Have a pleasant night, Lady Richmond. We will begin in the morning."

We exited as we came, retracing our steps through the gardens to a small shed in the back corner, a building I missed earlier. We stopped at the wooden door with metal grating studding the surface. A stout lock hung from a chain, wrapped around the little structure. Alexander fiddled with a ring of keys, muttering to himself. "So many places, so many people. How to keep them all straight?"

He peered at the lock. "Can you hold a bit of light for me? I cannot find the correct key."

The vicar yelled, "Bring a light!" Then he looked at me. "Maybe we should ask the witch to light our path."

I shuddered.

Lantern light swinging wildly marked the friar's path towards us. "Hold the light high," he directed. Alexander fumbled through the ring of keys, selecting a small one made of silver before fitting it into the lock. "Silver. Resists enchantment."

The door opened without a creak and darkness loomed in the opening. The smell of old bodies irritated my nose.

Strong hands pushed me inside and I stumbled over the uneven surface. I fell, landing flat on my face, and groaning with the impact.

"Sweet dreams, Lady Richmond. If you do not perish from cold tonight, we will wring a confession of the truth from your dirty lips in the morning."

The door slammed, and the key scraped in the lock.

Imprisoned. I, Julia Nesbit Richmond, was a prisoner.

Rolling onto my back, my hands began protesting over my weight and their bondage. I contracted my stomach muscles in an effort to sit up. It took three attempts.

I bent my legs, digging my heels into the ground to push my bottom across the dirt floor until my back hit the wall. I sidled along the wall until I was satisfied I was safely lodged in the corner.

My hands were numb from the tight bonds. I breathed deeply, blocking the pain from my face, my bruised body, and my hands. Pain could not help me escape. Clear thoughts and a solid plan were what I needed.

Chapter Twelve

I opened my senses to the night, now noticing the scrape and scuttle of small animals outside the wooden walls, the smell of dirty skin and offal wrinkling my nose.

"Hello? Is anyone here?"

A slight sound, the rustle of cloth, came from my right.

"I can smell you, even if I cannot see you. Please identify yourself. I know someone is here."

A dark shape, darker than the surrounding night, appeared in front of me. The shape bowed, almost toppling over. "Sorry. I am weak." Standing upright, he continued, "I am Master Daniel McGhee, last of my line."

"Your name sounds like you hail from the north."

"Scotland."

"I am Lady Richmond, of London."

"I gathered."

"Will you release my bonds?"

"No, ma'am. I've met the Bishop once before, and I do not wish to raise his interest in me again. What kind of witch are you?"

I sighed. "This is a great misunderstanding."

"They all say that."

I wiggled my shoulders to ease the ache building between the blades. I pushed with my legs, holding my back against the wall, leveraging myself to stand.

I counted my paces, starting in my corner, keeping my shoulder against the wall, the rough boards tugging at my clothes. Ten paces until I hit the back wall, where I repeated my survey. Father always said to escape from a cage, you had to know what kind of cage it was.

I ended where I began, the room ten-by-ten, with a pile of straw in the corner farthest from the door. I wedged my shoulders against my corner, balancing against the wall to slide down to the floor.

Daniel said, "That's it? No histrionics? That is the only relief out here."

I leaned my head back, closing my eyes. "I have had a trying day. I want to rest."

"I thought we might speak longer about your situation."

"No amount of talk will change my situation tonight, and unless you are offering to untie my hands, I have nothing further to say to you."

"It's because I'm a Scot, I know it."

I cracked open an eye. "Master McGhee, I do not care a whit where you are from, who your parents were, or your past transgressions as long as they do not involve crimes against bound women held captive in a garden shed."

"He thinks you will talk. Confess."

"I have nothing to confess, except the unholy thoughts as to what I will do to the person naming me a witch in the first instance."

"I would untie your hands, but he forbade me to help you. Please understand."

"Then goodnight." I turned from him as best my bound state allowed. I reviewed my position. I did not know if Richmond would offer help. If he truly captured witches for the church, my only hope lay in convincing him and the Bishop of my innocence, yet is seemed I was already convicted.

Chloe's whereabouts presented another conundrum. I prayed she escaped to safety, wherever that might have been on this night.

Daniel settled across the room from me. "I lied. Earlier. There are others, under the house. They are too afraid to speak."

I opened my eyes a little. "Maybe they will acknowledge themselves with the light of day."

"No. Last week, or last month, I cannot keep it straight, one of them refused to speak to the Bishop. He yelled and screamed for information, but Michael remained quiet. The Bishop cut out his tongue as if it were a roast, just so we could all see. Now, no one wants to speak. He is a terrible man."

I closed my eyes, thinking about the story. If anyone tried to cut out my tongue, I would blow them to heaven and get out of there.

"Master Daniel, as I said, this is all a misunderstanding. My husband will come and collect me on the morrow. The Bishop will likely be embarrassed by Vicar Morris's mistake."

Daniel scooted closer, his voice dropping lower. "They do not make mistakes, Lady. They make you want to agree to every depravity they accuse you of, for death is more welcome than the persistence of their tortures."

"Do not be melodramatic. Either untie my hands or go to sleep. Everything will seem better on the morrow."

I prayed my words were true.

The morning dawned cold. I called it morning since I dozed, but really had no concept of passing time. It could have been three hours or eight since Vicar Morris slammed the door to the shed. My body was stiff from the bonds, and I needed privacy for basic functions, but since I was housed with Daniel that would have to wait. I wiggled my hands again, twisting them a fraction within the thick rope. Needles of pain greeted my swollen fingers.

Daniel appeared at my elbow, his face speckled with freckles and dirt in the weak light. "They come."

I peered through a space between the planks, using my legs to push myself into a standing position. Without the use of my hands for casting, I was as useless as the poor, non-magical souls incarcerated with me. I wished I were back in my bedroom, dueling with Alistair. Or on Nevis, dueling Alistair. Anywhere, but here.

The Vicar appeared, his nose swollen and blackened. Richmond soon passed into view. My pulse raced at seeing him. "Richmond came!"

Vicar Morris rattled the keys in the lock. As the door swung open, I stumbled out of the cell, filling my lungs with air. I launched myself towards my husband, but Vicar Morris caught my arm by the elbow, digging his hands deeply into the flesh.

Richmond remained where he stood.

"Stephen, please, help me clear up this confusion and take me home."

He chuckled. "There is no confusion. One of my men has been inside your home for several weeks now, collecting evidence of your devilry."

I pleaded with Richmond. "There is no evidence. I am an innocent."

Richmond spoke, his voice devoid of emotion. "There was a book found in your rooms."

"I have many books in my rooms. I did not think there were things disallowed by the church since the Inquisition."

Vicar Morris rolled the words on his tongue. "It was a book of demons. The type of book a witch would have."

Sebastian's book. I forgot to return it to his rooms. "I do not own such a volume."

The churchman continued. "There is more, but that must wait until the Bishop returns." He turned to Richmond. "Please wait in the solarium. I must make preparations for the Bishop."

Richmond remained. "I wish to be present for any conversations between my wife and the Bishop."

"That is unheard of, sir. The Bishop will not like that at all."

"I insist." He refused to look at me still, but stared at Vicar Morris's hand on my arm. "Remove your hand from my wife."

Vicar Morris dropped my arm as if stung. "I do not want to touch her tainted flesh, anyway."

I looked at Richmond, wishing he would soften his gaze, and give me a sign he might listen to me instead of the Bishop. He stared at me, unblinking, his mouth pressed into a thin line.

Richmond pinched the bridge of his nose. "I want to fix this misunderstanding with the church and move on." He turned to me, and I saw hurt flickering in his gaze. "If we get through this, you can never go home. You must choose to stay here. With me."

My heart ached. "Please do not make my decisions conditional. Please give me the freedom to choose the right course for me, for us. Trust me, Stephen."

He continued as if he had not heard me. "Your family is suspected of witchcraft. If you were to travel to Nevis, when you placed your pretty, little toe on land in Dover again, the church would greet you with the Iron Maiden and crow their victory. That is why I have been so stubborn on this issue."

"It is my family. My father. Please understand me on this issue."

"What is really going on that you are so keen to cross the Atlantic?"

"I am faced with the prospect of my father being returned to the earth in a coffin before I can say good-bye. Before I can apologize to him. Before I can repair our relationship. We did not part on good terms, and I cannot let him take that to the grave with him. I cannot be left here on earth to deal with that guilt alone."

"You never wanted to see him before Alistair arrived."

"I have just learned of his illness! My God, man, how can you be so cold? Would you stay away from your mother if she needed you? Would you not rush to your father's side if word of his illness reached your ears?"

"No. I boarded a ship set to sail to India instead."

"Oh."

Hurt seeped into his words. "If you loved me, you would stay."

I shook my head. "I grew up in a house full of ulti-matums. Please do not push me on this."

Vicar Morris chuckled and clapped his hands. "Enough! Follow me, Lord Richmond. We meet in the solarium. Men, get the accused."

The man with the raspy voice grabbed my arm above the elbow, steering me after the others. We were a strange procession, the men ahead with their stiff backs and formal walks, and me limping along beside my cap-tor. We continued around the western edge of the house until the gravel path stopped at a beautiful hothouse.

A small sigh escaped my lips at the glorious ex-panse of glass sparkling in the morning sun. A lovely growth of winter roses arched around the entryway. We entered the solarium, and my uneasiness returned.

Two contraptions stood near the center of the room, leather straps worn from use, and metal spikes that failed to glisten in the sunlight from caked blood covering the surface. The stench of rotting flesh was overwhelming. The tile floor was swept clean, and stained with dark splotches no amount of scrubbing could remove.

My power thrummed inside me, pushing against my skin. I glanced around the room, searching for a source of water. In the left corner, a barrel stood, and the floor around it looked wet. *Fuel*. I had no further illusions about the need for my magic. It was just as Daniel McGhee said: there were no misunderstandings, and no amount of talk could get me out of this mess.

Vicar Morris paused before a gilt chair, resting his frame on the padded velvet seat. "Lady Richmond, welcome to our interrogation chamber."

I twisted my hands in their restraints, the rope never giving, but only biting deeper into my skin.

"We will not start until the Bishop arrives." He motioned towards a large wooden machine with a platform of wood illuminated in a bright shaft of morning sun. "The Bishop prefers to start with a few stretches on the plank, but I rather prefer to begin with more persuasive methods."

"You are making a mistake. I am ashamed to have offered you comfort and counsel in the past, knowing the depraved man you are now."

He spat at my feet. "You are the one to be ashamed, living a lie, disobeying the common rules of decency and bewitching all around you."

"That is enough. My wife has not been convicted of any crime as yet," Richmond said.

The Bishop entered the solarium, leaning heavily on his cane, the click of its tip on the stones sounding like retribution for all my lies and half-truths. "Good morning! I hope each of you slept well last night. We have a special situation today." His voice quivered with excitement.

"We have a noblewoman accused by one in her class of practicing witchcraft." The vicar jumped up, vacating the Bishop's chair.

"Yes, we understand that," the Bishop responded. "Who is her accuser, and what evidence do we have against her?" He steadied himself into his chair, patting the cushions to get comfortable. "These old bones need a bit of support. Hope you don't mind that I sit in front of you all."

Vicar Morris cleared his throat. "Lord Sebastian, her brother-in-law, stands as her accuser."

Richmond swore in a language I have never heard, his hand reaching across his coat to finger the pistol at his belt. "That sod-off of a brother, he will pay for slandering my family name."

My power rolled in answer to his anger, coursing down my arms to rest beneath the skin of my fingertips. If I weren't careful, I would start glowing blue in front of the holy men. I pulled it back. No good came of me blasting myself out of this predicament. *Yet.*

The Bishop continued, "I cannot authorize any interrogation of Lady Richmond until I hear the crimes against her from her accused. Bring me Lord Sebastian."

Vicar Morris groaned. "But, sir, I protest this delay."

"If she is innocent, she deserves to go free. If she is guilty as charged, the Lord will punish her if we here on earth cannot."

Morris sighed. "I will send a man to him immediately. While we wait, may we proceed with another investigation?"

He waved his hand. "Proceed. I have a meeting in an hour."

I spoke. "Bishop, may I have my hands unbound? I fear I have no life left in my limbs."

He waved his hand again. "Untie her."

Morris protested. "I disagree, sir. She can use her hands to cast witchcraft."

"She is no threat to me. I am a man of the Church. Untie her."

Vicar Morris slunk across the floor to stand behind me. His arms shook, his voice too low for the Bishop to hear as he cut through my bindings with a small knife from the folds of his robe. "You'll wish you were on the rack when this morning is done. One crook of your finger, witch, and I'll gut you."

Morris breathed heavily, inhaling with each swipe of the knife against my bonds. With the last of the ropes released, I flexed my arms. Tingling pain, like a thousand needles piercing my skin raged from my fingers to my shoulders. My arms felt as if there were no bones within them. Shaking my arms only accentuated the painful sensation.

The men returned with Master McGhee between them. I recognized him from the freckles on his cheeks. His eyes were wild. He sobbed incoherent primal sounds that echoed in the room before settling in my marrow.

Bile rose in my throat, but I did not know what to do. Blast everyone to China and reveal my true nature? Try to talk myself out of this mess and keep my powers secret? I wanted to preserve a chance to salvage my marriage, and that meant no spells. So as they placed Daniel in the torture device, I held my power in check with iron resolve.

They strapped Daniel to a chair, the seat made of wood, but the arms were covered with metal spikes. He resisted, holding his arms above the sharp projections.

"No, please, I tried to get information from her, but all she did was walk around the shed. Please, I will do better the next time. No!"

His breath came in short pants. He squirmed on the seat, unable to twist free of the two leaning their heavy bodies on top of his thin arms.

Inexorably, his arms inched closer to the wicked armrests. "No, I beg you, no," he cried, his voice rising to a high-pitched keening when the first spikes breached his skin.

As the first drops of blood ran down the dirty spikes, he crumpled in the chair, his head lolling against his chest, sobbing incoherently. One man buckled a leather strap across his chest, holding him tightly to the chair.

"Do it," he commanded.

Each man, one at each arm, fitted a thick wooden plank over Daniel's arm.

"On my mark,".

My power bubbled under my skin and my gaze darted among those in the room. Everyone was focused on Daniel. Except the Bishop. He was focused on me, his watery gaze unwavering.

Not a time to practice magic.

"Steady," the vicar said, his hand raised high.

Each man hoisted a mallet high above his head.

"Go!" He dropped his arm, like starting the races at Ascot.

I jumped. Daniel screamed. Blood flowed anew as the spikes pierced deeper into the skin of his arms, the men raising mallets high above their heads, to bring them crashing down with a horrid thump against the trapped human flesh.

Vicar Morris yelled, "Shut him up! I cannot abide his caterwauling!"

As the men stuffed a leather strap into his mouth, I asked the Bishop, "If you gag him, how can you hear his confession? Unless the purpose if this exercise is merely to torture a young man."

The Bishop of London blinked twice. The vicar turned, slapping me on the cheek. The force dropped me to my knees, the taste of blood salty in my mouth.

"Your opinion is not needed, Lady Richmond. Remember your place."

I rose, casting hand clenched, ready to hit him back. Richmond rushed to my side, fingers probing my cheek.

"Are you hurt?" he asked, concerned.

"No."

The Bishop held his hand up. "She is correct. Do not gag him."

Richmond positioned himself between the vicar and me, placing his hands on his hips, displaying the brace of pistols in his belt. "Do not touch my wife again."

Daniel thrashed on the chair. "Help! Help me! Please, do not maim me! How can I work as a cripple?"

I hated them in that moment. All of them. The Bishop for allowing and encouraging this macabre show. Vicar Morris for enacting his master's wishes. The men for their blind loyalty. My husband for not shooting someone and stopping this nonsense.

Daniel's words broke my heart. There was no future for a broken man in the British Empire. He did not realize that he had no future. Morris was not interested in the truth. He wanted blood and bowels to run in the gutters for his sadistic pleasure.

The men fitted a wooden lever above each of Daniel's arms, the plank attached to a press above. The intent of the machine now became clear. With each crank of the wheel, the lever drove the metal spikes further into Daniel's arm.

"They must be tired of pounding the spikes into his arm." I wanted to vomit.

Daniel saw me. "Lady Richmond! Please! You can help!"

I moved closer to him. Richmond grabbed my arm, glaring at me. "Do not do anything foolish. He is dead anyway."

I stared at him, wondering how I could love this man. "What a cold bastard you are."

"I am as affected by his screams as the next man. But my goal is to help you out of this mess, not give the Bishop reason to post notice for your hanging."

"Stop dawdling! To your posts!" the vicar cried.

Daniel blubbered as the men positioned themselves at the crank. They pushed up the sleeves of their robes before laying hands to the crank. They shoved, the muscles on their thick arms bulging with the effort. Morris hopped from foot-to-foot. I bent over to retch, but there was nothing but a few bits of bile to clog my throat.

Daniel screamed again, and the sound of blood splattering on the floor rang in my ears.

The Bishop waited a moment, then asked, "Do you recant all forms of witchcraft, young man?"

"I am not a witch! I have never practiced witchcraft!" Sweat beaded on his forehead. My power reached out, probing. *Not a witch.*

The Bishop waved his hands. "Then we must continue, for you either admit to witchcraft, and recant, or we continue until the truth is revealed."

Daniel keened and whimpered. The men flexed their hands, preparing for another turn at the crank. I looked at Richmond, my heart breaking with my choice.

"Stop!" I commanded.

The men paused, looking for guidance from the vicar. He motioned for them to continue. "She does not give orders here; I do. Continue!"

I shook my head. "The boy knows nothing. Look at him. He'd call himself a woman if you promised to relent. His mind is broken." The men looked at Daniel, slumped and bleeding, babbling in the chair.

Vicar Morris turned to me. "You are not in charge. I am! We are slated to interrogate today, and interrogate we will! The Bishop has refused to allow me to wring the truth from you, so it must be from him."

I held out my tingling arms. "Release him. Take me instead."

The Bishop gasped. "You would take his place?"

Richmond, skin pale, added, "Julia, no! This is not your battle to fight."

"I cannot stand for an innocent to be tortured. Put me on the chair."

The vicar laughed. "We use other items for women, Lady Richmond." He jerked his head, and the larger man unwound the wheel, the lever above Daniel's arms receding inch-by-inch. They unbuckled the belt holding him upright. With the last tug of the spikes from his skin, Daniel fell from the chair, crumpling to the floor.

He grabbed my arm, and we headed toward the left of the room, to the barrel of water. Vicar Morris grabbed my neck, pulling my hair. "We will see what confessions we wring from you."

I filled my lungs with air, steeling myself for the feel of the cold water on my skin.

"Excuse moi, but are we too late?"

We turned. Madame Oualie picked her way among the machines to give a pretty curtsey to the Bishop. "I could not miss this for anything. Please, let me be of service."

I trembled, my power thrashing at her entrance.

Another voice followed hers. "Yes, let us see how you can be of service." Sebastian stood behind her, two pistols visible at his belt.

He stroked her back. "Tell me, sweet, what evidence do you have of my sister-in-law's witchy ways?"

"Yes, Madame Oualie, what evidence do you have against me?"

Madame Oualie left Sebastian's side, sashaying across the room to stand in front of me, a picture of French perfection from her coiffed head to her satin shoes. She pinched her nose. "You stink."

"Your opinion means nothing to me."

"It should, dear Lady." Raising her voice, she began, "I had a young girl under my care, Miss Chloe Longood. While out for an evening of entertainment with my charge, Lady Richmond lured Miss Longood to a retiring room, where she practiced dark magic against the child, cutting her arms. These cuts were evident to three of Lady Sutton's servants, as well as the coachman who drove the young miss home. After I confronted Lady Richmond over her harsh treatment of the chit, I demanded her return. She refused. I fear for the young girl's health."

"These are all lies, Bishop. Madame Oualie was the person torturing Miss Chloe Longood!"

The Bishop nodded, fingers steepled in front of his mouth, ruby ring twinkling in the sunlight. "Lady Richmond, where is Miss Longood to verify these claims?"

"I do not know. She fled after the good vicar took me captive."

"I see. So in the absence of Miss Longood, we must hear other evidence. Continue, Madame Oualie."

My power seethed at her deceit. I felt the answering call of her power, and her eyes widened as a tendril of red escaped from her hand. She clenched her fist, narrowing her eyes at me.

Madame Oualie continued. "Due to my suspicions, I inquired of my dear friend, Lord Sebastian, if he would allow the placement of one of my loyal servants in the household to provide surveillance for me of Miss Longood's condition. My man found a book of demonology in Lady Richmond's rooms, as well as observed her practicing witchcraft with the young lady."

Sebastian added, with a satisfied look upon his face, "I searched her rooms myself."

"That is odd, dear brother, because I retrieved that book from your rooms."

Sebastian laughed. "You just admitted to being a thief, and you think we will listen to your protestations of innocence?"

Richmond said, "It must warm your heart, brother, to assure yourself of inheritance."

Sebastian replied, "You are the picture of health, but you have dangerous occupations. Fighting the French, the Spanish, on a boat at sea. Capturing witches. I shudder to think what type of accident might befall you, and I will do my duty as the second son to forward the family fortunes if misfortune befalls you."

"I know you ordered the attack on me at the opera, brother. I only chastise myself that I thought you were a man and would limit your attempts to me. I did not think you would accuse a defenseless woman."

"Stephen, come now, your wife is as defenseless as a tiger."

The Bishop turned to me. "Let us return to the matter at hand. I have another engagement this morning. Lady Richmond, what do you have to say about these claims from Madame Oualie?"

I turned to my husband, searching his face for some thread of truth, knowing what I was about to do would change our lives forever. "Stephen, is there any chance for us?" I whispered.

His skin paled. "I love you, Julia. Whatever you are about to do, please stop. I will fix this. We can be happy, here, in London."

"I love you. Please understand I do not have a choice in this."

"This is all very touching, but what is your comment in your defense, Lady Richmond?" the Bishop demanded from his perch.

I looked once more at Stephen, then lifted on tiptoe to place a gentle kiss on his cheek. "I suppose what I have to say in my defense, sir, is this."

Blue magic sizzled along my arms, light so bright, the Bishop shielded his eyes. I pulled water from the barrel behind me, forming a glowing fireball in my palm.

Madame Oualie stood, uncertainty showing in her features.

"We will start with you, Madame. This is for torturing Miss Longood." I threw the blue fireball at Madame Oualie. It landed at her feet, flaming upwards, reaching out for fuel. It licked the bottom of her low-cut, silk dress, catching the hem of her gown on fire.

"Mon dieu! C'est un feu!" She stamped her feet about as the flames climbed higher on her gown, dropping to the ground to snuff them out. Sebastian pushed her away from him, drawing a pistol. He pointed the barrel at Richmond's chest.

"This is for you, dear brother, for betraying your family." I energized another round of magic, flinging it at Sebastian's head.

He yelped, ducking the fireball, but not before it grazed his scalp.

"Think twice before entering a lady's rooms without her invitation."

He flapped his hands about his head, screaming in pain as the fire lapped his ears, reaching around to singe his eyelashes.

The Bishop hid behind his chair, his eyes wide with terror. "Bishop," I called. "Your faith will not protect you from me. I, too, am a child of God." I threw a bolt at his chair, setting it ablaze.

Vicar Morris ran towards me with a wooden beam raised above his head. I flung energy from both hands, freezing the air around him, Sebastian, Richmond, the whole lot, into solid ice.

Oualie threw a red shield, deflecting my spell from her. She stood, surveying the assembly, from the shocked look on the Bishop's face to the amazement in Richmond's eyes. "Tres magnifique, Lady Richmond. Your spell does not disappoint. It is unfortunate you are not adept enough to counter me. I am distressed that you forced me to reveal my nature."

"They only know you are a witch. I know you for what you truly are: a practitioner of the dark magic. Where is your blood-slave now? Or have you not had enough time to find a new one in the Bishop's dungeon?"

Her face contorted into an ugly snarl. "I do not need a slave to best you."

Her wrist exploded with red light, multiple tendrils arcing for my face and throat. I formed a thin sheet of water, power stoking it until it glowed blue hot. In the space of a heartbeat, I commanded knives of water to hit its mark on her putrid spell, cutting it from its energy source until the ground was saturated with red strands floating in water, twitching in their last bits of energy.

I pointed at her spell lying on the floor. "It appears you may need some help."

"Oh, but you would like to best me, non? I will make you grovel at my knees and then I'll kick you in the teeth. As you lay on the ground crying, I will take your husband to my bed."

I snarled. "I do not need to enchant a man before he beds me. Can you say the same?"

She yelled, a torrent of French and English spewing from her lips, and drew her hand back, red light licking her skin, racing towards me. I blocked her blow with my arm. Her words were a flurry of French as she stamped and tossed her arms about. I blew her off her feet with a shield, flinging her body into the rack. She collapsed, groaning.

I gazed at my husband, seeing the ice starting to melt around his face. "I am sorry, Stephen. I wanted to tell you myself."

"Good morning! Am I late?" Lord Botetourt stood at the entrance from the garden, his cloak billowing around him.

"Lord Botetourt!" I exclaimed. "What are you doing here?"

"Rescuing you. Anyone who thinks you are a force for evil is quite mistaken. He pointed a finger at Madame Oualie as she picked herself off the floor. "You have displeased me greatly, spreading gossip and slander."

He surveyed the dripping forms of the Bishop, the vicar, Richmond, Sebastian and the friars. "It is rather like a macabre ice sculpture garden."

He picked his way over the floor to the Bishop, pulling a thick vellum envelope from his vest pocket. "I have here, dear sir, a letter of pardon for Lady Richmond. I would hand it to you, but you seem indisposed. I'll lay it on the cushion for you to peruse as you melt."

The Bishop's eyes squinted under their icy crust. Lord Botetourt moved to kneel beside Daniel, laying his hands on the boy's still form.

With him occupied, Madame Oualie flung a ribbon of red at my throat. I ducked the slow-moving spell, bending the water on the floor into a cage for her, producing thick ropes of fluid, which held her arms to her body.

I stalked across the room to stand before her. As she opened her mouth to protest, I stuffed a gag from the torture machine into her mouth. "Really, you need to learn when to keep quiet."

Botetourt rose, supporting Daniel. "Master McGhee has agreed to work in my stables on a trial basis. He seems quite a fit stable hand." Daniel's head lolled to the side, his eyelids fluttering. "Come, Lady Richmond. My carriage awaits."

I paused in front of the frozen form of my husband. "I am sorry that I deceived you. I truly loved you. I hope you can forgive me one day."

Water had refrozen around his mouth, preventing him from answering. I did not know if I would want to hear his response, anyway, if the cold in his eyes was any indication of his feelings for me.

I hurried after Lord Botetourt, out of the solarium and into the chilly air.

He strode quickly across the garden, making for a small gate in the back wall. He glanced over his shoulder at me. "We must hurry to reach my house. Your spells will not last long."

I hesitated among the winter stalks of shrubs. "There are others. Beneath the house."

"We do not have time for them now. I will return for them if I can. Hurry, Julia."

Chapter Thirteen

He threw me into the open coach, vaulted into the cab, and rapped on the ceiling. The coach sped into the flow of traffic, swaying from one side to the other. I settled on the leather squabs, my arm braced against the window so my head would not slam into the frame. A vicious bump sent me careening across the bench, hitting something... solid. I screamed, "There is someone here," pulling magic into my hand.

"Stop!" Botetourt commanded. The air beside me shivered and melted, colored in patches like a quilt without a backing, until the form solidified into the shape of Chloe.

"Ah!" I sighed. "Chloe, you startled me!"

She blushed, ducking her head. "Lord Botetourt said if I were to accompany him, I needed to stay out of sight."

"You did an admirable job," Botetourt added, pulling back the curtain to view the traffic outside.

"Julia, I am so glad you are all right!" Chloe exclaimed, hugging me close, with her arms tightly wrapped around me, and burying her head in my neck. Waves of comfort from her power lapped at the sore edges of my soul.

"Oh, I am so happy to see you whole! I feared for your life." I held her tightly, reveling in her energy. "I prayed that you would escape."

She pulled away from me. "I hope you are proud of me, Julia. When I ran from the friars, I was scared, and not thinking. But then I stopped, and thought what you would do in a similar situation, so I went to Lord Botetourt."

"That turned out to be an excellent decision."

She continued. "No. I mean, I told Lord Botetourt about me. About what happened to me in the church, and about Madame Oualie." Her gaze pierced mine, worry creasing her brow. "Please do not be cross with me, but I did not trust Lord Richmond. All he would demand is a lot of explanations, and gnashing over how he was duped by his wife for so many years. I needed a man of action."

I remained still, too exhausted to think. "Chloe, I am proud you were not captured, and I agree. In this instance, it is better to go with the devil you know."

A smile lit up her face. "Then you are not cross with me? I am not in trouble?

I patted her hand. "How can I be cross with you when you helped me escape?"

"In regards to the King's pardon," Lord Botetourt interjected, "it is not exactly a pardon."

I sat straighter at hearing his words. "Whatever do you mean?"

"It is a forgery. The King is at Balmoral now, a fact the Bishop will discover soon enough."

Panic imbued my limbs with energy. "I need to stop this coach! I must get out of London!"

"All in good time, dear lady. You need a bath, some food, and rest before you sail for points unseen. The high tide has passed for today. No ships are leaving port tonight."

I chewed the inside of my cheek. "Richmond will know where I am."

"Yes."

"Do you have any intelligence on what he does once he captures a witch?"

Botetourt thrummed his fingers against his crossed legs. "Ah, so you can plan an adequate defense? Intelligent of you, Julia, but unnecessary."

"He will melt in an hour or two. I will not be on a ship by then. It seems reasonable to have a plan." I cast my gaze at my abused hands. "He will be awfully cross with me."

Botetourt eyed me, the brown of his eyes deepening in his agitation. "He helped you in his own way."

"Only because I froze him before he had the opportunity to do anything else."

We arrived at Botetourt House ten minutes later. Botetourt pulled two pistols from his belt. "Julia, Chloe, allow me to exit first. I am in better condition to respond to any possible pursuit than either of you."

He flung open the door, alighting from the coach like a great bird of prey swooping upon a piece of flesh, his cloak flapping in the light breeze. We followed closely behind, and I resisted the effort to turn and see if anyone took note of our exit.

Hadgi stood on the front stoop, ignoring Chloe and me as we entered the house, his focus directed on the street outside.

"I need a bath, and food, in that order." I added, "Please."

He laughed, a cheerful, hearty sound at odds with the gravity of my situation. "Of course, Lady Richmond. I will meet you in the study when you are ready. We have much to discuss."

• • •

I stayed in the bath until my fingers were wrinkled and the water long tepid, scrubbing my skin and hair until my hands were raw. I cried in the solace of the bath for all that my marriage could and should have been. Richmond would not want a witch for a wife, or a mother to his children. All of the last three years of my life now were seemingly wasted on a man who, in the end, could not love me for the person I really was.

When I had no more tears, no more angry words, and was no longer mad at myself, I climbed out of the bath, feeling empty inside. I endured the pain of sorrow before when my father excommunicated me from the clan. But losing your only happiness and realizing you may never have it again? That great emptiness was like a bottomless hole where light cannot penetrate.

I slipped on a soft robe, rolling up the sleeves, cinching the belt tight, and moving automatically through the mundane tasks. I ignored the tray of food on the bedside table, along with my muddy, bloody shoes. Instead, I rang for the maid to get directions to Botetourt's study.

Five minutes later, I rapped on the study door.

"Come in." Botetourt sat behind a desk, his shirtsleeves rolled to his elbows, a fire crackling in the hearth. I paused in front of him, scrunching my toes in the plush carpet.

"Sit down, Julia."

I sat in the chair he indicated, a comfortable brocade close to the fire. He began, "I cannot take full credit for your rescue today. Neither can Chloe. Your husband formulated the plan, and asked for my assistance."

"Richmond? But he hunts witches."

"Let us speak of a subject more interesting to me. When you duel Alistair Dupont, if you win, I expect something in return."

I gazed at the fire. "That seems to be a common theme."

He continued, steepling his fingers in front of his mouth. "I want exclusive trading rights with the sugar output of all plantations under your clan."

"You surprise me. I believed you would want the clan rings, or perhaps a few witches in exchange."

"I do not need larger numbers in my clan, and I am uninterested at this time in wresting from you what you have fairly earned. But I am putting myself in a disadvantageous position by helping you, and a few barrels of molasses will go a long way into alleviating the stress of dealing with the church."

"Nevis has the largest sugar output of any of the Caribbean islands. An exclusive trade with you would jeopardize the sugar industry, not to mention, how it would outrage the agents of the West India Company, as well as the American states."

"Yes."

I gazed at him, sitting so smugly in his chair. "What if I say no to the deal?"

He shrugged. "Why would you? You are intelligent, and although your mental faculties may be strained by the recent unpleasantness, you are practical enough to realize you have no other option."

"You are a cold man, Botetourt."

"I am a practical witch, one who has gone to great lengths to assist you."

"Thank you. I will accept your offer, although I must let it be known that I would rather you asked for the clan rings than to affect my financial standing. I will not have a husband to rely on anymore."

He extended his hand, without a twitch of power as we shook on the deal. "Speaking of which, your next visitor is arrived."

He opened a drawer in his desk, removing a small pistol, checking the chamber and clicking it closed. Handing it to me handle first, he said, "Use this at your discretion. I will be in the house, but not immediately available. You have one bullet to do with as you wish."

I took the proffered weapon, placing it in my lap. "Why would I need this?"

The corner of Botetourt's mouth twitched. "Consider it my unusual sense of humor." He left the room, and I heard murmuring outside the door.

I stood, unsure of what to expect, when Richmond entered the room, shutting the door with a soft click.

My heart thudded. "What are you doing here? I thought I would never see you again."

He took three steps closer to me, then stopped, his arms outstretched, pleading, "Julia, please listen to me."

I rubbed my thumb on the pistol stock. "Fine. Say what you feel you must, then leave. I know you do not want me any longer."

He remained where he stood, his speech measured. "I first learned of witches on my travels in the Caribbean, for the Navy. I had an exchange with a band of witches on Martinique before you and I met. The things I saw those witches do on Martinique were terrible, just awful. And I was powerless to stop the suffering. We were lucky to escape with our lives."

"Martinique has a clan of fire witches, known practitioners of dark magic. It is no surprise that you saw their atrocities. Anyone with a shred of common sense avoids Martinique."

"I was not privy to that information. I heard the rumors around your family, Julia. I knew there was a good chance you were a witch."

"You married me anyway."

"Yes. Because I loved you. I met a woman of charm and grace, a woman uninterested in my fortune, or title, or how many houses I owned or what my listing in De-Brett's said about my grandmother. I met a woman who loved me for me, Stephen. And I did not care that she could be a witch. Because a woman as wonderful as that would surely tell her husband something so vital. Right? But the months passed without a word from you."

A single tear leaked out of the corner of my eye. "I am sorry, Stephen. I thought you would reject me if you knew the truth. I chose to recant my heritage. I never planned to practice again. In my mind, I was no longer a witch. I had everything under control."

"Julia, you glow blue sometimes when you sleep."

"Oh." I played with the belt to my robe. "So you knew the entire time."

"Yes."

I pondered his words. "So any estrangement in our marriage is my fault?"

"No. I could have forced the issue. My ego hurt each time you failed to confess your true nature to me. So I volunteered to work at the Admiralty to assist in relocating witches. I wanted to keep you safe, Julia. I thought if I were an insider, I could protect you. I thought if I gave you enough time, and enough space, you would realize how much I love you and tell me the truth."

"God, what a fool I have been."

He continued. "In the beginning, we searched for bad sorts. You know, witches who were aiding street gangs, or militants in the Highlands. We moved to hunting for families on nothing more than a word from a jealous neighbor. I started to investigate what happened to the witches after they were turned over to the church, or the government. I was not happy with the results.

"That is when I enlisted Lord Botetourt's assistance. We have smuggled several families to other parts of Brittania, even some to America. Sebastian became involved. Things changed. I just wanted you to be safe, Julia. I never intended for things to go this far."

"I have to go to Nevis, Stephen. Alistair has taken over as clan leader and infected my father with a demon.

If I do not go, the taint will spread to me. I have no choice. I want to stay here and repair the damage to our marriage, but I cannot."

"I know. Just as I must stay here and deal with Sebastian, and Madame Oualie."

"Why were you involved with her, Stephen?"

"She was a source of information on missing witches the government was hunting. Nothing more."

"You let me think you were perhaps unfaithful for the prospect of information? You were willing to risk our happiness for a chance to impress the admiral?"

"I'd have gone to my grave never knowing from my wife's tongue that my children were half-witch. I felt it was an even trade in dishonesty."

"I never planned on practicing again. Now, I am forced to embrace a life I never wanted. NEVER! Do you ken?" My voice quivered. "All my father ever did was teach me spells: how to hurt, how to fight, how to kill. How to lie. Because I am powerful, and that makes me useful. No one ever wanted to know what Julia wished. When we married, I gladly swore to lead a life free of magic, free of manipulations, and ultimately, free of home."

He poked a finger towards me, and I raised the gun. "I am the one who has been manipulated! Used between two witches, my country, and I am now left with what? A resigned commission in the Navy? A job at the Admiralty I no longer have the stomach for? And a wife who is estranged enough from me to pull a gun and point it at my chest?" He held out his arm, pushing the barrel of the gun away from him. "I am sorry, Julia. I need time to think of what I want."

"What you want? Stephen, have you ever thought about what I might want?"

"Yes. Many a night. I am afraid I am not the man who is best for you."

I stood there, feeling the breath tearing through my chest, and a thousand barbs of hurt as his words ripped through my soul. "I agree, Richmond. I do not think you are the best sort for me. But we cannot choose whom we love, and I, alone, must suffer for that emotion."

He bent, his lips brushing my cheek in a gesture of tenderness. "I am glad you are without injury. I wish you well, Julia."

He turned and took two steps towards the door before facing me again. "Julia, I knew what your family was; I knew your father was a witch. That is why I did not want you to travel to Nevis. I was scared of the island's allure on you, and feared it might awaken some primitive power in you. Or take you from me. What I failed to realize was there was never any chance of my winning that competition in the first instance."

"Goodbye, Stephen." A tear slid down my cheek.

He left.

Chapter Fourteen

"We will head in a coach to the West India docks. *The Loire* has moored and is ready to sail."

Chloe and I stood in Lord Botetourt's study. Our clothes were freshly laundered; my eyes were dry; and our bellies were full, even if my soul was empty, and dark with sorrow. Chloe fingered a leather pouch full of dirt at her waist.

"I plan to enchant two servants to appear as Lady Richmond and Miss Longood, and have them board the vessel as a distraction."

"What other vessels are in port?" I asked, shaken from my brown study.

"Hadgi reports a small slaver, about fifteen guns, named *The Constant*, intends to leave today, as well as a merchantman headed to Jamaica."

"We will choose *The Constant*."

Botetourt adjusted two pistols in his belt. "Really! I had a bet with Hadgi you would choose the merchantman."

"A merchantman is a target for any galleon, Navy vessel, pirate or privateer on the water. No one touches a slaver. The cargo is not as portable, and requires food and water, which means little to anyone other than a few ports of call. We will take the slaver."

Botetourt pulled his belt tighter, adjusting the buckle another notch. "We will travel in a cab, as the coach will take the decoys to *The Loire*. We leave in ten minutes. I need to transform the ladies into likenesses of you."

"Can I observe you? I have never seen an illusion of that magnitude, lasting for the space of a voyage, cast in person," I inquired.

"Flattery will not succeed. No, dear lady, you and Chloe need to wait for me here."

Hadgi remained impassive by the door, his arms crossed. "Hadgi," I asked, "can you give me any more information about the slaver? How many slaves in the hold? Number of crew?"

"No."

Chloe giggled. "He never speaks more than a word or two. I do not think he is capable."

Hadgi replied, "I am."

Chloe giggled again. "I wonder if I can get you to speak three words next time."

He answered, "No, you can't."

Chloe clapped like a small child with a toy. "I did it! You said three words!"

I inspected our bag while Chloe entertained herself with Hadgi. We had two thin wool dresses for me, my newly laundered dueling clothes, and a small pouch of willow bark. It was difficult to obtain in Nevis, and ships were known sources of all types of pestilence. I also had my gold wedding band in the pouch.

Botetourt returned with two women behind him. The woman on the right appeared to be Chloe's twin, moving as she walked, and swinging her arms enthusiastically just the same way as Chloe did.

"Magnificent."

"Yes, it is." Botetourt answered. "How do you like your twin, Lady?"

I blinked, espying a perfect copy of me standing in the hallway behind Botetourt. "I think she is a little taller than I."

He squinted his eyes, looking first at one figure, then the other. "Rubbish," he argued. "She is a perfect copy."

Hadgi said, "It is time."

Botetourt opened the front door, staying behind the portal, and out of view. "Remember, ladies, at the first sign of trouble, run. Hadgi will be there to offer protection."

"Yes, sir." They chorused as one, following Hadgi out the door. Botetourt sealed the portal with a shot of teal from his hand, the spell sliding into the lines marking the door, glowing bright for an instant, then receding. "Hannibal's army could not get through that door without the key," he said.

"No need to use the door, sir, when a broken window will suffice," Chloe added.

"The spell extends to the windows as well, cheeky miss. Now, let us go."

We hurried through the maze of halls to the back of the house, out the side garden, and into the busy intersection of Seymour Street. Botetourt carried our valise, and stuck his arm out to hail a cab. He was dressed in a nondescript, brown cloak. In all, we appeared to be poor travelers.

Once we were settled in the cab, Botetourt peered out the windows, a vigilant guardian. *He should be*, I thought, with all the money he would make off my lands in the coming months.

I reviewed our plan with Chloe. "Once we are at the docks, Chloe, we must not be known as Lady Richmond or Chloe Longood. Remember, we are indentured servants traveling to Nevis to work on Pinney's Plantation."

"I will remember. Do not worry."

The sounds outside the coach changed from the shouts of other carriages to the whips and yells of commerce, signaling our arrival at the mercantile docks.

"Botetourt, I do not like this. It is too easy. Where are the pursuers?"

Botetourt kept his eyes at the window, peering to the outside world through the sliver of glass. "I sent Lord Richmond to book passage on a trade ship headed for Nevis. Another layer of deception, and another lead for your enemy to unravel. Perhaps your husband is playing his part well."

"He spoke nothing of his participation in my escape to me last night."

Botetourt glanced my way, then returned to his post. "He is not all bad, you know. And it pains me to offer him support, because in another time, perhaps we could have been something, you and I. But I believe in a man taking responsibility for his sins, and his alone. Believe what you may, but he is risking himself to help you escape to safety."

"Not really to safety, Lord Botetourt. She has to duel a head master and exorcise a demon," Chloe reminded him.

"I stand corrected, Chloe." He placed is hand on the handle to the cab. "We are arrived."

Nothing looked out of place. Men called to each other, boxes and crates were loaded and moved, and huge horses strained to pull the weight piled onto carts. Everyone had a purpose, and a reason to be there at this time. Botetourt remained in the cab as we climbed out of the interior. Chloe exited first, and I handed her our bag.

"Do you see the ship?" I asked.

"Yes. Third down on the left side of the dock."

"Wonderful."

I prepared to exit as well, when Lord Botetourt grabbed my hand. "Julia, remember our agreement."

"I will."

He kissed the knuckles of my hand, his lips barely grazing the skin. "Stay well, be bold, and do not surrender."

"Thank you."

I removed my hand from his grasp, following Chloe into the chaos of the docks.

The cab rumbled off. I picked up the cloth bag, nudging Chloe ahead of me. "Let us go."

Barrels full of goods stacked higher than my head hugged each side of the docks. The streets were full of men rushing to and fro, each with a cargo destined for points west. I paused beside a stack of barrels. This close, I could smell the sweet, tangy scent of molasses. I inhaled deeply.

Chloe wrinkled her nose. "What is that smell?"

"The smell of money."

"Money does not smell like that!"

"I meant, it is a cash crop for the West Indies. These barrels will support a plantation throughout the year." I put my hand on Chloe's arm. "Do you see the two men across the street?"

Chloe peered through the crowd. "Yes. They look familiar, but I cannot place them."

"That is enough for me. I feel their magic and it is disturbing. Like Madame Oualie'."

Chloe bent to the ground as if to check the laces on her shoe. She placed one palm flat on the dirt. When she stood, she said, "Yes. I can feel it as well."

"Then let us proceed." We walked down the dock, picking our way through the loose boards, cargo piles, and ropes to stand at the gangplank of *The Constant*.

"Oh, by the tides, I do not have any money! How are we to pay for our passage without coin!"

"Well, I have plenty of money." Chloe hefted a small pouch hanging from a thin cord around her waist. "I made coins from rocks in a garden behind Botetourt House, while waiting to see when you escaped." The coins tinkled in the pouch.

Encouraged, I wrapped my arm around her elbow. "Then let us approach the ship's captain."

Apprehensive, I edged out into the open, my shoulders taut, and my ears tuned to acknowledge the slightest hint of danger or changes in our surroundings. Chloe followed, walking on my left, protecting my weak side.

The Constant bobbed up and down, its masts swaying in the gentle breeze. A thin line of African slaves, still dressed in tribal scraps of clothing more suitable for warmer climates, trudged up the gangplank, shackled hand-to-hand and foot-to-foot. A thickly set man boomed orders from the deck. "Hurry home, lads, if we are to make the tide. Good fortune in America awaits!" A whip hung at his side, the end encrusted with dark bits of blood and flesh.

The man on the deck, the captain, I presumed, espied us standing on the dock. "You there," he called. "State your business on my dock!"

I called back to him. "We are looking for passage to the West Indies. We are indentured servants, bound for Pinney's Plantation. We missed our packet earlier in the week. Can you take us to Nevis?"

His eyes narrowed. "Pinney's Plantation? That is where this cargo is headed. Come up the gangway and we can discuss payment terms."

Chloe whispered. "Do you trust him?"

"No," I responded. "But in a day, with rest and food on the open ocean, I'll have my strength back. Then it will not matter who trusts whom. On a ship surrounded by water, I am the master."

"Then let us hasten up the gangplank." She hurried up the crooked, wooden slats.

"It is called a gangway," I mumbled.

The deck of the ship was crowded with bodies: men scuttling about fixing ropes and hoisting sails, while the human cargo of the ship folded into the hold below, link-by-link of the iron chains. Most held their heads bent, but for one woman. Her hair was gray under the half-sun, and she held her frame erect, staring about the decks, spearing the sailors with her unblinking gaze. When her eyes met mine, I did not turn away, but instead, tipped my head in deference to her power that rolled over the deck and threaded amongst the wind. A tribal shaman, the African counterpart to my powers. A sailor jerked the chain when she hesitated, appearing still so regal in her scraps of tattered rags. He began hitting her with a rope flog.

"Get below, old woman. There will be a flogging for you if we miss the tide."

We stood before the captain, who stunk, and stains marred his tattered coat. He spat between a gap in his teeth. "Now, let us discuss payment. I am Captain Dobbin, captain and proprietor of this ship. I set an honest fare for passengers. Forty pounds for passage, ten pounds for a cabin, and another ten pounds for food and water."

Chloe's hand curled around the pouch of coins. "Thirty pounds now, and the rest payable when we land. A bonus for clean sheets in the cabin."

He held out his calloused hand, the dirty lace cuffs falling over his wrist. "Done." He shook Chloe's hand, and she transferred the requisite amount of coin into his palm. "Now, let us show you to your cabin. Stay there until we are underway, then you may move about the deck to get some air each day. You are not allowed out any other time, as I cannot guarantee your safety at all hours."

We wove through the piles of provisions and ropes to the aft of the ship. Three steps led to two cabins. He opened the door to the left cabin. "This is normally the first mate's rooms, but he will sleep with the crew. Dinner is at six. We will bring you a tray. Stay out of our way until we are at sea, then we may discuss chores to pass the time in the doldrums." He pushed us into the room, and the door shut with a soft click.

The room held a small bunk against the outside wall, and a small desk piled high with papers and charts. A single lantern hung near the door. Chloe wrinkled her nose at the messy room. "It will take us two weeks to clean this desk of papers."

I climbed onto the bunk, balancing against the pitch and roll of the ship to see the docks outside. Despite the messiness of the room, the sheets appeared clean. "It will give us something to read along the way."

Chloe held a map, twisting and turning it in her hands to orient it correctly. "How long does the crossing take to complete?"

"About a month, if we do not hit a calm."

She giggled in return. "Not likely with our deadline."

"Not likely with a water witch who has a deadline."

Weariness weighed down my bones. "I want to sleep, Chloe. See if you can find a basin for water in this mess while I rest." I lay on the bunk, and in my need, it felt more comfortable than any bed I had ever slept in before.

Someone was screaming. I blinked the sleep from my eyes, utterly disoriented. It was dark outside the porthole window. Still night, then.

"Are you awake?" Chloe whispered from her bunk.

"Yes." I sat up, rubbing my sore arm. Another scream echoed in the night. "What is happening?"

"It started a few moments ago."

"I am going to investigate. Close the door and lock it behind me after I leave. Do not open it for anyone but me."

"How long will you be gone?"

"I do not know." I pulled on my boots and walked over to Chloe, bending to give her a hug. "I will return, do not fret."

"I will be brave, I promise."

I trod softly to the door. Opening it a crack, I peered outside. The corridor was deserted. "Remember. No magic."

"There is no dirt here anyway. Be careful."

"I will."

I threw an invisibility spell over me, following the sounds of the screams to the main deck.

Lanterns swung from their hooks in the ropes above the deck. A light breeze lifted the hairs at the back of my neck as the ship pitched and swayed with the rhythm of the waves. I glanced about, searching for the twinkling lights along the shoreline, but there were none.

The crew gathered in a large circle around the main mast. I could not see what captivated their attention, so I crept as closely as I dared. Crouching down a few feet behind the closest men, I could peer through their legs at the macabre sight.

Captain Dobbin was perched on a molasses barrel, a bottle of rum to his lips. Master Slocum, the first mate, stood at his side, a lewd grin on his lips, his hand in the front of his pants. Another man, one whom I did not recognize, stood in front of the main mast, his shirt open and wet with sweat. A cat o' nine tails hung limply at his side, and his arms bulged with muscles.

"Again!" the crew roared. The muscled arm reared high into the sky, bringing the whip down. Another scream pierced the night.

I shook, my stomach turning at he sight of the crew getting so excited and aroused at such torture. From my vantage point, I could not tell who was being whipped. Maintaining the invisibility spell, I crept around the perimeter of the crew until I could spy the victim.

She was a young girl, stripped to her waist and lashed to the mast. Her small breasts were criss-crossed with cuts. Her head lolled on her chest, her thin frame shaking in her bonds.

"Again! She needs a few more before she knows not to hit the first mate!" yelled the captain. "Be gentle this time, Mister Lawson! I do not want my cargo reduced by one!" The crew shouted and stamped, clapping their hands for the blood and humiliation of the slave girl.

I did not think. I did not pause to consider the impact of my actions; but reached out, pulling water from the ocean. Blue light blazed from my hiding place, but I did not care.

I shaped the cold ocean water, delving deep into her waves, forming a wall of water. I pulled up, both hands moving in concert, drawing the water away from the surface of the ocean to stand thirty feet above the decks.

Screwing my eyes shut, I concentrated on the next portion of the spell. I let the water crash down in a wave, sweeping my arms across my body to control the flow of the enchanted tsunami.

I probed the water, pushing it about the unsteady knees of the crew, and pulling it away from the open hold, moving it ever closer to the captain.

Circling my hands, I encouraged the water to swirl about the crew, knocking them from their feet, and sweeping them across the deck to crash ruthlessly against the skuppers.

I let the flow carry the wave of water over the edge of the deck to rejoin its brethren waves in the ocean.

The night erupted in sound, as the crew shouted to one another, "Rogue wave!" and "Man overboard!"

Two crewmen worked to cut through the girl's bonds. As the last of the rope fell away, she collapsed on the deck. One of the men picked her up, slinging her over his shoulder, and carried her into the hold. Pausing only a moment over the gaping hole in the deck, he dumped her still form into its depths.

It was the best I could do for now. I pulled my invisibility spell closer around my cold body and headed back to Chloe. Our choice for passage on this vessel did not seem so intelligent now.

Chapter Fifteen

Chloe crouched over a metal pail, retching and moaning. The smell of vomit burned my nostrils. "If you look at the horizon, it helps."

Chloe retched again, her sides heaving with the effort. She wiped her mouth with the back of her hand. "I did not want to leave you alone."

I crawled over to her, holding her lank hair back from her face as she heaved again. "Then let me help you to the deck. Fresh air and the sun on our faces will do wonders."

We shuffled onto the deck. The skies were overcast, with a cold wind blowing from the north. I shivered in my thin dress. The captain presided over the wheel, conversing with a tall, thin, sour man of thirty or so, who must have been the first mate. Spying us, the captain motioned to the man who hurried across the deck to greet us.

Chloe hung onto the rail, big gulps of air filling her lungs. I stood to meet the first mate.

"About time you crawled from my cabin. I am first mate on this ship and you will address me as Mister Slocum."

I parodied a curtsey on the pitching deck. "Pleased to meet you, Mr. Slocum. I am Mrs. Frasier, and this is my niece, Miss Frasier. Can you direct us to where we can find water or a bit of food?"

His lips curled, moving about until he spat a glob of spittle on the deck, missing my shoes by inches. "The line for grub and water forms at seven in the morning, one in the afternoon, and six at night. Miss the line, miss the grub."

Chloe started to protest, but I interrupted her. "Thank you, Mr. Slocum. You are very helpful."

He narrowed his eyes. "You speak fancy for an indentured servant."

My mouth dropped opened in surprise. Fumbling for an answer, Chloe instantly supplied one for me. "We have just come from London, working in a right fancy house." She giggled, the sound adding emphasis to her words. "My aunt always gets in trouble for her loftiness and airs."

Slocum seemed appeased by her excuse. "See that those airs don't interfere with my ship." He made his way back across the deck to speak with the captain again, both men bending their heads over the compass.

"Chloe, while they are occupied, let's go below and search for water and a bit of biscuit. By the sun, it is nine in the morning, and I cannot wait until one for food or water."

Chloe stared at the tossing horizon. "I'd like to stay here a bit longer, if possible."

I surveyed the deck. All hands appeared to be concentrating on their tasks, with not so much as a glance in our direction. "You would think two women on a ship would cause a stir, but everyone seems to be deliberately ignoring us." I related the events of the evening to her. "Maybe we can locate the slave girl when we go below and offer her some comfort."

Chloe nodded, her gaze distant, and her shoulders set firm. "They beat her, Julia. Which makes them no better than the heathens in Madame Oualie's home." She studied the gloomy horizon, nodding her head at the crew. "They will leave me alone, or I will make them pay, I assure you! There is enough dirt on my person alone to cast a spell after wallowing in that cabin for a night."

"No witchcraft, Chloe. I can command water, but I cannot sail a ship. We need to stay out of trouble until we reach Caribbean waters. Understood?"

"Yes." Her face was set in stern lines.

"Good. I will meet you back in the cabin in an hour."

"Agreed."

Most slave ships carried up to three hundred slaves in the cargo, because half of the slaves usually perished on the Middle Passage. Higher numbers were needed to make the run profitable. *The Constant* only held fifteen cannons and fifty slaves. Her hold was small in comparison to the larger ships. There was much less room for loss of life on the crossing, which could have been a sign of weakness if Chloe and I needed better terms for negotiation.

I picked my way along the deck, ducking under the main sail set. At the hatch to the hold, I turned around. The captain and first mate were huddled over the wheel of the ship. The other sailors avoided looking my way.

I swung onto the ladder leading into the hold, pausing as my head broke the surface of darkness beneath the deck. Below deck, casks of food and water were locked behind a wooden door, with only a few mates who had access to the key. Empty hammocks swung with the motion of the ship, tied between the great timbers comprising the skeleton of the hull. Tables littered with tin cups and stained with spittle lined the center of the room. These were the quarters for the crew.

I climbed further downward, into the levels beneath the waves. Here, my breath moved with the push and pull of the water against the hull, only a few feet separating us. My power, quiescent for the last day, awakened with the sudden proximity to its energy source, rolling like molasses through the marrow of my bones. I climbed farther downward, until I reached the door to the lowest hold. The smell of human stench told me I was in the proper place.

I made quick work of the latch on the door. The men and women were chained together inside, so there was no need for extra security. I opened the door and entered the dismal compartment.

Bodies were stacked one beside the other against any available surface. Men and women were chained to the beams, the support pilings, and any immovable object in the room. Offal and urine sloshed amongst the bodies. Little consideration was given for space or privacy. I closed the door behind me, and the room pitched into darkness, the sounds of water mixing with the broken-hearted sighs of the human cargo.

I remained near the door. "My name is Julia Richmond. I want to help. I heard there was a girl abused last night. I would like to help her. Do any of you speak English?"

There was a greater likelihood one of the slaves spoke French, but my French was not passable for conversation.

No response, except for a collective stilling of the bodies. "I want to help," I repeated.

"We do not need your help." The words floated from the back of the room, the voice old and wrinkly at the edges, like the person had not spoken in a long time.

"I will come back tomorrow and offer my services again."

A murmur from the slaves answered me, the language a beautiful mix of sounds, clicks, chirps and trilling melodies. The ancient voice answered again. I thought it was a female speaking. "If you help, they will hurt you too. Leave us to our fate, and you to yours."

"Our fates are intertwined, as we are traveling on the same ship."

"Leave us." The murmurs increased.

"I will come again tomorrow."

"There is no help for her."

"There is always help."

"Save your efforts. Leave us." A thick, acrid roll of power hit me in the stomach, swelling my skin. I stilled under the shaman's inspection. A few breaths, and the power retreated. I remained poised at the door, awaiting my verdict. The raspy voice said, "I know what you are."

"I know what you are as well. I am not the enemy."

Silence.

My hand fumbled in the dark to find the latch on the door. "See you tomorrow, then."

My stomach growled with hunger as I stood in line for food and water at one o'clock. I had no opportunity to tell Chloe of my visit with the slaves.

Chloe was standing beside me, the color now returned to her face with the morning spent outside the cabin. I felt odd. The last days in London were pressured for time, both to meet my deadline to duel Alistair, as well as deciding what to tell Richmond. Now, on the boat, time felt suspended, doled out in aliquots defined by the will of the captain. In truth, there was not a thing

I could do now, but wait until the shores of Nevis were visible to enact my escape onto the island.

That presented another problem entirely: how to get a ship to land on the opposite side of the island than it intended?

Chloe and I waited patiently in line, ignored by all but Captain Dobbin and Mr. Slocum. As we held out our tin cups and plate for our ration, Captain Dobbin informed the bosun, "Do not be giving these two extra rations because they are women. Just give them their fair share."

The bosun, a short, squat man, tanned by the sun, nodded his compliance, doling one ladle of water from the rainwater cistern each, and plopping two pieces of hardtack on our plates. We moved off to a quiet corner of the deck to eat our meal, away from the groups of sailors loitering over their rum pots.

I tapped the biscuit on my plate, knocking off the weevils before taking a bite. Chloe followed suit. Her mouth worked patiently to chew the hard bread while I scanned the horizon for sails. The water was dark gray, frothing at the surface with the brisk winds, and the currents called to my power. I did not think it would be so easy to leave London. I still worried about pursuit from the church, or Oualie, or maybe even from Richmond, but not a speck of white appeared on any horizon.

I waited until we had almost finished our meal, and the deck around us became isolated, before breaking our silence.

"I saw the slaves. They did not trust me to help the girl. I promised to return tomorrow. You are a better healer than I, Chloe. Do you want to go there in my place?"

"I do not think I am well enough to sneak about the ship, Julia. I cannot stop the sickness."

"Then I will go again tomorrow, and you can help keep watch from the deck."

"I do not want to be alone, Julia. I do not feel safe, and if I cannot use my witchcraft to protect myself, what am I to do?" Her voice trembled, and she clasped her unsteady hands together in her lap, looking miserable.

"No one will hurt you, Chloe. I have kept my promise to keep you safe."

"I know. I will just feel better when we are on solid land again."

"I can understand that. I feel the same way underground." I tucked a strand of hair behind my ear. "I have a plan that will allow us to arrive safely in Nevis."

Chloe stopped chewing. "I thought this ship would carry us there."

I rubbed my hands up and down my arms. "Nevis is ringed by reefs, and the only safe passage is from the south into Charlestowne Harbor. Fort Charles protects the southern portion of the harbor, and Fort Ashby the northern. I fear with the head start Alistair has, he can hold this ship at bay, and prevent me from landing, thereby, winning the duel by default."

"So, how do we get around the problem?"

"I plan on asking the slaves for help. This is where I need your assistance. I will visit them each day, until I can gain their trust. You will provide a diversion or cover story for my absences as necessary. If we keep our heads about us, no one will be the wiser if we go missing for a few hours." I knew the risks involved for Chloe, and I hated having to ask that of her, but it was also necessary.

Distressed, Chloe answered, "Lady Richmond, I cannot stay in that room! The moment the door shuts, my stomach opens. I have only begun to feel better with constant walks along the deck."

My voice dropped to a whisper. "Remember, I am

Mistress McGhee. And I am ashamed to ask this of you; but I do not see another way."

"You, there! Down below now! Captain's orders!" First mate, Slocum, hailed us from the bridge, jerking his thumb in the direction of the stairs. "Weather's changing. May be a storm coming."

On the horizon, dark clouds bunched together, blocking out the sun. The wind increased, whipping my hair across my eyes. My skin pricked, tingling with the energy of the strong winds. An energy no one ever taught me how to harness, as my mother died too young for her to help me. If I remained on deck, I would not be able to control my powers when subjected to the influence of the elements. Turning to pick my way across the pitching deck, I raised my voice to be heard over the wind. "Come on, niece. Let us retire to our cabin."

We hurried into the cabin, where the air was dank and still. Chloe paced the small patch of floor area, her arms clutched about her stomach. I lay on the bunk, bracing my legs against the frame to keep me ensconced in the bed, without toppling onto the floor with the next toss of the ship. My power quickened, fueled by the approaching storm.

There was a reason my clan was the most powerful water clan in the Americas: we lived at a prime energy source. Governments wanted Nevis for the trade winds and rich soil, prime assets for growing sugar cane. We, however, wanted Nevis for the frequent winds and steady rains.

Blue light blazed from my fingertips, the push of power strong enough to make me wonder of my skin would crack under the sudden expansion. My arms tingled, the power increasing its push on the limits of my body with each intensifying moment.

"Can I help?" Chloe asked, huddled over the pail again in the corner.

"No," I croaked. "I need to go below." I pulled myself to standing, blue light coloring all of my skin.

"You must not! You may be seen."

I struggled to grasp the door handle, wrenching the door open. "I need to be closer to the water. I'll find a place in the hold. No one will see, I promise. Lock the door behind me."

I shut the door before she could protest, and made my way into the nether regions of the ship. There, the wind was mute, but the water crashed relentlessly against the hull. I stumbled and climbed into the deepest parts of the hold, my power at a crescendo, demanding a release. The door to the slave hold stood quietly on my left, and a locked storeroom on my right. Fearful of capture if I remained in the open, I scooted into the slave hold, slamming the door behind me.

With the door shut, I released my power, blue light bursting from every inch of my skin, pouring from my fingertips, lighting the room several feet below the ocean as brightly as if it were midday.

The excess energy siphoned away, I gazed at the bound women and men staring at me. "I am so sorry to disturb you." In the light of my power, I could see the ravages of the trip on them: the cuts, the sores, and my nose detected the smells.

"I was expecting you," the old woman with gray hair finally spoke. "Do not be afraid; they cannot understand what we say."

"How did you know I would come in this way?" I stepped amongst the bodies to sit at her gnarled feet.

"Power calls to power. I felt you since the first day I saw you."

I remained silent.

She continued, "In my tribe, we have gifted ones. People hand-picked by the gods to help ease suffering here on this earth. You are blessed to have such a gift."

I tried to cover my hands. "In truth, I do not feel gifted. But rather, cursed."

She clucked, the chains around her wrists clanking with her movements. "People always get it wrong. They value the wrong things: money, land, power. These things mean nothing to the gods. Imprisonment cannot lead to freedom. Godliness does not condone or encourage the slaughter of those different from you."

With her simple words, something inside of me gave way, like a dirt embankment suddenly slides into the sea with a heavy rain. Tears began to fall down my cheeks. "I have spent many years ashamed for what I am."

"And what are you, child?"

My words were low, audible only to myself and the old woman. "I am Julia Richmond, daughter of Malcolm Nesbit, heir to the water clans of the Americas, last of the wind witches. I am returning home."

The woman answered. "I am called Pauline in your language. You cannot speak my tribal name. I am healer to my tribe, and imprisoned three times now. I am headed into a future I cannot control."

"I am not really a wind witch. I cannot cast wind spells." The awful truth, the thing I feared most to admit, the words were finally out in the open, and spoken to a strange woman under weird circumstances. With the utterance of those words, my heart felt free. "There are people in this world who value me because of my heritage. They believe I can cast spells that no one else can. They believe if they can control me, they can gain more power, more money, and more land. But I cannot cast a single spell! My mother died before she could start my training."

"You can call on the wind."

I shook my head. "No. I have tried. And failed."

She leaned closer to me, the stench from her body intensified in the close quarters. "The wind cannot be bottled up. You, you try to control everything. Your life. Your power. You come in here running from your own gift. Breathe with it. The wind, it goes in and out, up into places where no other things can reach. It is not at the mercy of the sun or moon. It flows freely. You cannot control the wind. The wind guides you where it wants *you* to go."

Her words seemed more like that of an old woman suffering the stresses of an ocean trip than any insight into my difficulties. I placed my hands on the hull beside her head, closing my eyes, feeling the thrum of the water against the wood, soaking the dampness into my clothes. We remained thus until the rocking of the ship subsided.

I stood, and she wiggled her hand in the shackles.

I inspected my hands, now only a faint blue in the blackness of the hold. "I will come again tomorrow."

She closed her eyes, resting her head against the rough wood. "We will meet when we meet."

"How is the girl?"

Pauline shook her head. "Her body I can heal. It is her mind that is broken. We will do what we can for her. It is our problem to fix."

I stood, my knees popping from the immobility. "I will try to bring you more food or water."

"Just keep us out of the doldrums. I will keep us alive."

Chapter Sixteen

" Sails to the east, by your leave!" the sailor called from the crow's nest. Today was the first clear day in weeks. I took my walk near the aft deck, to eavesdrop on the captain and the first mate and determine our progress in the journey. By my estimation, we were seven days out from Nevis. Chloe did not move from her perch over the pail in our cabin.

The sun shone brightly, and I felt warm for the first time in years. It soon became hot, causing me to sweat in my woolen gown. I squinted my eyes, searching the horizon for any shapes of land. I did not know our approach, but most English ships sailed on the east side of the islands, then turned sharply at the northern tip of them to sail in the channel between Nevis and St. Christopher's Island. There, the ship was guaranteed protection from the English cannon on the hills. Until then, we were at the mercy of any nation's pickings.

I needed to finalize my plan.

I mentally reviewed the island: roughly thirty-six square miles, encircled on three sides by reefs. Surely, Alistair lay in wait for me if I sailed into Charlestowne. I nibbled my lip as I took another turn on the deck. The closer we came to the island, the more effects of the demon I should have felt. But I felt fine. No dark stirrings of the soul, at least, no more than usual.

That fact bothered me a lot.

What if this were all a lie? What if my father was healthy? Impossible, I chastised my persistent inner voice. Alistair had my father's clan ring. There was no way he would relinquish his source and symbol of power without a fight. That led me back to wondering why Alistair preferred me alive in the first place.

The slaves were sitting on the opposite end of the deck, receiving their few minutes of sun for the day. I met with the old woman every night since my night in the hold during the storm, but none of the slaves indicated by their actions that they had any acknowledgement of my illicit visits.

The calm of the day was shattered by the trilling of the bosun's pipes. I veered clear of running men and loose ropes, snapping from above. I caught the sleeve of a passing sailor. "What is the commotion all about?"

"It's a Spanish galleon, tracking to the weather side. We are adjusting course to keep out of her way."

My heart thumped at the news. If we were close to enemy ships, we were close to Nevis! All the major routes from the West Indies passed near the island. I was almost home!

Relieved shouts mingled with the clanging of iron shackles as the slaves were led back into the hold. The captain yelled with his speaking trumpet, "Mistress Mc-Ghee! Down below! Avast up there! Reef the tops'l an' pull in the mizzen! Keep to the weather side of 'em!"

I peered into the bright haze of the horizon, unable to see the ship. A boom sounded like a peal of thunder, but no clouds marred the skies. To the right of the bow, a spray of water shot up into the air. Yells from the crew accompanied the next boom. Men took their posts at the cannons, our few small cannons, and strained to run the muzzles out past the edge of the ship. The guns were small, and although I was no naval marksman, I suspected we were out of range.

"On my mark!" the captain bellowed, and the decks stilled.

Another boom, but this time, there was no answering spray of water, just a high whistling noise, sounding louder by the second. With a crash, a red hot cannon ball smashed onto the deck, sending wood and splinters flying. I ducked behind the deck railings, shielding my face from the airborne debris. Screams filled the air. I crouched, holding my hands over my ears from the unbearable noise. Men ran about, some gesticulating towards the horizon, others pointing to the deck. I turned, searching for clear passage to get below deck and check on Chloe.

Wood and splinters lay about the deck, like a child just flattened a building of sticks. A few sailors lay closeby, groaning. Some were dead.

"Please, help me!" A young man close to me held out his hands. His leg was pinned to the deck by a large splinter. Dark blood seeped into the wood around him. My power lapped, encouraging me to get closer to the young lad.

I told the young man, "I will go for help."

Clutching the deck railing, which was blessedly still present, I used it to haul myself onto my feet. I picked my way amongst the chaos, both hands clinging to the railing for support against the pitching of the deck. Another boom in the air sounded, much closer this time. I dropped to the deck as another cannon shot whistled overhead, bursting thorough the rigging.

"Secure the ropes!" the captain screamed. I risked a glance skyward. Bodies moved among the tattered sails, pulling in lines, and securing ropes.

"Pull in the topsail! Reef the mizzen. To the lee! To the lee!" the captain yelled through his speaking trumpet, and the tiny forms, like ants, scurried through the rigging to obey his commands. "Keep to the lee!"

I was thankful there were still sailors left to obey his commands, for I had no idea what he was saying. Another cannon boom answered the captain.

Ocean spray showered the deck. That shot missed hitting below-deck by a few feet. We would not be so lucky again. I peered across the waves at our pursuer.

She was a magnificent ship. Three masts rose heavenward, every sail unfurled, bow leaping above the waves before crashing into the white water around her decks. She was travelling fast.

We did not stand the slightest chance of escaping her.

I crept along the rail, motivated more than ever to reach Chloe. The ship was too big for me to guide along in the water, especially with all the witnesses that would see my betraying witchlight.

I just hoped Madame Oualie or Alistair were not aboard that vessel.

I inched my way along the deck. I now stood five feet from the stairs leading to Chloe. I pictured her sobbing, curled up into a ball on the floor, praying for a surcease from the shelling.

A shot crashed through the railing, destroying it, and skipping across the deck like a stone across a stream. It disappeared into a hole in the deck.

The same hole the slaves had entered through only moments before.

Adrenaline fueled my legs and I sprinted for the stairs, dodging crying boys and injured men. The ship shifted, leaning to the right, throwing me against the wall as I ran down the stairs to the hold. When I reached the lower level, my feet landed in water. Fresh seawater was rising to my ankles in the moments it took to

reach the slaves' door. I pulled on the handle, but floating debris prevented the door from swinging open on
its hinges.

"By the tides!" I exclaimed. Here was a good use
for my power.

I inhaled deeply, filling my lungs, and opening my
nostrils to the salt air. Pushing power into my hands,
I imagined a barrier funneling the water back into the
sea. Mentally manipulating the fluid, I moved the water
away from the door, opening it with a flick of my wrist.
Water rushed from the room, and I pushed more power
into my hands to move this new volume from my path.

I stepped into the hold, now flooded with light,
water towering above my head in a wall, and ready to
drown us all if I lost my concentration. "Is everyone all
right?"

No response.

Water rushed into the hold from a breach in the
hull, three meters from where the old woman was
chained. I tried to push the wall of water out the hole,
but more water simply rushed in. The boat shifted a
few feet farther to the right. In a matter of minutes, we
would sink. Blue power blazed from my hands; the light
so bright, I had to turn my head from the glaring intensity. Dark gray salt water from the ocean met my power,
and still, it rushed in. The intensity of the water pushed
me down to my knees. I knelt on the ground, holding my
hands outstretched, both hands blazing blue light, and
focusing every bit of energy into the rushing wall.

The ship listed again.

Frustrated, I pushed again at the wall of water, my
light extinguishing under the ocean's incessant flow.

"Lava and ashes! I cannot stop it," I sobbed.

"Do not try to stop it."

The old woman, her face bruised, and bleeding
from a cut above her eye, knelt beside me in the cold

water. "Do not push the water. It will always resist you. Bend it to do your will."

I filled my lungs with air, closing my eyes to the nervous screams of the Africans, and the clanks of the rusty chains, and the booms of cannon fire above. I opened my mind to import the sound, flow, and movement of the water, forcing my terror into a small corner deep inside. I released power from my hands, not as a wall of energy, but rather, as a set of feathered fingers, pushing through the water, moving the mass from within, and bending the flow in reverse, to seek the greater ocean and rejoin its larger entity.

The flow lessened.

I tried again, the encouraging grunts from the slaves encouraging me to continue reapplying my power to the problem, and driving the water back to the depths of the ocean.

The flow diminished.

I do not know how long I labored in the hull, as my sense of time was measured only in the ebb and flow of water. When I finished, the ocean raged outside the hole, but no water entered it. Power pulsed from my hands, the blue twined with gray to stopper the breach in the hull.

I could not release my power, or water would again rush into the hull. But I could not stay there for the remainder of the voyage either. I giggled when I imagined the look on the captain's face at the sight of me, a sight that would, no doubt, land me right back in the clutches of the church again.

I turned to the old woman. "I've stopped the water. Now what shall I do?"

She held up her hand, her wrist crusty with grime where it met the iron shackle. "I will mend the hull. Close your eyes against the light."

I obeyed. A warm rush of words, in a language I did not comprehend, filled the space. Clicks, chirps, and the sounds from deep within a forest rose and fell. I lost myself in the primal flow of raw power rushing past my elbow like a breeze ruffles the stalks of grass under a summer sun. I felt warm, imagining the heat against my skin. The resistance of the water against my power halted, the sudden cessation threw me onto my back. I landed against a coil of chain, the links digging painfully into my skin.

The sounds stopped. "You may open your eyes."

I cracked my eyes open to see the hull now solid in front of my eyes. I sat, rolling my shoulder, and testing for damage. I looked at the old woman. "If you can fix the hull, why did you not free yourselves and take over the ship?"

She chuckled. "You, always about overcoming problems with more power! Who here can steer a ship?"

I gazed at the men and women, their gaunt faces lacking any animation in the darkness. "No one, I suppose."

"No one," she agreed. "It is best to wait until we approach land, then we may make our escape."

I surveyed the hold again, thinking of how I planned to reach land. "I intend to disembark from the ship on the windward coast of my home. I can help get you off the ship. After that, you will be on your own."

She shook her head no. "We are bound for Haiti." Haiti had been rebelling against French colonial rule for years. Any slave wanting freedom in the Caribbean dreamed of reaching Haiti.

"No," I answered. "Haiti is not my destination."

She remained silent and I rose. "Consider my offer. I will return tomorrow to discuss this further."

I turned to leave, picking my way along the damp floor.

"Wait."

I paused, the darkness like a breathing thing settling on my skin.

"We want freedom."

"I have no need of slaves," I answered.

"But your plantation neighbors have a need. We must consider that before we agree to any terms."

"There are freed slaves that settled in the hills. You would not be alone."

Chapter Seventeen

I found Chloe in our cabin, bent over the floor with a sliver of wood held in her hand. She clawed at the ground, scraping bits of dirt into a small pile by her knees.

"Chloe, what are you doing?"

She concentrated on her task. "I am collecting dirt to replenish my supply. With the ship blown to bits, I found this shard from the mizzenmast works well to scrape dirt from the cracks in the floorboards." She straightened, her gaze piercing mine. "I want off this ship, Julia. I cannot abide this nonsense anymore."

I clapped my hands together. "Capital! Because I have just calculated that we make Nevis in two days."

"How are we going ashore? I cannot swim, and you have promised to miraculously get us off this boat. Perhaps we are exiting through the hole in the hull?"

I was taken aback by her clipped words. "Chloe, are you upset with me?"

Her bottom lip trembled. "Why would I be upset? My *protector* left me to my own devices while we were under *fire* from a Spanish galleon!"

"I am sorry. I had to go below to stop the ship from sinking!"

"You have left me to my own devices on this ship long enough. I am tired of relying on others for my protection. You have not taught me a single spell, In fact, I think you are sorely under-prepared for your duel. And if you lose the duel, what happens to me then!?" Her last words were difficult to hear through her sobs. I bent to hold her, my arms encircling her thin shoulders.

She pushed me away. "I do not need your help to cry."

I sat with my back against the bunk, my legs straight in front of me, talking to her huddled form. "But I need your help, Chloe. I need your help to get off this ship. I need your help on Nevis."

"I may want to go by myself when we reach land."

"You are free to go as you wish. There are several clans to consider approaching, if that is what you want. I would caution you to avoid certain areas of the island."

"Like what? Is there a volcano I must remember to avoid?"

"Actually, yes. There is."

"Oh."

"I want to tell you all about Nevis, if you will hear me."

She did not look at me, but curled into a ball on the floor.

I continued, "My father was, and is, an awful man. When we were young, he did not show love to his daughters; he only showed us how to fight. If we scraped our knees falling from a tree, he did not kiss our tears away, he taught us how to heal ourselves so we would not be taken advantage of in a fight. As we matured, he taught us how to block emotions, and to do what was right by the clan. Our feelings did not matter. Who we were, who we wanted to be, did not matter. His plans, his dreams of an empire, they mattered. I have hated that side of him for years."

My voice roughened with emotions I refused to acknowledge for most of my life. "When I fought my first duel, I was appalled at what I had done, what my magic accomplished. What my father encouraged me to do."

I stopped, remembering the hot summer day.

We were in the dueling pits, a circular area cleared in a fallow sugar cane field. Tropical trees graced the north edge of the field, while a stream, called a 'ghout' by the islanders, trickled through the stands of cane to form the eastern border. The cane itself was dead cane, blackened husks from the controlled burn of the fields the previous season, and stood five feet tall.

Alistair, Penelope and I were standing in the flat center of the ground. Lazy bugs circled aimlessly in the air, and monkeys perched in the trees.

"I think we should have a real duel," Penelope said, tossing her auburn curls with a nod of her head.

"Do not be an idiot, Penelope," Alistair answered. "We must wait until the proper time. Any outcome from today would not matter anyway."

Penelope rolled her wrist, green mist twisting among her fingers. "Just because you are scared, Alistair, to let us see the three spells you know, do not take away our fun. What do you think, Julia?"

"I think I do not want to duel. Ever."

Penelope smiled. "I knew you would say that! Your father can crow about your talent all he wants, but in the end, you will quit."

"No, I will not. I will fulfill my duty to the clan."

"Does that include marrying Alistair?"

Alistair paled under his tanned skin. "We are decidedly off the subject. Now, we came here to practice. So let us practice."

"I do not want to. You and Alistair can work together," I said.

Penelope answered, "Really, Julia, you need the most practice of anyone. I mean, when have you actually fought anything that had a chance to fight back?"

"*Fine.*" Her comments needled me, getting under my skin. I forgot all the words of my father, especially his words of caution. All I wanted was to blast the smile off her porcelain-skinned face.

"*Capital! Then let us begin.*" She circled to stand opposite me, ten feet away, closest to the stream. *No matter,* I thought. *I can call water from the ocean a half-mile away if necessary.* "*Alistair, you be the referee.*"

He spaced himself equidistant from us, his casting hand at the ready. As referee, his job was to ensure any errant spells did not damage the fields. Or kill anyone.

"*Let us lay down the rules,*" I said. "*No spells intended to cut, break, or otherwise damage anyone.*"

"*What is the fun in that?*" Penelope pouted, the green mist darkening around her fingers.

"*Fine. We can cut, but no maiming.*" I turned to Alistair. "*Can you heal well enough to prevent any serious injuries?*"

"*Yes. I think so.*"

"*Good enough.*" I did not intend for any of Penelope's spells to land on my person. "*Then let us begin.*"

Penelope flung her hand at me, green fire erupting from her fingertips. I threw a shield of blue to block her spell.

"*Curse it, Julia. You cannot stand there and just deflect my spells. You need to fight!*"

"*No, I do not.*"

"*Then deflect this.*" She moved her hands in concert, in a casting pattern I had never seen.

"*That is not an approved spell,*" Alistair warned.

"*It is meant to test Julia's defenses. Nothing more.*"

I crouched, knees bent, ready to dodge the spell if necessary. Penelope's hands moved faster, a ball of green developing in the space between her palms.

"Penelope, stop it. Now. This is not what we had planned," Alistair commanded. His casting hand glowed green.

Penelope stopped her hands. "I just want to have a little fun. I want to see if the heir to all of our destinies is capable." The spell glowed, pulsating in her palm. It felt malevolent, like an animal waiting to pounce on a passing mouse.

"I am not heir to your destiny. Each of us is responsible for our own choices, and our own destinies."

"I meant the clans, Julia. Father says you are the heir. If you are anointed, then Alistair and I are subject to your whims."

"My father is the picture of health, and a young man still. He may remarry and sire a son."

Penelope did not answer. We stood thus, a triangle of teen witches, the spell in our midst. An eastward breeze ruffled the small hairs on my neck.

"Now!" Penelope yelled.

Her spell whizzed across the clearing, its outlines a blur. Scared, I threw a shield, then pulled water from the stream, commanding it to knock the spell off its trajectory. My water spell cut through the humid air, hurtling towards its target.

The green glob bobbled, avoiding the column of water.

"I knew you would try that, Julia! You cannot protect a clan without a sense for fighting!" Penelope taunted. "You are a failure!"

The spell hit my shield, the green glob shattering into a thousand little pieces. I pulled as much power as I could, throwing a wall of water to engulf the remnants. Concentrating, I pulled the disparate pieces closer, re-annealing the spell within its cocoon of water.

Sweat beaded on my brow, and the spell fought my control. With a great heave, I envisioned the spell *lobbing over Penelope's head to land behind her on the trampled ground.*

I released my control of the spell, the wall of water falling to earth. Raining down on Penelope. Bits of green mixed with water hit her skin.

She screamed, clutching her arm. "You hag! You idiot! Look at what you have done!"

The green bits coalesced over her casting arm, a green casing that stretched from her fingertips to her upper arm. The spell rotated a half-inch.

Blood spilled from her arm, running down the green cast to pool on the ground. Alistair rushed to her side, his hand glowing. He laid his hands along her arm.

"Get away from me!" Penelope cried.

"Let me help you!" Alistair demanded.

"You cannot help," Penelope whispered. "It is a black spell."

Alistair pulled his hands away from her body. "Penelope, what have you done?"

She screamed again in answer, the spell rotating another quarter-turn around her arm.

I hurried to her side. "Penelope, what type of spell is it? Maybe Alistair and I can both help you."

Her eyes glazed with pain. "Get away from me. You have done enough. What spell did you throw at me?"

"It was just a water spell to throw it out of the way. I did not add anything to it!"

"You must have. Look! Look at me!"

She held her right arm up, the green spell glowing under a thick crust of blood. Puckered flesh appeared at the upper junction of the spell and her arm.

"It is cutting off your arm. By the tides, it is cutting off your casting arm!" I cried out. "I am going to get my father. He will know what to do."

"I'll stay here with Penelope. Hurry, Julia."

"*I will.*"

I fidgeted on the hard floor. Chloe rolled over, peering at my face. "What happened next, Lady Richmond?"

I continued, "I raced to find my father. When I told him what happened, he agreed to help, but not before telling me how proud he was. Of me! Of what I had done! My father was thrilled. He said to me, 'Julia, you have the instinct of a warrior with a lack of conscience to match.'

"His words were the highest praise he could give me. But hearing his words describe me was awful. I tried to talk with him, to let him see reason, but he pushed me. He wanted to groom me and prepare me for taking over the clan. He began to walk about the house and loudly proclaim that I would be the first female clan leader in the west."

Chloe remained still on the floor, her gaze riveted on my face.

"My father insisted I was a natural. I have to agree. I do not think I will have difficulties in the duel, Chloe. I will defeat Alistair and reclaim my father's clan ring for him. You will have your protector. Everyone will benefit in the end."

"I am sorry. I was scared, I was not thinking of what this could mean for you," she said.

I continued, "You will benefit, Chloe. The clan will benefit. Everyone. Except me. I will die a little inside. Each time I do something horrid, I feel like I shut down the nice part of my soul. I am pushed away from the parts of me that I think define me as Julia, the very nice woman who saved a ship, and took in a foundling witch, and fled her home, rather than having her soul shrivel to nothing under her father's plans. I am reminded of the woman who threw a man overboard with a wave because he was mean to a defenseless girl. Of the woman who would curse her enemy if it meant protection for those I loved."

"Do not talk like that! We will find another way, or hatch another plan."

My throat constricted, preventing any further speech. Chloe moved, her clothes rustling as she sat up, mirroring my perch on the bed. She flung her arms around me, hugging me tight.

"I think you are wonderful just as you are. Please do not be cross with me. I was just scared."

Her words did not thaw the iciness frosting my soul. I pushed her away. "We need to plan for our exit from the ship."

She released me, her teeth biting her lower lip. "What do you have in mind?"

I smoothed her pile of dirt into a smooth surface, and rubbed my finger in it, drawing a crude map of Nevis. "The island is roughly circular, with reefs on all shores except the Caribbean side." I marked an X on the circle at roughly nine of the clock. "Here is Charlestowne, the capital and harbor."

Chloe creased her brow. "We are not going to jaunt off the boat in the middle of the capital, are we? Alistair may have spies positioned to watch for you, and blast you on the spot when your foot touches land."

"Exactly. Or he may have the batteries fire on any ship arriving from England. Which is why we need to wreck the ship on the Atlantic reefs the day before we make landfall."

Chloe gasped, "Oh! But I cannot swim."

I continued. "You will not need to swim far." I indicated an area opposite of Charlestowne on the circle. "This is Indian Castle. The reefs are close to land, and the water is the most shallow on this side of the island. Here is where we need to wreck the ship on the reefs."

"   H   o   w   ?   "

"My power. If we strike the reefs as the tides are high, I can use them to force the ship against the rocks. If we approach the area at low tide, I will need more power to drag the hull against the rocks. Did you feel the pull of land when we passed Barbuda?"

"No."

I thought about her answer. "Then you cannot help pull the ship towards land."

"If we were closer, maybe I would be able to help."

"I hope so. I do not want to deplete my energy so close to the duel, but if we are not successful, there may not be a duel at all."

Chloe regarded the map on the floor. "It is a rather small place to try and hide from your enemies."

"I agree. But I can find shelter until it is time to approach my family."

The ship shuddered to a great, shivering stop. We fell against each other, our arms and legs tangling together on the floor. Shouts and yells sounded from the upper deck. I heard a great scraping sound, like metal against wood, each time causing the ship to shudder and sway.

"I do not like the feel of this, Chloe."

"Me either. At least, it is not cannon fire."

"Cannon fire is always from a distance. This appears very close."

A wave of energy hit us, knocking my breath from my body. Chloe lay beside me, gasping for air. "What was that?"

"Another witch scouting the ship," I answered. "I think the galleon has returned."

Chloe and I crept up to the porthole to peer outside.

The great ship rested a few feet away. I could see the scars on her sides, evidence of earlier battles at sea. Cannons remained jutting out their ports, smoke wafting from the heated barrels. The smell of sulfur entered the cabin with the next breeze.

"Chloe, I think we are being boarded."

She cowered in the floor, sobbing. "I knew it! We are about to trade one awful fate for another."

"Not necessarily."

I pulled her into a standing position. "Let us see what is happening above deck."

Confusion clouded her dirty face. "How?"

"With an invisibility spell, of course."

"Oh," she answered. "Of course."

"Hold onto me. Do not lose contact with me or the spell will be broken."

She clutched my arm as I pulled energy from the water. I loved casting with the ocean; my tiny pull of water would not hurt the fishes in the depths. I started the spell, satisfied when we disappeared from view. Chloe giggled. "I can see the bunk through you, Julia."

"Quiet, Chloe. I cannot make us mute, just invisible."

She giggled once more. We trod carefully, picking our way across the mess of the floor to stand at the bottom of the stairs that led above deck.

"Do not break contact with me or you will be seen."

We crept up the stairs, Chloe clutching my hand, me dragging her along the narrow treads, both of us knocking against the railings. We wiggled through the small opening, crouching against the wall behind a pile of shredded sail, and behind the line of sailors.

The attacking ship towered above us, its masts shrouded in mist. Great grappling hooks held *The Constant* fast to her side. Wounded men lay scattered amongst the ropes, jumbled in amongst the detritus of cannon fire and splintered masts. A disparate collection of men held our crew at bay. They were well-fed, clean, with no tears or tatters in their clothing. Each clutched a knife, gun, or sword as a weapon. None looked our way.

"Captain, please make yourself present." A thin man with a bald pate of average height spoke. He wore cream breeches and a navy jacket, more suitable for an afternoon tea than an act of piracy. "By order of Lord Gladstone."

The captain limped forward, aggression still etched in his dirt-smeared face. "State your intention for blasting my ship out of the water! We have the proper letters of marque."

The thin man continued. "Lord Gladstone wishes to search the vessel for a fugitive."

The captain laughed. "I lost the lives of my men for a fugitive! I have a hold full of slaves bound for the Caribbean. I do not take fugitives in my employ. I have no need of them."

The thin man tutted. "Lord Gladstone understands, but there is a considerable bounty on this particular fugitive's head."

"What is this person's name?" the captain queried.

I shifted beside Chloe. My legs were tingling from the unnatural position, but I was riveted by the thin man's words. If Louise were here, she would have torn that ship apart searching for her husband. I did not even know what he looked like. I hoped I lived long enough to see Louise again and tell her of this day.

"The name of the fugitive is Lady Julia Richmond and her companion, Miss Chloe Longood."

The captain slanted a glance at Slocum, the first mate. "We have two women on board, indentured servants, bound for the islands."

"What are their names?"

"Mistress McGhee and her niece."

"Let me search the ship. Lord Gladstone would be unhappy if he missed an opportunity for a bounty."

The captain waved his hand. "Search all you like, and I thank you for asking permission," he sneered. "They have stayed in the aft cabin. I have not seen either one since the action started."

Three men, dressed in long pants and dark shirts, moved to the aft of the ship. They each held a pistol and bandoliers full of ammunition. Cutlasses hung from their belts, bobbing with their steps.

Chloe breathed into my ear. "What do we do?"

"Nothing."

The men slunk past us. In the aftermath of the cannon noise, it was eerily quiet, with only the sound of wounded men and the lap of waves against the hull to mark the passage of time. The thin man made a great show of pulling a watch from his pocket, consulting its face, then peering at the position of the sun.

"Captain, by the sun, you will miss the tide for tomorrow into Nevis if we delay much longer. Perhaps you can remember more clearly the appearance of these ladies?"

Captain Dobbin spat on the deck. "Do you have any rations of rum for me injured crew?"

"Perhaps that can be arranged with Lord Gladstone."

The search party returned, climbing over coils of rope to reach their leader. "No signs of anyone, sir. We even checked with the cargo."

The captain smiled. "Then you must be on your way. After the rum is sorted out."

The thin man bowed, a quick bend at the waist. "Sorry for the trouble, but Lord Gladstone is especially diligent in his tasks. We must wait for his decision on the matter. Now, about that description of the women?"

"They are of a size, neither too tall, nor too short. Both are thin. The one has blond hair, the other brunette. Neither struck me as having airs like a grand lady."

"I will communicate this to Lord Gladstone, as well as your wish for rum."

"Look at my ship! All this for a turn of coin in your pocket!"

The thin man replied, "Would you care for us to finish the job? Many a slaver is lost at sea in the storms of the Atlantic. Your fate could be no better."

The captain stepped back. "No, no, sir. Look at whatever you like, and take whatever you wish. Then get off my ship. She may be small, but she is all I have."

The thin man replied. "We will be as expedient as possible."

"What do you mean?"

"Lord Gladstone himself will wish to inspect the ship. Your description fits exactly with whom we may be interested in."

Chloe nestled closer to me. "Is that really Lady Gladstone's husband?"

I whispered, "I do not know of any other relation sailing about the Caribbean."

The captain replied, "Then let us get on with it. I have a cargo of slaves bound for the islands and I want a good price at the market."

"I will be quick." Every head turned to the galleon. A stunning man, a full six feet tall, perched on the railing of the larger ship. His hair appeared framed with gold, the sun glinting off light brown curls.

The captain stuttered, all bravado lost in the sight of Lord Gladstone, "Thank you."

Gladstone stepped onto the deck of the conquered vessel.

"I feel something different," Chloe said.

"I feel it too," I replied. An energy, witch in origin, oozed over the deck. My power roiled inside, not recognizing the foreign magic.

Like water unleashed from a dam, a wave of energy broke over the deck, surging towards our hiding place, and shattering my spell.

I retaliated, throwing another spell over us, stronger this time, pulling my energy from the ocean. A red and green parrot circled overhead, swooping from the rigging of the galleon to perch on the quarter house above our heads.

"Squawk!" it cried.

Gladstone cocked his head, like a hawk listening to the breeze. "I may have found your passengers for you, Captain." He pointed to our vantage point. "Leopold, collect them and bring them onto my ship."

The thin man marched towards us. We remained huddled on the ground, the parrot screeching above us. Chloe clutched my hand.

"Steady," I cautioned.

The thin man stopped three feet from us. He glared at the bird. "Toulouse, cease that caterwauling."

A wave of energy hit me, knocking my breath from my body. "Oh!" Chloe exclaimed.

My spell dissolved like sugar in the rain. We were visible.

The thin man, Leopold, pulled his watch from his pocket, consulting the dial. Placing it back in his waistcoat, he stated, "Eight minutes. I had hoped for a more sporting time." His gaze flicked over us, taking in our disheveled appearance, and finding us lacking. "It is unreasonable to resist. Come with me, ladies."

We shuffled past the collection of sailors. Chloe clung to my arm. I gently removed her hands. "If you must hold on, please hold onto my *left* arm."

"Sorry," she mumbled.

"Keep 'em on your ship!" Mr. Slocum chortled as we passed him. "They were nothing but bad luck!"

The thin man ignored them, ushering us to stand before Lord Gladstone. He remained still, gazing over the tiny slaver. The aspect of the sun in the sky prevented me from properly seeing his face. With a nod, he stated, "Keep the crew at the ready. Bring the women on board."

The ships were tethered together with grappling hooks and ropes, but it was a movable, flexible bonding that allowed independent movement of each ship along the waves. The single solid surface spanning the gap was a thin, wooden plank. With each bob and dip of the ships, the board banged about its moorings.

I peered at the frothy ocean below, wishing I wore pants instead of my skirts. If I fell, at least, I stood a better chance of swimming in pants.

"I cannot cross that plank," Chloe stated. "I will not."

"I will help you," I reassured. "I will hold your hand."

"No," Lord Gladstone said. "One at a time. The young girl first."

"No," Chloe repeated. "Do to me what you must right here."

A third wave energy lapped at my ankles. This time, I concentrated on it, dissecting the flavors of the magic like a sommelier judging a fine wine.

The magic seemed a mix from multiple individuals, not just one source. I glanced behind me at the odd collection of pirates.

I had an idea.

"Go ahead."

Chloe glared at me. Dropping to all fours, she tested the strength of the plank with her hands, pushing up and down on the narrow strip of wood. Crawling a few feet across the plank, she stopped. A wind had risen, whipping her skirts about, and it was difficult for her to move forward as her skirts caught in her legs and blinded her vision. "I cannot go on."

Lord Gladstone, standing on the galleon, pinched the bridge of his nose. "Oh, for God's sake. Leopold, make it right."

He raised his Navy insignia-covered arms, muttering beneath his breath. I saw no light, no sign of magic, but as his muttering continued, Chloe rose above the plank, then hurtled through the air to land in a heap at Lord Gladstone's feet.

Leopold turned to me. "Will you require assistance, ma'am?"

"Not from you."

I touched the plank with my right foot. It did not feel enchanted. My destination, a mere six feet away, seemed like a mile. Each lap of a wave pushed the ships together and apart, like an accordion. I closed my eyes, feeling the pitch and roll of the ships. I waited, poised on the plank, for a wave to push the ships together. Feeling the ship adjust, I opened my eyes, staring at my goal, hiking my skirts high and scampering across to land with a jump beside Chloe.

Closer now, I peered at Louise's husband. She called him a gambler and a bastard, but the man in front of me appeared impeccably dressed and clean-shaven with his hair groomed into a low queue. His clothes were cream and black, and seemed recently laundered.

Gladstone nodded. "Well, played, Julia. I gambled that you would reveal your witchcraft in helping the chit. Now I owe my crew an extra ration of rum."

"How did you know?" I inquired. "Was it your parrot? I always had a loathing for birds, and now I understand why. They are horrid creatures."

"My bird can sense magic spells, which is a useful asset, but I did not need my bird. Richmond sent me."

"What!"

He placed his thumbs in the pockets of his waist-coat, rocking back and forth on his heels. "Let us go to my chambers. I need to explain things to you."

Chloe and I followed Gladstone across the deck to his cabin in the aft of the ship. A Persian rug covered the wooden floor, the bright reds and blues echoed in the rich view from the windows on three sides of the room. The furniture would have been as appropriate in a drawing room as it was in that chamber. The parrot flew into the room behind us, landing with a great flapping and clacking on a perch near the east window. Gladstone rested on the edge of the desk, crossing his legs in front of him. He appeared at ease.

"Julia, Richmond hired me to track your voyage. He was concerned you would meet with an early grave if left to sail on that slaver."

"I can take care of myself." I opened my power, searching the room for any water to use as a weapon.

"Of course you can," he soothed. "But your husband was concerned, and I wanted money. It was a mutually agreeable plan."

"I see. So now what do you do?" My power probed, finding an ample amount of urine in a chamber pot to my right.

"Why, I cut ties with the slaver, sail you into Nevis, guns blazing, if I must, and ensure you get on that island safely. After that, my mission is ended."

Chloe added, "Lady Richmond, that sounds wonderful. Look at what this ship did to ours!"

I edged a few feet closer to the door, standing with my back to the exit and facing Gladstone. "When did you speak with Richmond?"

"I sailed into London docks the night before you left. He knew of my location, and sought out my help. He felt my talents could be of assistance."

"You mean, he knows you are a witch?"

He blinked. "Yes."

"He must also know that your crew are all witches as well."

Gladstone hesitated. "Yes."

"I find it interesting that such a disparate group can cast cohesive spells."

"I agree. Earth and air tend to cancel each other out, as well as the usual problems with fire and water, but we have come to rely on each other out at sea. Part of that reliance is learning to coexist with our magic, as well as our manners."

"I am curious. Did you see your wife while you were in London?"

"No. And my wife and I are none of your concern."

"She is hurt by your petition for a divorce."

"It is better this way. You have tried to live without witchcraft, so you know first hand how hard that is to do. I tried, and did not last three months. I need to cast. It is a part of me I naturally embrace." He gazed out the window at the sea, the sky, and the fluffy clouds, a man alone. "Louise deserves a better man than me."

Chloe said, "I think you are both nice people. Thank you for helping me over the gap. I do not do well when my feet are not on solid ground."

He appeared surprised. "You think it was I who assisted you?"

"Yep," she nodded. "I know it was you."

"Interesting. We can discuss this talent of yours, Miss Chloe, as we continue our voyage."

"I am afraid we cannot accept your offer of hospitality."

Blue light, like mine, misted from his fingers. "I am afraid you have no choice."

"I gave my word to the slaves in the hold that I would help them. Are you offering sanctuary to them as well?"

"No."

"Then I will have to decline your generous offer."

He considered me for a moment before nodding as if to agree with himself on his next words. "All is not as it seems. Richmond is not the devil you think he is, nor is he the enemy you cast him to be. I have regularly been transporting captured witches for him, taking them to safety, here in the Caribbean or in the American colonies. The ones he can spirit out of the church's hands."

"Are you suggesting he is a.. a double spy? That he plays one side against the other?"

"He is a man with a firm moral compass and a conviction of what is right. When you speak to him again, give him a chance. Listen to him."

"Marital advice is not what I thought I would hear coming into your office. I guessed it would be more on the lines of preventing me from going to Nevis, or stopping some dastardly plot to take over all the witch clans with demon infestations, the usual witch politics."

"Actually, that is exactly what your husband wanted me to debrief you on, but I have taken license to bend your mission a bit." He gazed at me for the first time, the intensity of his emotions palpable. "I am related to you by blood, something I did not know until three years ago. I need for you to banish this demon as well. Do you not feel the pull of the underground as you sail closer to Nevis? I could not stand on deck for more than a few minutes before the sun blinded my vision. I need tinted glasses to go about the deck in broad daylight. How can I be a pirate if I can't see what ship I am blasting? And how long would I stay in command of this crew?"

I stood there, processing his words. I felt none of the symptoms he suggested, and doubted his sources on the related argument. But time was of the essence, and I had spent enough in his company already.

"I plan to duel Alistair, whom I suspect is already infected with the demon taint. That should release you from any infestation. So I must leave your company, and be on my way."

"I command you to stay here, let my ship be the one that takes you in to Nevis. We have witches here that can help you fight."

"I have my own resources."

"I cannot allow you to traipse into Charlestowne, or get captured, and then all our plans are lost."

"I do not intend to fail, and I do not take orders from pirates. Nor do I rely on armies whose allegiance is not with me."

He stood, witchlight gathering at his hand. "I will take you by force if necessary."

"Then I bid you a good day and a bon voyage." I threw a spell at him, fueled from the chamber pot, while yelling, "Chloe, run!"

My spell hit him in the chest, soiling his clothes with the urine. He hesitated.

It was enough.

We ran. As my foot hit the deck, I pulled water from the ocean, preparing my attack. Chloe ran across the plank, no trepidation in her steps now. I followed, pulling the water into a rogue wave that toppled the plank and ripped the grappling hooks from their moorings.

We collapsed onto the deck of the slaver. Chloe raised her dress, running for the relative safety of the cabin. I reached with my power down into the warm waters again, pulling another wave up and over the deck railing, washing overboard the pirate crew.

"To your posts!" the captain yelled. "Blast 'em with a broadside!"

To a man, the able crew scattered to their places. The deck lurched under my feet as the two ships parted, the wind opening the remaining sails. I hurried to the back of the ship, dodging wounded men, flying ropes, and gaping holes in the deck.

Our cannon fired in unison, the report pushing the slaver a few feet further from the pirate vessel.

"Another one, lads! We need five hundred yards to be out of range! Fire when ready!" the captain yelled from his post at the wheel.

I crouched on the rear of the ship. Wind ruffled my hair with its increasing velocity as I peered at the froth from the rudder.

Five hundred yards. Even now, Gladstone worked to pull his crew from the waters, blue light flaring. We had little time left to escape.

Breathing deeply, I cleared my mind. I had never tried to move an object in space as large as the slaver. Typically, three to five witches were necessary to accomplish large tasks. I had to try alone.

I opened myself to the pull of the ocean, and the turbulence of her waters. I imagined the ship sailing faster and faster over the surface of the water.

Nothing.

I tried again, furrowing my brows with my efforts. Sweat pooled in my armpits as I worked over the rudder, coaxing every bit of speed from the little ship.

Nothing.

I glared at the galleon. Gladstone stood in counterpoint to me, hands working over the gulf between the ships. His parrot squawked.

I attempted my spell again. As soon as my power reached the water, the parrot squawked and cried, "Witch! Witch!"

"That bird is an unfair advantage, Lord Glad-stone!" I yelled over the boom of the cannon; but I did not think he heard me.

Fine. Be difficult. I turned my spell from the rudder of my ship and aimed it at Gladstone's chest.

It was a direct hit. He toppled overboard, crying out as his body hit the water with a smack.

When his head vanished beneath the surface, I applied my spell again. The slaver seemed to move faster in the water. I cajoled the water again, squinting at the rudder.

The slaver frothed a little more.

I applied myself again and again, until I was satisfied when the slaver skimmed over the water. I sat in the corner of the ship, monitoring the galleon as it faded to no more than a speck in the distance.

We were free. I was exhausted.

Chapter Eighteen

The next few days dawned hot and windy, with no signs of pursuit. I fidgeted, knowing the sands in my hourglass were fast approaching the day when I would have my reckoning. I knew Gladstone would eventually catch up to us, but I could not battle him and get the ship and slaves off safely at the same time.

As I stood on the deck, the scars of battle were evident in the mended sails and broken boards. The ship traveled slower than usual, the ripples of waves against her hull failing to break into whitewater. Nevis was a dark smudge on the horizon, two miles off to our starboard side. By the height of the sun in the sky, and the distance from the spot of dark on the horizon, we would miss the high tide at Indian Castle, the next point in our navigation to get closer to Nevis.

Chloe stood at my side, her pockets weighted with dirt. She collected her weapons most of the night. "We will miss the high tide."

"Low tide works just as well for my plan."

She added, "I think we should take over the ship and force them to do our wishes. Maybe we don't have to wreck the ship, or the crew."

"Are you saying, that after all the horrid things we have seen, I should spare the crew?"

"I just think we would be no better than they are if we, like, killed them." Chloe fidgeted under my stare. "I don't doubt you have the ability. It's just the reason for why to do it that I have a problem with."

Her words made me uncomfortable, and I turned in a huff. "I could possess the captain, maybe the first mate as well, if I could call a demon. Which is not possible over the water anyway. That still leaves the remainder of the crew unaccounted for. If I forced the captain to give an order to 'sail for the reef,' they would simply ignore him." I sighed. "This is the only way."

Chloe waved to the bosun's mate, who was scowling at us from the bridge. "I will take the sun on deck until you return. Think about what I said, Julia. There is a way out that you don't have to feel sorry about later. It just takes the courage to choose that option."

I grumbled, "If I am not back in one hour, move to our second plan."

I made my way to the hold, placing an invisibility spell over me as soon as I was out of sight of the main deck. I moved quickly through the levels below the surface of the ship, now familiar with each twist and stair of the route. My invisibility spell was much improved since I practiced it almost daily. Now, I could move among the men without a ripple in the air, or the slightest distortion of perspective that would indicate my position.

I felt small at Chloe's words. She was right. It was easy to claim that circumstances dictated certain choices; and even if I did something bad, as long as it was for a good reason, I should incur no taint on my soul. But that reasoning was precisely why I was upset with Richmond. I was being a hypocrite, and Chloe called me on it.

I entered the dark hold, my pulse quickening with my pace. The sights of the chained slaves and the smells were common to me now.

I stopped before the old woman. "What is your decision? Will you help in exchange for freedom?"

She drew herself upright, the chains clinking around her ankles. "We do not want to trade one master for another. I need your word we will be free."

"There are former slaves on the island who live in the hills. Join me, and you will have an opportunity to find them and embrace freedom. Or, you can work on my plantation as independent servants, earning a wage. Stay here, and I cannot speak for what may happen."

Her eyes narrowed. "What do you plan to do, child?"

"I plan on sinking this ship in a matter of hours." As I spoke the words, I felt the call of the warm waters lapping against the hull. My waters. Signs of home.

She spoke to the others using the language of the forest. My power built slowly, wave-by-wave, echoing the lapping of water against the wooden hull.

"We will assist. What must we do?"

"You will help me. The rest stay here until the ship is on the reef. Then we move for freedom."

"Then let us go. My limbs are eager for action with the smell of freedom so near."

She stood, her shackles melting off her wrists and ankles in a burst of green light. I supported her unsteady legs as we exited the hold.

We made slow progress to the main deck, stopping often to allow Pauline to rest. Standing under the last ladder to the deck, with the sunlight warming my skin, I said, "Wait one moment." I placed the invisibility spell over us, and we crept up the last ladder, holding onto each other, her old skin dry under my hands.

She shrank from the sun when we stepped onto the main deck. Men were scurrying about with the brisk wind capturing the sails.

"Are you all right?"

"I will be fine, child. Where is the best place to stand?"

"Over here, near my ward, Chloe."

We negotiated our way to a spot on the rail near Chloe. She swayed with the movement of the ship, gazing at the green slopes of Mount Nevis. I whispered, "We have returned, Chloe."

She started at my voice in her ear. Gazing at the larger mass of land looming off the starboard bow, she spoke into the wind. " I am glad you are returned."

The old woman clutched the rail, bent at the waist and snuffing the air. "We have passed here before."

I leaned over the edge of the rail, peering at the water against the hull. "Can you use that to help me pull the ship against the reef?"

The break in the water looked too far away, the white, frothy plumes beautiful against the bright blue of the sky and waves. "Yes," she replied.

"Chloe, please keep us out of view."

"I will try my best, Lady Richmond." She pulled a handful of dirt from her pocket and let the wind whisk it away, popping a shield into place over our forms. "All the men will see is the coastline. I made us transparent. They will only detect our presence if they touch us."

"Good." I turned to the old woman and said, "I will start to cast my spell. Please feel free to help as you see a need."

She nodded, her eyes fixed on the shores of Nevis. "The bones of my ancestors are calling to me."

I released the spell, my arms spread wide, the power bursting from my hands. I plunged the blue energy deep into the water, pushing and bending the waves to hit the hull at a different angle, turning the ship towards the shore. It was slow work; too fast an adjustment, and the sailors would realize the change in course and have to reset the sails, which would have worked against me.

Inch-by-draining-inch, the water hit the hull, pushing the ship closer to the reef. The old woman started chanting when the wave break was five hundred feet away. Her voice rang loudly, the chirps and clicks harsher than those in the hull.

Chloe murmured in my ear. "Hurry, Julia. The captain called to readjust the sails."

All subtlety lost, I threw myself into the spell, draining my reserves. Water rose in a thirty-foot wave along the port side of the ship. I allowed the water to crest, pushing the mass away, my arms trembling under the weight of the spell before yanking the wall of water down and pushing the bow of the ship closer to land. I ignored the panicked shouts of the crew, and focused instead on the attitude of the ship in the water. I wanted the ship to hit the reef sideways, thereby ripping open a larger hole in the hull. Concentrating, and ignoring the steady drip of sweat off the tip of my nose, I pulled the ship closer to the reef, imagining the water on the starboard side melting away under the force of the rogue wave. I gasped for air, as pain lanced through my body and the spell pulled more energy from my marrow.

Chloe warned, "Julia, stop the spell, It is too much of a drain."

"No," I gasped. "I will not fail."

Chloe yelled at the old woman, "Help her!"

Yellow light, as bright as the sun in the desert, twinkled on the sandy shore. It grew larger and bolder, its beam sweeping out to grab the bowsprit. As the light touched the wood, the ship hurtled closer toward land, the old woman swaying in the same rhythm as always, her words unchanging in her chant.

Chloe shouted, "The rocks!"

The reef was a dark stain in the water, easily seen now with our fast approach. We clutched the rail as the ship crashed onto the rocks, the wooden hull peeled away by the sturdy fingers of coral. Water rushed into the hull, and the ship shuddered to a jolting halt, the timbers screaming and popping. With the winds blowing stronger, and the hull immobilized, the force was too great on the main mast, and it broke, the whistles of untethered ropes whizzing over our heads. I felt invigorated as salty spray jetted into the air to cover the deck.

The old woman stopped chanting, opening her eyes to look at me. "I must free my people." She turned, as if making her way back down to the hold.

"Wait!" I called. "I have a better way." I held up my casting hand, and the waves halted their progress towards the hull. "Rip a larger hole in the hull, and they can walk right out."

Where I held back the tide, the coral was exposed, revealing fish lying on the sandy floor, their gills working to capture a last breath. I did not see her move a muscle, and I was sure she did not utter a sound, but without notice, the whole side of the ship ripped off, allowing the slaves to crawl out of the hold, their shackles gone, as they shielded their eyes from the bright Caribbean sun.

They made slow progress across the rocks. Chloe bit her lip beside me. "Julia, I do not know if I can keep this spell going much longer. The wind has carried away most of my dirt. We will be seen in a few moments."

"Wrap a rope around the railing of the deck and use it to drop to the ground. I will stay until everyone is safe."

Chloe quickly threw a rope over the edge, holding onto the hemp strands. "When I go over the side, I won't be able to maintain the spell."

I kept my eyes on the progress of the slaves. By my estimation, only a few were left in the hold, still to escape. "When you hit the bottom, grab a handful of sand to cast a spell. I just need a few more minutes."

She disappeared over the side, and I continued to hold the wall of water at bay. "Now, you go," I directed the old woman.

She shook her head. "I do not need your rope. We are leaving." Yellow light erupted beneath her feet, spreading toward me. We flew through the air, landing with a thump on the wet, sandy ocean bottom. As soon as our feet touched the ground, she withdrew the spell and hobbled over the slimy rocks towards land. Chloe hurried in front of her.

My feet flew over the sucking sand, the wave of water crashing behind me as I released the spell. Once I cleared the reef, I dissolved my hold on it and a wave hit me in the back, dunking me under as I swam to the surface, turning and treading water. The ship listed again, the crew screaming as the waves tore apart the hull.

"I will offer you as much compassion as you offered the slaves, as much compassion as you gave to the poor girl you ravaged, as much solace as you offered to the ones you abused for your base needs." I flicked my wrist, and took satisfaction in a wave sweeping the first mate over the rails and into the ocean's depths. I imagined the wave carrying him further out to sea as I headed for the safety of land. The rest were on their own.

Chloe waited for me on the sandy beach, smiling. "Julia, what an exhilarating day! What cracking magic!"

I staggered from the surf, water streaming off my clothes. My power surged as my feet touched the sandy shores of my home. "It is good to be home. And to wash the stink of the ship from us."

I surveyed the beach. Indian Castle lay just south of Eden Brown Estate. My lands were to the north of the island. Alistair lay in wait at his home on the south-facing slopes of Mount Nevis. "Let's head into the hills."

The slaves paused at the edge of the foliage, melting into the jungle. The old woman stood at the boundary, her skin bagging at her knees and elbows, but her head held high and straight. I approached her, stopping for cover in the shadows of the palms.

"Thank you." I extended my hand, unsure of the proper way to show her my appreciation. Should I curtsey? Or clasp her hand?

She smiled, the action creasing her face and hiding her eyes in the wrinkles from her cheeks. "Oh, child. You are welcome." She threw her arms around me, holding me close. I buried my head in her nape, not smelling the skin of a woman dirty from living in the cargo hold of a ship, but breathing in the comfort and acceptance she offered me in her simple embrace.

She pushed me away to hold me at arm's length, keeping her hands still curled around my upper arms. "I am proud to call you friend, Julia Richmond. Your mother must be smiling from heaven."

I bit my lip at her tender words. Never in my life had anyone praised me with such sincerity for using my magic the best way I saw fit. Tears pricked the corners of my eyes. "I would like to think she watches over me."

The old woman released me. "I will help you if you need it, friend."

"I appreciate the offer." I pointed upwards, to the summit of Mount Nevis, covered in white clouds. "The hills are your best chance of survival. Stay away from the sugar cane fields; they will be patrolled. When I correct the situation in my house, I may be able to offer more help to you."

She melted into the jungle. "We will be watching. Good day."

I raised my hand to wave goodbye. "Good luck."

Chloe shivered beside me. "Did you see her power? It was yellow. I wonder if I'll ever be as strong as her when I mature."

"Time will tell, Chloe. Now, I propose we get off this beach before the ship attracts the notice of the inhabitants. Let's head towards Eden Browne. There is a stream close to the estate where we can wash."

"That sounds wonderful." She remained crouched beside me, covering her arms with dirt, rubbing it into her skin, and sighing with pleasure.

Nevis was covered in foliage. On the slopes of the mountain, it was mostly tropical plants, a combination of the ferns and palms that were native to the island. Green vervet monkeys pounced in the trees, introduced to the island by the French many years ago. The remainder of the island was covered in a different vegetation, and the green stalks of sugar cane reached for the sky.

"We will keep off the main trails, and stay in the jungle until nightfall."

Chloe smiled, her hands kneading the rich, black dirt. "Lead the way."

We traveled through the jungle, shielded from the tropical sun by the same palms shading the ferns and hibiscuses. The dirt floor was alive with insects and budding leaves. This part of the island was never cultivated because of the steep slopes. Every time Chloe's hands touched the ground, yellow flashed like sparkles. "Oh," she cooed. "What wonderful soil."

"Many seem to think so. The French, Spanish, and English all share your sentiment. Nevis is so fertile, it grows more sugar cane than islands twice its size."

"You are lucky you come from such a rich place."

I bent to avoid a large spiderweb. "My mother's family settled here for the constant trade winds, but most succumbed to tropical fevers. My father's family settled here for the regular hurricanes."

We climbed, ascending higher and higher into the hills. As the sun sank lower in the sky, insects emerged, buzzing around our heads, and biting our flesh mercilessly.

"Ow!" Chloe exclaimed as she swatted a large mosquito from her arm. "I thought they would leave me alone with all the dirt on my skin."

I laughed. "As if they care." I glanced at the sun through the canopy. "We should be close to Eden Browne, but I do not see their fields. I would swear by the tides that this land should be covered in cane."

"Maybe they rotate their crops each year."

"I do not think crop rotation is a concept sugar plantations have ever embraced. Certainly not here, anyway."

We continued through the tropical forest, swatting at bugs and jumping when the monkeys screamed in the forest canopy. Shadows lengthened among the leaves.

"Chloe, we need to find shelter soon. I must be remembering incorrectly. We should be standing in the shadows of the Eden Browne windmill. There should be activity all around us."

Chloe bent down, placing her hands on the dirt floor. "I feel a stone structure about ten feet to the east."

I followed her directions. Five minutes later, we stood at the base of a stone conical structure. It was a windmill, but the blades were broken, one hanging bent and limp at its tip. Vines climbed a few inches up the sides of the stone base.

I pointed at the vines. "This is recent."

Chloe said, "If you say so."

"Time in the tropics is measured by decay. You can tell when anything happened by how much jungle has overtaken the structure. This small of an encroachment means it was fairly recently that the owners stopped up-keep on the windmill. Which is odd. You can not process the cane without the mills."

"Well, we did not pass a single field. Maybe they do not need to process cane."

"Everyone needs a working mill."

"Can we camp here tonight?"

"Yes."

I crept through the jungle for a mile, staying off the paths, and keeping to the darkness. Small, carnivorous bugs feasted on my tender flesh, but I ignored them, thinking instead of the broken windmill, and Chloe slumbering inside.

Ahead, a wooden structure with gingerbread moldings painted pink stood in the center of the clearing. Eden Browne Estate, one of the few not owned by witches on Nevis.

A stone structure off to the right smelled of cooking and old fires, the kitchen, if I remembered correctly. To the left, aprons, shirts and dresses hung from a line tied between two trees. So people still inhabited here, but why were the fields left untilled?

I crept across the clearing, avoiding the pools of light emitted by the main house. The kitchen remained busy at all times, with servants rushing in and out of its open doors, their arms laden with trays of food as they headed to the big house.

I crept to kneel in the shadows beneath an open window, its sill full of loaves of bread, cooling in the night. I heard the voices of servants chattering inside.

"I do not like that man! He is arrogant!" The voice sounded like it belonged to a young girl.

"Hush, child. He is powerful on this island. What made you so upset?"

"He wanted a lemon custard instead of the one you made. I told him, in my pretty manners, we did not have a lemon custard. He told me to find him one. How are we to make a dessert appear from thin air?"

"We do not do anything, child, except offer him the bread pudding, and the sweet pie I made today. He can have his own servants make a lemon custard if he wishes."

I reached my hand up to the window sill, feeling for a loaf of bread, and paused, my hand steady. No sound from the kitchen. I pulled the loaf down into my lap, both ears straining to hear if anyone noted the loss.

"I do not like him coming here for dinner. It makes the mistress nervous."

"She is a good hostess. It distresses her that our fields lay fallow, the cane dying faster than we can plant it."

"I bet he is the cause. Jonah says our water runs from his lands. I bet he poisoned the streams to bankrupt the plantation."

"Jonah! And what does that man know except rum and women? Now, take this tray and be kind in your offers. No attitude."

I remained still, clutching my bread and stolen clothes. Who were the slaves talking about? And why was the cane not growing?

"Marjorie! Did you take a loaf of bread from the sill? I know I put out five loaves. I am not so old that I cannot count the loaves in front of me!"

I did not hear the answer as I tucked the bread under my arm. I paused, waiting for a moment until the servants were serving dinner in the great house before melting into the jungle, and heading to my makeshift home with Chloe. I felt certain Alistair was the man they were entertaining for dinner.

Chapter Nineteen

"How much further?" Chloe tramped along behind me in the cane field. It was early morning.

"At least another mile. Same as the last time you asked."

In my estimation, our lands were some of the best on Nevis. We were located on the northern coast, where the Caribbean meets the Atlantic. The steady winds and quick currents were constant sources of energy for our casting. My house stood on a plain several hundred yards from the ocean, with our sugar cane fields backing up to the slopes of Mount Nevis. One of the few good things my father did was using indentured servants for working his lands. Of course, they were really witches under his protection, but as a cover for our life, it proved to be a good one. Their houses were scattered along the plain between the house and the sea.

"If Alistair is the head of your clan, wouldn't he want all the clan at his home?"

"I don't think so." I stopped to swat at a winged insect on my hand. "He needs money like everyone else. Pulling workers from a healthy plantation is not the way to remain unnoticed."

"Why does his clan live so far up the mountain?"

I stepped around a bent stalk and stopped. Ignoring Chloe's question, my gaze and mind were transfixed by the scene below me.

My home, the rock-and-wood, lovely house of my memory, stood in the same spot as I remembered, but that is where the similarity ended. The porch, once a majestic skirt, featured on three sides of the house, sagged on the east end. The lawn, a beautiful green carpet extending from the porch to the drive, now grew in shaggy clumps and starts. The crushed shell drive was clogged with weeds. I could not even recognize the kitchen garden on the west side of the house.

"What happened?" I said.

"Is there something wrong, Lady Richmond?"

"The house is a mess. I know father has been ill, but that is no reason to let the fields go, or have the house crash down around your ears."

"Maybe there wasn't anyone to take over. That happens a lot." Chloe fingered a brown cane stalk, turning a section green with her touch.

"I have two sisters as capable as I am of running a plantation."

Chloe tutted. "The younger siblings never step up to responsibility."

I sat, uncaring of the dirt and cane stalks, and plucked a length of grass to chew on as I mulled the situation. Sucking on my grass, I yearned to be welcomed back into my family, and to make peace with my father. Yet my house appeared empty. Desolate even.

We remained thus, small insects buzzing in our ears. "I want to watch the activity around the house before we knock on the front door."

Shadows lengthened to point at the eastern edge of the island, the heat of the sun slipping behind the mountain. I stood, brushing the dirt off my borrowed dress. "Let us go inside."

Chloe dogged my footsteps, as I marched out of the fields and up the steps to the front porch. I allowed my power to flow into the ground, searching and prodding for the thrum of energy supplying spells. I pushed my power as far as my ability allowed, with no signs of another witch. No warding spells, even.

The area appeared safe.

"I do not understand," I murmured to myself as I pushed open the front door. "No guards, no wards on the house. No legions of witches arrayed in warrior circles to spring out of the bushes. This is not Alistair's style at all." The front door opened with my gentle push, and I walked unimpeded into the seat of power for the water witches of the West Indies.

I giggled in shock. "Here I worried over how to find my father, how to sneak into my old lands, and Alistair fooled me in the end. There is nothing left here."

I searched the first floor of the house, looking again for signs of illusion, or any clue to reveal the truth of what could have occurred to drive a thriving home and plantation to desertion. It was like the people simply stopped coming back. The furniture was there, covered in a thick layer of dust and grime. There were signs of rats in the dining room where a full buffet table displayed rotting food.

Mother's parlor, a room I always loved with its pink wallpaper and views of the mountains, was the cleanest of the rooms, and even it was filthy. Chloe touched a crystal sconce flanking the mantel, wiping away the dirt. "Why would Alistair force them to leave?"

Chloe's question made me pause. "Something encouraged them to leave, or they wouldn't have abandoned the house."

Chloe glanced over her shoulder, as if the old threat would walk into the room behind her. "I think we should leave as well."

"No." I ran my finger over the dust and dirt, caking the mantel in the parlor. A picture of my mother still hung above the lovely carved wooden piece, her kind eyes and brown hair resembling mine. "This is my home, and I will stay here, if for no other reason than to have a bed to sleep in instead of the jungle floor."

Chloe wrinkled her nose. "It must be a trap." She looked at the empty room. "And I doubt there is a bed."

"I agree. But I must meet Alistair soon by the terms of the duel. Here is as good a place as any."

"I'll go outside and see what plants we can use, maybe find something in the garden to eat for dinner."

"I'll search the house for more clues. Perhaps I'll find a wand or spellbook lying around." We kept those in a magically warded safe. Only my father knew the combination, and the counter spells to the wards. I was sure that at least those items were still present.

Chloe hurried outside. I crossed the empty hallway, standing at the entrance to father's study. I hated this room, the place where the miseries of our mutated relationship played out in macabre regularity. The old, wooden floors creaked and moaned under my feet. So much heartache, so many lives twisted. I despised the duplicity of it all. No daughter wants to believe her father is a monster among men, so I like to think it was the stress of the position that wrung every shred of humanity from the man I called "Daddy."

I turned the knob, throwing open the door and stepping boldly over the threshold.

The room was just as I recalled. No bookshelves or mighty desk, just an innocent collection of spindly-legged chairs centered around a small tea table. A few paintings hung on the wall beside a political map of the Caribbean.

Not threatening. Innocuous, really. My father loved to disarm his opponents by sipping tea in the delicate chairs as he talked. When he finished his cup, if he were displeased, he would flay the flesh from bone with spells fueled by the scalding water in a porcelain pot. A trick I used in London. Perhaps we were more alike than I cared to admit.

I pushed a small amount of power to my hand, running the palm over the surface of the walls, searching for hidden caches of wands, or a magical lever to open the portal to the library housing the spellbooks. Starting at the furthest corner, I flattened my hands against the cool plaster, concentrating on my task, focused on the smallest fluctuations in the walls and joints of the room.

"Did you really believe I would let you set up house, Julia? I believe we have a prior engagement."

I turned, casting hand at the ready. Alistair stood at the door to the study, the only exit from the room. Round, mirrored rims perched on his nose. His skin was covered, from his fingers to his head, leaving only his fingertips exposed. Three witches flanked his sides, all old acquaintances from my youth, and red light flared around their hands.

Odd, since Alistair had green light. "What happened to your powers? Traded green or blue for red?" I peered at the faces of the witches arrayed behind them. Any passerby might have thought they were headed to a garden party, attired in silk pastel gowns and buttoned vests and coats. I greeted them one-by-one.

"Hello, Forester Pinney. I am shocked to see you standing with Alistair. I do not recall you being very good friends when we were young." A tall, blond man in a lavender vest blushed, ducking his head under my scrutiny.

"A lot has changed since you left, Julia."

My gaze slid to his right, where a thin woman stood, her brunette hair pulled into a severe bun, dark circles ringing her eyes. "Augusta Fleming, how nice to see you again. I passed your fields yesterday, and I must say they look lovely. Congratulations on what must have been a successful year."

Her thin mouth twisted into a cruel line. "No thanks to you and your family."

"I do not know what you are talking about." I kept my right hand out in a defensive posture.

A pretty woman pushed to the front of the group. Her features were a copy of mine, except for a dusting of freckles across her nose, and our coloring. Her hair and eyes echoed the lighter complexion of our father, where I always favored our mother. A lump formed in my throat. I swallowed before continuing.

"Caroline! What a delight to see you looking so well. Will you give a welcoming hug to your sister?"

Red light flashed from her hand, and I ducked as the spell hit the wall beside my head. Hatred dripped from her words. "When you left, you ruined everything! Father, Alistair, everything!" Another spell escaped from her hands to land harmlessly at my feet. "You were always more concerned about stupid things like morality and the consequences of actions. But you never thought about what your departure would do to the rest of us!" A third spell from her landed off to my right.

I kept my voice level, ignoring the anger of her words. "If you would calm yourself, you might have a chance of landing a spell. Although, I would have a difficult time bespelling any blood relative of mine. You must have a decided lack of conscience to even try."

Tears tracked down her cheeks. "Do not chastise me for making decisions that were necessary for my survival."

Her words gave me pause. Alistair remained standing, but he did not enter my house with spells blazing. He could have killed me with my back turned at any time before I was alerted to his presence. Pinney and

Caroline hated Alistair as children, but they stood with him now in my house. Augusta was always a neutral party, known for her logic and cool decisions under pressure.

"It appears there is more to this saga than meets the eye. Would any of you care to explain the situation to me?"

The witches stood silent, red light still flaring from their hands.

I nodded. "So be it. Alistair, I will meet you at the old dueling grounds, the cane field west of here. Name your time."

A crooked smile crossed his face, highlighting his yellow, pointed teeth. "Ah, a return to the scene of the crime."

"Yes."

He flicked his wrist, and the three witches around him circled the room, effectively surrounding me, not that I had an escape route anyway. I flared the magic in my hand brighter, hoping to scare the intruders in my home.

He laughed. "Intimidation does not work when you are outnumbered." He paused as sounds of a scuffle from the hallway interrupted his speech. The witches parted, and another threw a protesting Chloe to the floor. Alistair continued, "Especially when your cavalry is an untried witch of uncertain heritage."

I did not take my gaze from his face. "Chloe, get behind me."

She picked herself up from the floor, momentarily blocking Alistair from my view.

"Get out of the way!"

A bolt of red sizzled through the air, catching Chloe in the side. She screamed, the sound stopping as red fingers of magic crept across her body, up to her mouth, and turned black as they entered her mouth. She crumpled to the floor, her eyes staring at me, full of fear.

I crouched beside her, watching her terrified eyes as the red-black flickers moved like snakes over her skin. I glared at Alistair. "A nice variation on the water spell."

He bowed to me. "Consider it a boon to your reputation that I heard tell of your spell and thought it meritorious enough to utilize myself. Unfortunately, the terms of our agreement do not extend to Miss Chloe Longood, so I will be holding her as collateral for your appearance tomorrow."

Panicked, I forced my voice to remain steady. "I will show. How is Father?"

"He is in as good a health as can be expected."

"I need to see him."

"Of course you do. Noon, tomorrow, at the old dueling grounds. He will be there to witness your defeat." Nodding to the witch on his left, they held out their hands, keeping me at bay. Gathering Chloe, they led her from the room. I called out, "I will see you tomorrow, Chloe. Fight it."

I turned to Alistair, jabbing my finger at his chest. "I will take pleasure in ripping out your soul and feeding your lifeless body to the sea if you hurt her."

"I look forward to that, Julia." He adjusted his glasses.

They melted from the room as quickly as they came. I collapsed into a puddle on the floor, the sounds of crickets chirping in the night my only company. I wrapped my arms around my stomach.

He had my father.

He had my sisters.

He had Chloe.

He had black light to his magic.

I rolled onto my back, staring at the cracked plaster on the ceiling, thinking of how I wanted to plan the morning of the last day of my life. Walking onto that practice field tomorrow was suicidal. I had not found father, hence, I did not have enough power to defeat the lot of them.

I was alone. What I wanted my whole life: to be separated from my clan, and from other witches, just to be left alone.

I did not cherish the feeling now.

Chapter Twenty

My back ached from sleeping on the floor. After searching the house for clues, books, spells, wards, or any item that may have helped me free my family from whatever infestations this demon caused, I still exhibited no symptoms. However, the mark of demon taint on my old clan, and in their magic, was unmistakable. For all my rummaging, I could only find an old dress of mine.

I bundled the garment under my arm as I walked down the trail leading from the house to the ocean. The warm breezes ruffled my hair and my stomach growled. I'd often wondered as a child why I could command the elements, but could not conjure a pastry to appear. My father used to laugh when I asked him that question, and would pat my head as he replied, "It is dark magic, indeed, when a witch can make a physical change occur to a solid form. Just content yourself with perfecting a good illusion."

I pondered his words as my feet touched sand. I disrobed, hanging my clothes from a small palm tree, and plunged into the surf. The soft sand of the beach gave way to the rocks and reef that protected my home from the sea. I swam until my arms ached, and the sun rose high enough to sparkle off the tips of waves. I pumped my legs, working to stay afloat in the rough sea.

Treading water, floating over the crests of waves, I opened my power. The water around me changed, bubbling with the exchange from my body to the sea. Its color transitioned from the warm blue, characteristic of the Caribbean, to a deeper shade, lacking translucency. It was like looking into a bottomless spot of ocean where light ceases to penetrate.

I pushed more power out of my core, exchanging and recharging the source of my energy. I had not felt this good since I left London. I stayed as long as I dared, the ocean washing away the physical evidence of the voyage, the arduous tramp through the jungle, and rejuvenating my body.

Nothing could lighten my soul.

I swam for land, my arms energized, my stroke strong as I burst from the water. I imagined myself reborn, renewed, clean, and pristine. The breeze dried my body with the aid of the sun. I put on the dress, its white linen shining like a beacon in the strong sun.

I liked the idea of dying in a white dress.

I stayed thus on the beach, contemplating the blue sea, the pale sand, and the hot sun in the sky.

"Strange way to spend your last moments before a duel."

I turned at the familiar voice to find the old woman, Pauline, was standing behind me. I patted the beach beside me. "Sit with me for a moment, if you please."

She sat on the beach, her hair braided and clothes different from the rags she wore on the ship. "I came to talk about our arrangement, child."

I waved my hand behind me, motioning towards the house and lands. "If I read the situation correctly, these lands will be up for the taking this afternoon. Feel free to work them as your own. There are a few plantation owners who may be willing to set you up under an indentured servant plan, giving you a way to sell the goods and keep a portion of the profit after a time. Call on Augusta Fleming."

"I did not come today to talk of these things."

I squinted my eyes at her. "Then why are you here? Because I give my odds at one in five hundred that I will not be alive at one o'clock today."

She clucked at me. "Where is the spirit of the woman who sank a ship against the reef and saved the slaves in its hold? If you do not think you can win, why try? Just swim for that island over there." She pointed to a dark slash against the ocean horizon.

"I do not want to run from my problems. Not anymore." I sighed. "I have done that for three years, and all it caused was a broken heart, a broken marriage, and a big mess." I scratched a pattern in the sand with my fingertips, enjoying the gritty feel under my nails. "The old Julia, the one who first left this home, would be packing up and leaving now. Discarding her responsibility because she did not think it worthy of her time, or finding fault with the mechanics of the issue. Any excuse for avoiding doing what every person around her wanted her to do, and needed her to do."

I continued, "I do not want to be that person. I want to do the right thing, even if it means I may not survive, or may not like what I have to do. Running away only created more havoc, not peace."

Pauline nodded, rustling in a small cloth bag at her hip and bringing out a stalk of sugar cane. "The past will always find you." She bit the end, chewing on the hard stalk to suck at the sweet juice inside. "All things need food to grow. This cane, it still gives me juice, but it is cut from the plant. It will only give me as much juice as it has, then it is done."

"Your analogy is a nice one, but I am up against something I do not think is alive.

But rather, immortal."

She spat the bits of stalk out to land in a puddle on the sand. "Unless you fighting God, you always got a chance. I'll visit on Tuesday to discuss the terms for my people."

I rose and brushed the sand from my hands. "Thank you for the talk. It made the time pass quickly." We walked in silence, our feet sinking into the hot sand until we reached the edge of the fields.

"See you Tuesday, Lady Julia."

"Talk to Augusta Fleming."

She strode into the darkness of the jungle. "I won't need to."

I peered at the sun in the sky. Time for me to head to the dueling grounds.

A witch duel is a strictly controlled affair. Stronger casters maintain a perimeter to corral any errant spells. A circle of witches of equal allegiance to the duelists keep close watch on the competitors. This makes it difficult to cheat, and difficult to win. Most duels end in a tie, and neither side reveals the true extent of their powers. This negates the need for a tactical retreat by either party. Elegant war games.

Unexpected outcomes only occurred in rare situations, like an out-of-control caster like me and Lady Penelope, or a duel with uneven spectators. Much like this event.

This part of the island was criss-crossed with underwater channels, and if I could tap into one of those, I could expand the repertoire of my spells. The ocean was too far from me at this point to provide unlimited assistance.

I heard the commotion long before I stepped from the tall stalks into the grassy ring. Loud chatter filled the dueling place, and witches crowded the perimeters, all wearing dark red cloaks with black toggles at the throat. The roar fell and silence greeted my short walk from the edge of the circle to the center. The wall of witches closed in around me.

Alistair stood, his round glasses in place, wearing a long-sleeved black shirt and black breeches that reached the ground. His hands were covered in black gloves, so only the tips of his fingers were bare. He bowed when I stopped before him.

"Welcome, Lady Julia Nesbit Richmond, previously of the water clan of the West Indies, descended from the wind clan of the north."

I parroted his bow, keeping my eyes raised to survey my surroundings. The rules of a duel forbade any active spells from the crowd, but that did not mean such action never occurred. To my remembrance, the largest threats from the crowd would be Caroline and Augusta. Caroline was angry with me and may have chosen to ease her dissatisfaction with a spell or two. Augusta was smart enough to try and turn the tide of the duel if she thought she would profit from it. They both stood directly behind Alistair.

I answered him. "Welcome, Alistair Dupont, of the earth clan of the West Indies, new leader of the water clan of the West Indies as demarked by your rings, and human harbor to a demon."

His mouth quirked as a gasp arose from the crowd. "I wondered how long it would take you to figure out that little piece of the puzzle."

"The glasses were the nidus for the thought." My gaze scanned the crowd. "Where is my father and Chloe?"

Someone hissed, "She is more concerned for a half-breed gutter rat than her own blood. Hit her!"

I kept my attention on Alistair, whose face remained impassive. "What is the true intention for bringing me here? Really, you have all that you want. You are the head of the only two clans of consequence in the area. You control sixty percent of the commerce on Nevis by having that position. You have money, power, and influence. I fail to see how I figure into the equation."

Alistair clenched his hands, his fingertips blistering in the noon sun. "Bring out her father. Let us show her."

Caroline and Augusta parted, and my father hobbled to stand beside Alistair. His back hunched over a thin cane, his wobbly legs failing to support his thin frame. His face drooped in haggard lines, as if all the flesh from his body was sucked away, leaving only the skin and bones. His hair lay thin and gray along his scalp.

His blue eyes remained sharp with cunning as he addressed me. "Julia, we do not have much time. I love you, child, and always will. I have faith in the decisions you must make."

A flurry of French erupted from behind him. "Step aside! Mais oui! Must I do everything myself?"

I recognized that particular accent.

A familiar form burst through the crowd, her auburn hair shining in the sun, black silk dress cut low over her bosom. Chloe cowered at her side, fresh cuts along her arms. She kept her gaze down, refusing to look at me, her fingers clawing at the dirt.

"Ah, Julia. How nice for you to come. I am a *leetle* angry with you for leaving me with the Bishop of London. It prevented me from making it to Nevis until yesterday. Naturellement, I do not care for interruptions to my plans." Looking at the assembled crowd, she raised her voice. "Show the proper respect to the leader of your clan!"

The witches, including Alistair, sank to their knees, their heads scraping the ground. Only I remained standing, glaring at Oualie.

"You always did have a flair for the dramatic. What do you wish me to call you, by the way? I confess I do not know which name to choose. Should I call you Oualie, or just a simple demon prostitute?"

She screamed, throwing a spell at my feet. I jumped, pulling my legs high, and the spell sank into the rich volcanic soil of the island.

Landing on the balls of my feet, I held my casting hand at the ready.

"You will call me master by the end of the day." Pointing a finger at Alistair, she commanded, "All rise. Monsieur Dupont, if you please, duel Lady Richmond. To the death."

Chloe gurgled beside Penelope. I focused on Alistair. He needed to protect his skin from the sun if he harbored a demon. His casting was limited by only the use of his fingertips, instead of the fullness of his palm. His first spell flew from his fingers, aimed at my left shoulder. I dove to the ground, throwing up a shield, and the crowd screamed when the spell hit the spectators behind me.

That was one way to gain dueling room.

Keeping my shield in place, I scrambled to stand. My power demanded to equal his spell in kind, rising like sap in spring to infuse my limbs with energy, but I held it in check.

"Alistair, dear, the purpose is to hit me, not your own clan."

The corner of his mouth twitched. "Ever the astute observer, Julia." He threw another spell, this one to the right, and I dodged it, deflecting the spell with my shield. I advanced, closing the distance between us.

"My father seems to be in poor health, but not under demonic control. Explain this, please."

"Alas, it is not my story to tell." He raised his arm, but I threw a spell first, hitting the ground beside him, spewing dirt and grass into the air. The explosion beside his feet threw him to the ground. I rushed to land on him, pushing his stomach on the ground, while forcing my knees into his back. His hands were caught under him as my knee dug into his spine. I flung a rope spell around his neck to squeeze his throat. I threw a second spell, one to rip the cloth from his body, thereby exposing his vulnerable back to the sun.

His throat glowed blue from my rope spell. Each flick of my wrist tightened the noose around his neck. But when the sun hit his pale flesh, he screamed. Great oozing blisters erupted over his skin; and his flesh appeared to melt under the lesions, exposing raw muscle.

I lowered my head to his ear, whispering to him, "Why me, Alistair? What is your game here? You intentionally missed."

He grunted, "You are the only one to save us, Julia. I am at war with the demon within."

A bolt of energy hit me between the shoulder blades, tossing my body ten feet into the air before slamming me into the ground. My vision clouded, turning black at the edges. I struggled to take a deep breath in, certain my ribs were broken.

Another bolt of black hit my body. I felt the impact of the blast to my core. *Move, Julia!* I scrambled to stand on shaky legs.

With my hands in front of me, I struggled to maintain my thin blue shield. I pulled power, turning to face my new threat.

Oualie stood over Alistair, whipping his back with lengths of black magic. Blood oozed from his skin, and blisters popped along the ridges of torn flesh. She raised her arm, prepared to slash his back again.

I was low on power to maintain my shield without a nearby source of water. Then I heard a bubble of water at my bare feet. Looking down, a puddle gurgled from the impact my body made with the last spell. Thanking God, I drew the water into an orb in my palm, breathing in its essence. It was water from deep in the earth, water familiar with the dark caverns and chambers beneath the island.

It moved and rippled in my hand, and an inner part of me, a part long dormant, stirred. It directed me to ask the water to stop Oualie from harming Alistair again. Not *demanding* it to accomplish this task, but guiding it to do my will, bending it to identify my enemy as its enemy.

I raised my right palm, the water flowing through the air, gurgling and churning as it went, to transform into a thin line.

Oualie ignored the bit of fluid, intent on flaying the flesh from Alistair's back. The water spell met her left arm at the elbow. She halted her swing. I thought the spell may have gone wrong, for she stood as before, her magic whip at the ready, her minions cowering around her, feeding her energy to hurt one of their own.

My spell twinkled in the light, flaring blue, the light brighter than the sun. I shielded my eyes from its intensity. The spell moved, and in the space of a heartbeat, it sawed through her flesh, amputating her arm.

I stood in shocked disbelief at the result of my spell.

Oualie screamed, grabbing her arm as blood, black with demon taint, rained to the earth. Chloe shivered, clawing the ground beside her before crawling away from her captor.

Caroline threw her cape at Alistair. He whimpered, huddling beneath it to protect his skin.

Oualie turned to me. "God damn you, Julia! Why can't you leave well enough alone!" Her casting hand, the only hand remaining attached to her body, shriveled and transformed itself into a blackened stump. She raised it, waving the useless appendage in the air. "This is what the great and wonderful Julia Richmond did to me! This useless stump! Before our duel, I was the most powerful, and the prettiest, the catch of the island."

She paused to breathe deeply, blood still dripping from her severed arm. "I had no choice. Dark magic returned these things to me."

"Penelope? Penelope Pinney?" I shook my head, my eyes disbelieving the transformation. "You did all this because of our duel?"

I walked backwards over the uneven territory, increasing the distance between us. "I am sorry, Penelope. I apologized then, and I apologize again. I offered your family restitution. They declined."

"They declined because Alistair told them I was at fault! He said I cheated. He wanted you to be his wife, not me, because he thought you would be more manageable. But he always wanted me. Until he betrayed me. He betrayed both of us."

Alistair swayed to his feet, his face contorted with pain, and clutched his chest. "You did cheat, Penelope. You cast a spell to rob Julia of her powers. It backfired, and you lost yours instead. Your own spell prevented you from blocking an immature cast."

Shocked, I glared at Penelope. "So you were angry with me and took it out on everyone else?"

She responded by throwing a massive black spell at my shield, the energy coming from the stump of her arm. The force was powerful, and cracked my shield. "I made everyone pay, including your dear husband."

Fear for Richmond quickened my pulse. "What did you do to him?"

She cackled. "That is the beauty of the plan! You took everything from me, so I systematically took everything from you. Your house, your family, your clan. Your husband. All mine to control, all mine for the taking. I left you with the same things you left me: nothing. And now you will die."

I formed another shield, uncertain what kind of spell to expect from her. Irrational could not fully describe her thoughts; and if I could not predict her thoughts, I could not formulate a defense.

"I do not think I want to die today. I have a lot of things left to accomplish. Saving my family. Destroying you. Finding my husband."

"You cannot find him where I put him." She turned to Alistair, and a thin bolt of red energy flowing from her stump split open his chest. He collapsed, fresh blood gurgling in his throat. A dark claw, like that of a crab, appeared from his chest cavity. Alistair's form danced upon the ground, contorting and writhing in seizures as a monster, a demon, stepped from his body. It discarded the remains of Alistair's form like a dirty bit of clothing.

It was an awful thing, parts of its body solid flesh, covered in spikes and scales, other parts as ethereal as the mist in the trees. A thin line of smoky mist trailed from Alistair's chest, scrabbling across the ground to twine along Oualie's stump. The demonic form flickered, opaque to translucent, until the tail embedded in her flesh. The face was part human, part animal, with too many teeth in its mouth, and the proportions stretched into grotesque lines. The animal portion reminded me of a dog with half its muzzle rotted off, and the human portion was the terrible intelligence in its two black eyes. The body was a combination of a crab in its upper torso, with two formidable, serrated claws snapping in the air, the fat, armored bodies diminishing into a thin, single, smoky tether into the ground.

Alistair's chest closed, and his body lay limp on the ground, as he took shallow breaths, rising and falling in his abused flesh.

The demon crouched on scaly claws and knees, bowing to Penelope. It spoke, but the words sounded like the scratching of rocks and metal combined with rumbles of the earth. Chloe screamed.

Penelope grabbed Chloe by the hair and pulled her to kneel in front of the demon. "Tell me what it says, half-breed!"

Chloe sobbed. "It wants Julia's blood."

Penelope clapped her hands. "Tell it to take all her blood it wants. I will enjoy watching her do my commands."

My patience snapped. "You are such a coward, Penelope. You cannot best me on your own, so you call a demon to do your work for you. How common."

She ignored me, commanding the demon, "Take any form you choose."

The demon nodded its head, its skin reddening in the blazing sun, blisters popping from its scales. It crawled along the ground, sniffing the feet of each witch in its proximity.

It reached Chloe, who shrank from its heathen form. A forked tongue flickered from its mouth, claws clacking about her head. The tongue, red with the smell of brimstone, slickered over her jaw, delicately licking her face. Chloe sobbed, biting her knuckles at this invasion. The demon answered her fear with a spate of rumbles, moving its claws closer to her body.

It cannot be Chloe. Not her.

I threw a blue bolt, thinking of the warm sun and the pure water of the ocean, and the bolt struck into its protruding tongue.

It howled, the terrible sound echoing off the mountain to reverberate in the air. A breeze lifted the hair from my neck. A deep part of my soul wished the air could wipe away the sound. A stiffer breeze blew, tangling my hair in front of my face. The demon swung its head to me, a series of rumbles carried away in the breeze.

"Do not touch what is mine, beast. I am not afraid of you. You, who must cower from the sun and water."

The demon's lower half solidified, now standing on crooked hind legs, towering above me. Its claws clicked and its mouth moved, but I ignored its show. I threw a shield around the demon, hoping to trap it before it chose another vessel. It tore through the thin blue with its sharp claws to stride across the clearing, stopping in front of my father.

"Julia!" he called in his thin voice, his eyes never leaving the gaze of the demon. "Do what you must! I have always been proud of you, proud to call you my daughter."

The demon flicked its claws, cracking my father's chest open like an oyster.

"No!" I screamed as the demon's tail snaked inside my father.

My father's eyes, once clear blue, swirled and turned red. Alistair crept along the ground, blood oozing from his wounds, to offer him his glasses, taking the lenses from his face to place them gently on my father's nose.

"Malcolm, do not despair. I think our girl has a fighting chance. It is nice to be rid of that thing."

Father turned to me as Alistair collapsed behind Caroline. Father's frame expanded, gaining muscle and sinew to replicate his form as I remembered it. "Surrender, Julia. Do not make a father take the life of a child."

I circled in counterpoint to him as he twisted his shoulders, rotating his head upon his neck, limbering up for the battle to come. "I will save you from this dilemma by offering you one chance to surrender, beast, before I consign you to your fate."

My father's voice replied, strong under the demon's power. "I have taught you all you know. The student cannot defeat the master."

I circled around him again, bringing myself closer to Alistair. "Possibly."

When I was close enough to reach Alistair with a spell, I flung another rope spell at him. The spell caught him by surprise. It wrapped around his arms, preventing his movement. I pulled on the spell, maintaining my shield to my father, until I could smell the sweat from Alistair's body.

"Really, Julia, I have waited an eternity to be this close to you, but this was not the scenario I had in mind." His skin was blistered and pale, his brow sweaty. I could see his pulse beating irregularly at his throat.

I ignored his glib comment. "Give me the rings."

His face was blank. "What rings?'

"The clan rings on your finger. Give them to me, or I walk away and leave the nasty and Penelope for you to deal with."

He protested. "When I planned to bring you here, it was only for you to defeat the demon. Taking over the clans was not in the cards."

"By the tenets of the duel, you agreed to relinquish the clan rings to me upon your defeat. I posit you are defeated. The rings are thus mine."

Penelope cursed, stalking across the field towards us. "What are you two talking about? Demon, fight her!"

I held my spell on him. "Quick, Alistair. Which do you choose?"

He smiled, teeth perfectly white and straight, now that he was away from the demon influence. "You always were a cunning miss. Do not fail, Julia. Consider this a loan."

He pulled the two thin rings from his hand, placing them on my right hand in a caricature of a marriage rite. As the thin gold bands settled onto the joints of my fingers, power rushed from every member of the clan into my body. Overwhelmed by the onslaught of energy, I fell to my knees, breathing against sore ribs to stuff the energy into any available place. Blue light erupted from my skin, painting the dueling grounds cerulean tints. My former clan shrank from the bright light, disappearing amongst the cane.

My father cowered in the glare. Pain laced my every move, the normal motion of my muscles and bones displacing energy, energy that shuffled more energy to find a home. My hands clawed the earth, searching for surcease from the pain.

"Stand and fight, Julia."

My father stood before me, his hands at the ready. Blue light, like my own tinged with black from the demon, licked along his fingers.

I struggled to stand, stuffed too full with power. I gazed around, and saw witches clawing the ground.

I was draining them of their power. If I did not shut off the circuit, they would perish.

Breathing deeply, instead of trying to absorb all the power, I pushed it away, leaving my own power intact. The cries of pain dwindled, and the witches threw off their black cloaks, no longer needing to hide their skin from the sun.

"Enough!" Penelope bellowed, directing the demon. "Duel!"

My father raised his arm, throwing a spell at my head. I ducked, but it followed my movements, shooting bits of flame. I did not move fast enough. The flames bit into my skin, charring the flesh along my arm.

Pulling water from the ground, I threw it at the spell. Where my blue light landed, the demon fire extinguished.

One cut split my eyebrow above my right eye, sure to leave a scar. Blood dripped from the cut, blurring my vision.

The demon in my father's body spoke. "I will enjoy the taste of your blood when it nourishes me."

A bolt of blue erupted from my hand, aiming at my father's chest. "You have made your fatal mistake, demon. Before today, I did not know how to defeat you. Now, I know your secret."

My father laughed. "A thin slip of a girl bleeding from her eye defeating me? The leader of the third circle of demons! It is laughable."

I yelled at Chloe. "Chloe! Can you prevent the earth from opening?"

She answered, a confused look upon her face, "Yes."

I turned to the demon. "Father, I am sorry for the pain I have caused you. I am sorry for the pain I am about to inflict."

A shocked gasp rose from the crowd, the witches each shielding the other from any errant spells. I dropped my shield, standing in the center of the circle with the wind whipping around me, focusing all my concentrative powers on asking the wind to help me with my task.

As soon as I dropped my shield, the demon flung a spell at my defenseless form, flaying open the skin along my casting arm. I ignored the pain, closing my mind to the hurts of my body.

I needed to find a breeze among the cane stalks to help me. The wind is fickle, and hard to cajole. I reached out to the trade winds, the ocean breezes, begging for help.

Pain racked my body, pulling me back to reality. I collapsed to my knees, trying to throw a shield.

My casting hand did not work. Pain arced along the circuits of my brain, clouding my thoughts as blood poured from my useless arm. Closing my eyes, I concentrated all my power into my left hand, the motions awkward, and threw a shield to deflect the demon's next spell.

My shield was weak, and my energy low. I would not last much longer under the demon's onslaught.

"Julia! Use the clan rings!" Chloe screamed. "You cannot fail!"

"No," I whispered. "I cannot doom everyone with my defeat."

I pushed myself to stand, legs wobbly, and reached out to the winds again, dropping my last shield. I knew I was dead if I could not catch the wind. A shield would not help me now.

I felt separate from the world of the earth and trees, the form of my father standing in front of me, pelting my earthly form with spells to break my body.

I refused to feel the pain, concentrating on speaking with the wind. A warm breeze, smelling of clean earth and water eddied back around, away from the ocean, to swirl around me. I whispered in my mind, asking it to help me.

It swirled amongst the crowd of witches, ruffling hair and scenting the sweat amongst the bodies. It flowed along the demon's skin, rotating many times before returning to me.

"A puff of wind will not carry you away from death," the demon laughed. "I am through playing with you, little witch."

The warm breeze swirled around my body, rotating faster and faster. It picked my body from the ground, howling among the cane stalks.

The witches below sank to the ground, covering themselves from the fierce wind whipping at their hair, and pulling at their clothes.

I was cocooned in my ball of wind, supported six feet above the ground. The winds howled around me, but I was safe within its invisible shell. From this vantage, I called to the winds, concentrating them into the swirling ball of fury around me.

As one force, I commanded the swirling vortex to cover the demon. We moved through the air. Propelled by the winds. I hovered above the demon, staring into my father's face.

"Release my father, demon."

It laughed. "No. I can have the father and the daughter."

"Please." I asked, hoping it would offer the broken body of my father to me.

"No."

My energy ebbed. I had little time left.

I commanded the vortex to engulf the demon. We sank lower. When the wind touched demonic flesh, it propelled me back to reality, my body landing on the ground with a thump.

I screamed, the pain of the spells lacing through my body reducing my mind to nothing, and preventing me from thinking. Chloe crawled to my side, trembling.

"Julia, please fight!" A thin, yellow shield covered our bodies. Chloe reached out to touch me, her hands hesitating to meet my flesh. "Julia, how can I help? You are bleeding so much."

I groaned, pulling myself to stand. My right hand hung uselessly at my side, but my left hand worked. Without thinking, I channeled my power to my left hand, raising it in the air. The energy transfer worked better this time. The swirling vortex lifted my father's form high into the air, separated from the earth, and thus separating the demon from his refuge.

"Chloe, just prevent that monster from climbing into the ground. No matter what," I croaked.

She nodded. "I can do that."

I held my left hand high, my arm trembling with the force of my spell, and crooked my first finger of my right hand, the only finger that obeyed the commands of my brain. I pointed that single finger at my father.

I hesitated. *Could there be another way?*

I stayed thus, the demon scrabbling to reach the sanctuary of the earth, my finger trembling in the air. The demon, my father, pleaded. "I will give you the power you want. Just don't hurt me, Julia. I am your father. I love you."

I hesitated.

"You can have whatever you want, just let me live."

I thought about what Chloe said, racking my brain for another way, another solution.

"We can help find you a new mate, someone who can help run the clans. I can help you rule them all. Just release me. All this is yours. Just stop the spell."

I crooked my finger and a spell hit my father's chest.

The thin line of blue threaded its way among the swirling ropes of air to wiggle into the body of my father. The demon screamed, a mixture of my father's voice and the rumbles from the demon. It was a horrible sound, a sound that turned the stomach to cowardice.

"Be ready, Chloe."

Tears fell, stinging my cut face and lips. I made myself watch as my spell cut the skin from my father's flesh, draining his life's blood to pool on the ground below the spectacle in the air. A few witches, unable to resist the call of spilt blood, hastily crawled toward the offering.

"No," I commanded. "My clan does not take blood offerings."

They shrank back, humiliation and shame causing their shoulders to sag.

The demon erupted from my father's form, gnashing its teeth and tearing at the prison of air. A chasm opened under my feet, sulfur smells like the bowels of the earth assailing my nose.

Chloe moved her hands amongst the dirt, closing the hole. The demon slashed its claws through the translucent walls of its prison, the air swirling back upon itself to seal off any exit. It screamed its rage, howling, the sound rumbling among the vegetation deep into the ground.

Chloe panted beside me. "It calls for help, Julia."

I kept my gaze on the swirling, blood-soaked ball of air and evil ten feet above the ground. "Do not let the ground open, Chloe, or we all die."

Fissures cracked the earth. The ground shook. Witches worked to cover the holes, and deny the demon's call to its brethren, and keep it from breaching the surface of the earth.

As the blood of my father sank into the ground, the demon's form wasted, losing muscle and flesh, the bones snapping under the weight of its scaly skin. It called again, but the sound diminished, lost among the gusts of air. My arms grew heavy under the weight of the spell.

We stood thus until the cauldron of air was empty, my father's form and that of the demon reduced to dust.

I released the spell, the winds scattering the thin layer of dust over the sea.

My hands trembled. I wanted to vomit.

I had killed my father.

Alistair grabbed my shoulders, holding me, and supporting me from falling to the ground. I shrugged him off, my gaze searching amongst the crowd. "Where is Penelope?"

I staggered through the witches, pushing them out of my way. "Penelope! Come out, you coward! Stand and fight!"

"Julia! Stop it!" Alistair grabbed me by the arms, shaking me. "She is gone. Leave it."

Witches stood around us, in a circle, holding their left hands out in humble salute, to me.

I was now head of the water and earth clans of the West Indies. I was their master.

I pulled away from Alistair, addressing the witches. "Spread the word. I want Penelope Pinney captured and brought to me. Alive. I, Julia Nesbit Richmond, am head of the clans and make this decree on that authority."

The witches murmured amongst themselves, disappearing into the sunny fields of sugarcane. Chloe called me to her side.

I hobbled over to her. She stood in the center of the dueling ring, a small mound of dirt at her feet. "It is your father. I sorted it from the other bits. I thought you might want it."

I looked around the empty ring. The sun shone hot on my skin. Cane stalks rusted in the gentle breeze. I lay on the ground and wept beside the tiny mound of dirt.

Chapter Twenty-One

I hobbled back to the plantation house, Chloe support-ing me. She tried to heal my wounds as best as she could, but the demon taint resisted her attempts. The journey took well into the early evening due to my need for frequent rests.

As we approached, the smell of meat cooking on a fire caused my stomach to growl. We left the stalks of cane behind to see the house ablaze with lights, the porch repaired, and the smoke from kitchen fires dark-ening the horizon.

"I do not want to appear ungrateful, but where were all these people yesterday? 'cause that would have been nice to have a warm meal before confronting all that ugliness."

"I don't know, Chloe. But as long as they are friendly and want to share their dinner, I won't protest."

Pauline exited the house to stand on the porch, her arms open wide. "Welcome home, Lady Richmond, Miss Chloe. We have dinner waiting and hot baths, too. Which would you prefer?"

The house smelled of fresh beeswax, and the land was cleared around the house as I remembered it from my childhood. The gravel drive was newly raked, and the clumps of weeds removed. Order had been restored.

"Dinner, please!" cried Chloe, hurrying off to follow the smells to the dining room.

"I'll take a bath first." I limped up the stairs, following Pauline to my old room. I paused on the landing to catch my breath. "Did you know my mother's name was Pauline?"

She clucked her tongue and smiled. "I know, child. I know. Let's get you cleaned up."

I followed her to my old rooms, my mind at ease for the first time in years.

The next day dawned bright and sunny. The doors were opened to take advantage of the cross winds, and the house remained cool despite the heat. I stood in my father's study, my right arm in a sling, my right hand tingling with the pull of the clan rings. I directed two men, my newest indentured servants, to place a large desk in front of the window. Between Pauline's skills, the power in the rings, and my plan for a swim later, my healing was progressing rapidly. I may not even have gotten a scar from the demon fire.

"Yes, leave it there. I like the natural light from the window."

"Uncanny how you managed to acquire a bevy of slaves so readily," Alistair's voice sounded behind me.

I turned. "Actually, they are not slaves. They are indentured servants who earn ten percent of the profit from the plantation. They are free to come and go as they wish."

Alistair cocked his eyebrow. "Ten percent? Julia, has the battle addled your brains? That is unheard of."

I pointed my finger at him. "What is unheard of, Alistair, is a deputy of a clan entering a room without permission, improperly acknowledging the clan master, and having, in general, a loose way of speaking with his superior."

His mouth twitched at the corners, suppressing a smile. "My apologies, Lady and Master. I will do better next time."

"Please ensure that you do."

I sat in a pink upholstered chair behind the desk, motioning for Alistair to take the chair opposite me. "Thank you, Sam, for helping move my desk."

The former slave nodded and left the room.

When we were alone, Alistair motioned to the room. "How is this possible, Julia?"

I smiled, thinking of the magic Pauline and her followers had used to ready the plantation. "Magic, Alistair, of course. Now, about those reports."

His mouth dropped open. "That is it? After yesterday, you plan to waltz in here and start running things?"

"After the mess you and my father made of things? Yes. Yes, I do."

Alistair stared out the window. "It was not entirely our fault. It started on Martinique years ago."

I wrinkled my brow. "Martinique?"

"Yes. Where your husband and Lord Souter worked for the English government to overthrow the French government by using a certain witch as a spy."

Bile climbed up my throat. "Penelope?"

"Yes."

"That is a different tale than what he told me."

"From what I pieced together, Penelope used her witch powers to gain access to Martinique. Instead of helping overthrow the government, she took over the clan there with the aid of the demon. It was her first possession, I think, and many died in giving their blood to fuel the conversion."

I interrupted, "So she covered it up as an unsuccessful coup, and sailed to another island to repeat the process."

"Yes."

My hands shook, the awful pieces fitting together in my head. "She wanted me off the island to make it easier for her to return."

"I believe so. Once you left, she began her conversion of Nevis. It destabilized the power structure, and we were ripe for the picking. It took three years to get all of us under her control."

"The length of my marriage until she returned to London."

"Precisely."

With the sun shining on my new desk, the wind ruffling the hairs at my nape, and the demon vanquished, it should have been a lovely afternoon, but it felt dark and cold and empty. "When did you know she was Penelope?"

"In London. I had never met her on Nevis."

I doubted the truth in his words, but did not challenge him. "I think I need some time to think."

Alistair rose, placing the papers in his hands on the desk. "You will find the information about the lands in these reports." He reached out his hand, his fingertips brushing my cheek, then dropping away. "Your father would have been proud of you, Julia. You amazed even me, and I have admired you for years." He bowed, moving towards the door. "Send a messenger over when it is convenient for you to ride the lands. I have a few ideas for improvement."

"No attempt to wrest the rings from my hand, Alistair?"

"I am not a fool, Julia. I saw what you did yesterday."

"Did you love her? Penelope?"

He hesitated at the door, his hands clenching before replying, "I thought so. Once upon a time." He turned, gazing at me with sorrow. "I know now how hard it was for you to leave your husband. Not a feeling I wish to endure again."

I gathered myself together and sneaked out of the house to the beach. Plopping down in one of the new chairs beneath a palm tree, I sat in the shade. I flung off my shoes and dug my toes into the warm sand.

"By the tides. I loved him." Harsh sobs, which I thought were done when I left Nevis, and when Richmond left me in Botetourt's study in London, erupted from my core.

Wiping my eyes, I gazed at the clear blue water, a small square of white denoting a ship far out at sea. I turned, gazing at my lands lying verdant and fertile at the bottom of Mount Nevis.

I looked at my right hand, with the two bands of yellow gold around the one finger.

Pauline walked from the house with a tray full of glasses and a pitcher balanced on top. Reaching me, she placed her burden on a small table beside my chair.

"Lemonade?"

I nodded. She poured me a glass, then sat in the empty chair beside me and poured herself a glass. "I heard the conversation with you and Mr. Alistair. I would not put too much stock in what that man says. He'd tell God himself to doubt Jesus if he thought he could have the role of savior."

I drank my liquid, rolling her words around my head like the drink flavored my tongue. "You know, Pauline, I am tired of crying over things I cannot control."

She cackled, refilling my glass. "Now, that is the spirit I know as Lady Richmond."

I glanced at my hand, the gold bands sparkling in the sun. "I am wedded to a new master now."

"Yes, you are. But we will help you, Lady Richmond. You are not alone."

We sat thus until the sun sank below the top of the mountain. I gazed out at the Caribbean sea, wishing for peace and happiness and safety for the people I loved.